NOBODY LOVES
A GINGER BABY

Laura Marney

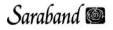

Saraband ◉

Published by
Saraband
Suite 202, 98 Woodlands Road
Glasgow, G3 6HB, Scotland
www.saraband.net

**FT
Pbk**

ISBN 978-1-908643-01-8

First published in 2005
This edition has been revised by the author.

Editor for this edition: Craig Hillsley
Cover illustration and design: Scott Smyth
Text design and layout: Marta Wawro

4 5 16 15 14 13

To Holly, Max and Ellen,
for making me laugh and making me proud.

Chapter 1

'No,' Daphne tells Donnie, 'stop worrying, I'm not going to chuck you.'

This is what she tells him to calm him down. It's not always what she thinks.

'But,' she says, only half joking, 'you'd better step up your antidepressants. You'll get arrested if you don't get a grip on the kleptomania and there's a good chance you'll be sacked when they find out who's putting soap in the sandwiches. You could even get evicted from your flat. I'm pretty sure squirting a piss-filled Super Soaker, even at deserving neds, is an evictable offence. Take your meds,' she gently encourages him. 'You don't want to be forcibly committed, you'll end up licking the windows in the laughing academy.'

Laughing academy, they both laugh at that one.

On the outside Donnie looks like an ordinary Joe, he isn't overly tall or handsome or different in any way. He wears his red hair short and tidy. He has two eyes, two ears, a nose and a mouth, all of average dimensions, all precisely in the right place. If he is exceptional it is in his symmetry. The second and fourth fingers of both his hands are exactly the same length.

If you walked past him in the street you wouldn't notice him, even a street where there were no other passers-by. If, on that same deserted street, Donnie walked past holding a smoking gun and a swag bag filled with pilfered sporting goods and novelty items, you'd be hard pushed to pick him out in any subsequent identity parade. He is very, very careful to be discreet; he is devious. This reticence extends even within his employment, which Donnie thinks of as his job rather than his career. He's good enough at it and that's good enough for him.

Apart from the men he plays football with Donnie has no friends of his own. With Daphne's friends he is polite, considerate, charming. They think he's a great guy. Little do they know that when, in the privacy of their own homes and after a few drinks amongst friends, they say and do foolish things, it is meat and drink to Donnie.

He keeps Daphne awake in bed by picking apart her friends' conceits and weaknesses, ascribing ugly motives to their good-natured buffoonery, reprising phrases they have used intemperately so often that they become, in Daphne's mind, her friends' signature tunes and she has to be careful not to say them out loud. Daphne's friend, Mark, diffidently recounts what his boss has recorded in his annual appraisal: 'Mark Leslie is probably the most popular lecturer in the department.' Donnie calls him 'Carlsberg'. He asks Daphne with his imitation of the gruff voice-over of the advert, 'Is Probably The Most Popular Lecturer In The Department coming?'

'Probably,' is Daphne's tired reply.

Donnie relishes inventing cruel nicknames and using them exclusively with Daphne, like a secret code. Joe, who so often earnestly affirms his heterosexuality, becomes Nancy Boy. Lucy, who occasionally recounts her once-only experience of magic mushrooms, is known, among other things, as 'Shroomhead. Probably worst of all is his name for Colette, shy about the disfiguring scars across her chest, who never talks about the childhood accident when she was peeled from the red-hot bars of an electric fire, her young bosom permanently desiccated. He calls her Char Grilled.

Donnie is high maintenance. He's not the type of man who can be left to himself at a party. Daphne would like to mingle but she stays by his side to keep him from becoming jealous of all the men who, given the slightest encouragement, would throw her to the floor and ravish her. She also has to guard against him visiting the bathroom and trousering their host's cute ceramic toothbrush holder.

'It's Tigger off *Winnie the Pooh*,' Donnie later tells her, giggling at his own daring, attempting to justify the theft.

Every time he has a bath he likes Daphne to wash his hair. She kneels at the side of the bath and rubs shampoo into his scalp, scrubbing around his carroty hairline. When she's ready to rinse she supports the back of his head and lowers him under the water. The kneeling hurts her knees and tires her back but Donnie seems to love this baptismal ritual; he closes his eyes and smiles.

Every few weeks she has to shave the twizzley ginger hairs that grow on the back of his neck. They stand at the bathroom sink and he takes his shirt off. She scooshes a blob of white foam into her hands and rubs it on his neck. Daphne thinks it's a pointless exercise; she's the only one who ever sees this secret part of his body.

If ever she wants to make a Spanish omelette she has to make two: one to eat that evening and one for Donnie to take to work the next day. It's a fiddly job getting the omelette in his plastic sandwich box and the box smells of garlic for days afterwards. How can he be bothered eating the same thing two days in a row? Daphne wonders. Donnie says he wants to make his workmates jealous with his home-made Spanish omelette while they eat their usual cheese, or occasionally, soap, sandwiches.

There are certain places Donnie will not go. He will not go to the theatre; theatre is 'a pile of wank' patronised only by poofs. He won't set foot inside any kind of museum; museums are for eggheads. Nor trendy coffee shops; they are taking the piss charging more than two quid for a tea bag dunked in a plastic cup of hot-ish water. Although he takes a keen interest in Daphne's undergarments he refuses, for fear of being branded a pervert, to enter what he calls a 'lingeree' shop. He doesn't do DIY shops or clothes shops or supermarkets, except of course for Asda. Even then, the Partick branch of Asda is out of bounds because his ex-wife, who he has not seen for six years, might be in there. He can occasionally be persuaded to go to the movies but he will not watch foreign language films, costume dramas, political thrillers, chick flicks, rom-coms or weepies, unless there is some kind of football content.

Donnie is obsessed with football. He pays for Daphne to have cable TV installed in her flat so that he can watch matches when he comes round. He takes pride in a comprehensive knowledge of the game and his team and laughs when Daphne calls him an anorak. He knows off the top of his head when, and by how many goals, his team has ever won a competition. He's intimately acquainted with players' details, their backgrounds and future prospects. He compiles databases of team statistics and applies complicated formulae to predict the outcome of each game. Sometimes he is right. Whenever he gives Daphne advice, for instance about one of her difficult students, it is always couched in footballing terms, counselling her to 'take control of the dressing room', or 'show them your championship medals'. One room of his flat is virtually filled with football memorabilia. Daphne sometimes finds him there, reading from his stack of fanatical fanzines, chuckling away to himself.

But Donnie chuckling is a lot easier than Donnie panicking. With drastically reduced medication his behaviour has been wild and unpredictable over the last few weeks. It is a temporary side effect and will stop when the chemicals settle down, Daphne tells herself, but it's embarrassing and often inconvenient.

They make arrangements to meet friends for dinner and half an hour before, Donnie decides he doesn't want to go. Daphne has to call off with a lame excuse that she knows they can hear in her voice. So, she makes a steak pie from scratch, and, just when she is cooling the perfectly golden crusted pie and transferring the buttery mash into an old-fashioned tureen, Donnie throws up and has to go to bed. Daphne brings him tea and he lies quietly sipping, only managing to get up when *Match of the Day* comes on.

They accept an invitation to go paintballing with Daphne's crowd. In the communal changing room the atmosphere is crazy. Everybody is talking loudly, bumping into each other, struggling into their kit: overall, chest shield and helmet, ammo belt and gun. Donnie is the first one dressed and ready to go. He produces a tube of something and carefully smears two even black lines under his eyes. One of the nicknames Daphne has given Donnie is Semper Apparatus, based on his predilection for being well equipped for every occasion. He is good to himself and spends many hours in sports shops eyeing, buying, and, when the opportunity presents itself, stealing pocket-sized products.

4

'Oh yeah!' says Carlsberg. 'Give us a shot of your warpaint, Donnie, that looks cool.'

Donnie hands it round and now they all look cool, even Nancy Boy. The battledress transforms Daphne's harmless pals into fierce warriors, handsome and heroic. Donnie looks especially sexy, Daphne thinks, as she imagines his face inches above hers in bed tonight. She makes a mental note to ask him to bring the warpaint.

As the instructor takes them down to the gate of the battlefield, Lucy starts a whooping rallying call and this is swiftly taken up by all of Green Platoon, as they have become. Their adversaries, Blue Platoon, a stag party of eight hung-over lads, are already at the gate. They have no enthusiasm for an opposing war cry and already Green Platoon have the psychological advantage. Striding forward, Donnie waves his gun in the air the way people do in the Middle East and the platoon follows his initiative.

After going through the tedious safety talk, 'protective equipment must not be removed at any time within the war zone,' the instructor tells both sides that the object of the game is to obtain the enemy's flag and plant it on the hill.

Exchange of fire is at first tentative and sporadic but quickly becomes reckless. Within ten minutes Daphne is grabbed from behind and pulled into thick bushes. She believes she has fallen foul of a kidnap attempt by the Blues and struggles as hard as she can, but her captor is Donnie.

She can tell immediately that something is up. He has taken a direct hit, his breastplate is splattered with blue paint but it's worse than that. The black under his eyes is wet, either with sweat or tears, Daphne is not keen to find out which.

'I can't do this, I'm just not …'

'Oh Donnie don't, please, not today. C'mon, we can't let the side down; we've just started! So you've been hit, it's okay, we've all been hit, I've been hit twice, I'm going to have a corker of a bruise tomorrow but we're winning! I got that big baldy guy a cracker, right on his side…'

'I'm going home.'

'What for? What's wrong with you?'

'I can't do this.'

'Okay, relax; nobody's making you do it. I'll come back with you to the changing room. Get a cup of tea or something out of the machine, you can wait for us there.'

'No. I'm leaving.'

'But Donnie, what about Mark and Lucy, how will they get home?'

'I don't give a shit about Mark and Lucy, I nearly took one in the eye, it missed me by a fraction.'

'But that's what the helmet's for! It's perfectly safe. D'you think they'd still be in business if their customers' eyeballs were regularly exploding? They wouldn't get insurance, the council would shut them down; think about it, be rational, Donnie. Lucy and Mark need a lift, how will they get back if we leave?'

'I didn't say you had to leave. Stay. Enjoy yourself.'

'How are you going to get home? We're in the middle of nowhere.'

'I'll get a taxi, I'll ...'

'A taxi?'

Everyone is gutted that Daphne has twisted her knee. It takes a few minutes to sort out alternative transport arrangements for Lucy and Mark, vital minutes on the field of battle. They wave them off as Daphne hops to the car with Donnie, who gallantly if a little inelegantly, lifts her poor twisted knee and supports her.

Although no one says it, Daphne feels like a deserter. Her comrades say nothing but suffer a humiliating defeat at the hands of the hung-over Blue Platoon. At college Daphne will have to wear an elastic bandage around her knee, and remember to hirple for a few days. Donnie nicknames her Gimpy. That night they have comforting, rather domestic sex. Daphne has forgotten all about the warpaint.

Donnie worries constantly that she will leave him. He talks about it all the time, more and more since he lowered the dose of the antidepressant. He mentions it at least once a day, saying she's bound to run off with someone else.

Daphne knows she's no supermodel but neither is she a toothless hag. She scrubs up well, her thick dark hair gathering in solid clumps around her heart-shaped face. With a push-up bra she can muster quite a respectable cleavage and hip length jackets work wonders on her chicken drumstick thighs. She favours pastel shades that don't try to compete with her high colouring: her cheeks are red and round like Santa's and with glittering green eyes and a flashing white smile she can be as vibrant or as irritating as a fruit machine. Before she met Donnie she had always suspected, although she would never say so, that she is beautiful.

Donnie says so, he tells her so often that she now accepts it as a given. But she's acting the innocent, he says, pretending to be unaware that men fancy her. Daphne concedes that she might occasionally encounter members of the opposite sex who are attracted to her, but what does he think she is?

He remains unconvinced of this argument and watches her like a hawk around her male friends. She makes an effort to be tactile with him in front of people so they get the message; so he gets the message. After sex he holds her so tight she can hardly breathe. As he kisses her neck and strokes her hair, she says soppy things to reassure him, waiting until he's asleep before unravelling his arms.

Sometimes she thinks: wouldn't it be nice to have a nice ordinary boyfriend, one who didn't constantly harp on that he was about to be chucked, instead of one who, if he were to keep up this unrelentingly needy, greedy, craziness, might find himself chucked.

And then he chucks her.

Chapter 2

Donnie arrives unexpectedly at Daphne's flat telling her they need to talk.

Daphne has occasionally used this expression and Donnie has always flown into a panic, taking it to mean that she is about to chuck him. She's even said it a few times purely for the fright value but Donnie has never played the 'need to talk' card. Daphne, now knowing how it feels to be the recipient, manages a smile.

With a sick feeling in her stomach she shows him into the living room. He won't take a cup of tea, thank you, or even a beer. He chooses a chair rather than on the couch beside her. In typical drama queen style he opens with a sensational statement.

'I love you. I'll always love you. But we have to stop seeing each other.'

Daphne holds her breath waiting for him to continue, to explain himself, but he has stopped.

'Donnie,' she says gently, 'what's all this about?'

This is the point where he should be pouring his heart out about a problem, with his health, or work, or with his family. Or even, surely not, thinks Daphne, some real or imagined problem between them. For instance, something along the lines of: he's just discovered he's impotent and can never give her children. Or, he has a wasting disease that will leave him in a wheelchair within five years, dead within ten. He won't let her witness his decline so, as painful as it will be, he's setting her free to find someone else, someone who isn't crippled. But if it is any of these, he's not saying.

'I told you. We can't be together.'

There is a long silence.

'I don't understand. What's going on? Are we splitting up?'

He replies immediately, no hesitation.

'Yes.'

'Yes? But why?'

'I can't have a relationship, not with you, not with anyone. I have to be on my own.'

'It's the pills. You're crashing off them, it's too quick.'

'It's not the pills.'

'But Donnie, I love you. There's no need for this. We can sort something out.'

'And *I* love *you*. We can't stay together.'

Daphne can't quite believe this, can't quite take it seriously, she feels like she's taking part in a rather ridiculous melodrama.

'But why not? Won't you miss me?'

'Miss you?'

The stage direction for the melodrama must read, *Donnie gives a harsh sardonic laugh*, because this is exactly what he does.

'Believe me, this is the hardest thing I've ever done. This is harder for me than it will be for you, you're the strong one, but we'll have to bear it.'

Cheesy as this sounds, it makes Daphne cry. Donnie hates it when Daphne cries. Now he tries to cheer her up.

'We've had a good innings, eh? A lot of good memories. You've been good to me, there's no doubt about it. We don't want to fall out, do we? Don't want to end up hating each other. Let's just leave it at that, D, shall we?'

Daphne sniffles, Donnie rams his fists deep into his anorak pockets and stares hard at the carpet. She doesn't believe it, and because she doesn't believe it, Daphne wants to be noble.

'If you love someone, set them free, that's what they say, isn't it?'

She has never actually heard anyone say this, she remembers it from a pop song, but it fits the situation perfectly. Donnie can only nod. He keeps pressing his lips hard together as if he's stifling an emotional outburst.

'Can I give you one last kiss?' he asks tenderly.

Daphne has a problem with this.

'Yes. No. Yes, but my breath stinks of garlic. I've just had my tea, I made soup and put in tons of garlic, I didn't know you were coming round.'

Despite her protestations Donnie sweeps her into his arms and gives her a long hard passionate snog. It is the first time ever in their relationship that he has disregarded Garlic Breath. In fact he appears to savour the fierce oniony tang of Daphne's mouth. After the kiss, he rests his head on her breast and listlessly runs his hand up and down her arm, fondly fondling her fleecy jumper.

*

Of course this is not the end of it.

The next day, in a daze, Daphne has to go to college and carry on as normal. The college where Daphne works is no ivory tower of stringent academic excellence. In the canteen there are laminated, wipe clean, place cards on the tables. They don't read, 'this table reserved' or, 'thank you for not smoking' they read, 'keep your feet off the table.' Not even *please* keep your feet off the table. This is the kind of place Daphne works.

Being the newest member of staff she doesn't get to choose which classes she will teach. She gets the classes no one else wants. Most of her students come from a background of drink or drugs, of crime or abuse. They are people of all ages who missed or messed up school, whose experience hasn't killed them yet and are starting over again. They are the most rewarding students Daphne has ever had.

They pester Daphne for essay results when she hasn't marked them yet, they complain if she takes too long a tea break and, except where they have a court appearance or visitation rights with their kids, they never miss a class. They learn fast and lap it up hungrily but the biggest challenge she faces is overcoming their illogical inverted snobbery.

God help the naive student who gets ideas above their station and uses a polysyllabic word. They are ridiculed, roasted, damned by the accusation of having swalleyed a dictionary. Last week she spent a long time trying to convince them of the power of a good vocabulary.

'In a few years when you need to have a lung removed because of all the fags you've smoked...'

A chorus of 'ooow' from the class interrupted her.

'Well, let's face it, every one of you smoke and you all know the consequences.'

Though she knew she shouldn't, as an ex-smoker herself Daphne couldn't help evangelising.

'You need to have confidence in the surgeon, to be sure that he knows what he's doing, don't you?'

'Too right, man,' Dan said, 'when ma brother got his leg aff he wis worried sick in case the guy took the wrang wan.'

'Heh Dan, tell him I'll buy his slippers aff him,' quipped Billy.

'Daphne, how d'yae know the surgeon's gonnae be a guy?' said Thomas, the shyest yet most astute member of the class.

'Oh, hands up to that one!' said Daphne, caught out. 'No reason why it couldn't be a woman.'

'Naw, but it wis a guy.'

'What was?'

'The guy that took ma brother's leg aff. He telt him it hud tae come aff, it was poisoned, aff a durty needle. It wis aw green and purple; pure stank man.'

Even without an extensive vocabulary Dan could paint a vivid picture.

'Anyway,' said Daphne trying to pull it back. She was beginning to lose the thread of what she'd been saying in the first place. 'So there you are, lying in hospital, coughing your guts up, spitting out bits of lung. They're getting you ready for theatre and the surgeon comes to discuss your treatment with you, to put you at your ease about the operation.'

At this point Daphne's shoulders sagged inwards, her hands were all chopping gestures and her voice became a nasal whine.

'Awright wee man? Waant me tae howk yir lung oot an 'at? Nae bother!'

The class laughed and seemed to take her point. While she had them on side Daphne asked, just as a matter of interest, if anyone maybe had a dictionary lying around at home. No one did. As far as they were concerned owning a dictionary was a pretentious affectation akin to holding your pinkie finger out whilst drinking tea.

'Y'know, you can get a dictionary out of these bargain bookshops for a couple of quid,' she told them.

'A couple of quid's a lot of money when you're on benefits,' said Jamie.

The nods and grunts from the rest of the class implied he represented a popular view.

'Och, your arse!' Daphne countered. This class appreciated plain speaking. 'How much do you pay for a packet of fags then, Jamie?'

'Eight pound.'

'Eight pounds? You'll get a not bad dictionary for eight pounds.'

'Aye, but you cannae smoke a dictionary.'

This is what Daphne's up against.

But today she is preoccupied with having been chucked and doesn't at first notice that the students are all present and correct, ready to begin the lesson, books and folders open, fully engrossed in studying their dictionaries.

Every one of her students has somehow managed to procure a dictionary. This makes her want to cry. Most of them have cheap pocket dictionaries but two lads have matching £12.99 ones. She doesn't enquire too closely about where these came from.

She introduces a game where everyone chooses three words from the dictionary and challenges the rest of the class to guess the meaning. The person nearest the dictionary definition wins the point. If no one successfully guesses it, the challenger gets the point but it has to be words they have a chance of getting. The atmosphere is tense with rivalry, and it's Daphne's job to guard against cheating: anyone surreptitiously looking up the word under their desk will be outed.

'Bumptious,' says Thomas.

'Bumptious. Good one,' says Daphne.

No one gets it.

'Never heard ay it,' says June, somewhat discouraged; she has been leading three points ahead up until now.

'Okay, fair enough, nobody wins that point then,' says Daphne, not wanting them to lose heart.

'But what does it mean?' everyone clamours.

Thomas, strictly adhering to the rules of the game, refuses to tell them.

'Eh, bumptious,' says Daphne. 'Well, it just means big-headed. Really it just describes a person who fancies themselves. Someone who's an arse.'

The class is going great. The students are getting their money's worth out of their dictionaries. After a few rounds everyone is skilfully wielding them to achieve maximum points. For a lovely half hour Daphne almost forgets that she has been chucked; that she no longer has a boyfriend; that she is not going to spend the rest of her life with Donnie, that she may never set eyes on him again. It is the mention of the word 'arse' that has reminded her. This can't be right, she thinks, not just like that, out of the blue for no good reason. She resolves to go round to his flat after work and sort it out with him. She must not dwell on it, now she has to get on with the class.

'If you're bumptious then you're arrogant, full of yourself,' she continues.

'Full of shit,' says Dan helpfully.

'Yes, something like that.'

'Hey Dan,' says Thomas, 'shut it, ya bumptious bastard.'

*

At afternoon tea break Daphne stays behind in class rather than face her colleagues. She gets a piece of A4 and draws a line down the middle: pros and cons. She can't think of a positive reason why she and Donnie should split up. Yeah, he's a bigot and an anorak and an old woman and a pain in the arse, but not all the time. The rest of the time he's interested in what she has to say, he always laughs at her jokes. Daphne never appears to bore him and he, except for his occasional bigoted rants, never bores her. He makes her laugh. He is the funniest man she has ever met, bar none. His conversation is fascinating and the main reason Daphne loves him.

She loves the way his brain is wired, his contagious crazy zeal for words and concepts, the way his thinking takes unprecedented routes and unpredictable jumps. In his eyes, shined and polished by his enthusiasm, she sees cerebral lightning crackling along unexplored pathways. She sees the lights clash and explode, the fireworks in his head. She knows he pays a price for this with his nerves and depressions and his borderline mental illness but this only makes the entertainment he offers her all the more valuable.

Daphne always feels sorry for the tired couples she sees in the pub with nothing to say to each other, both of them embarrassed, staring off or with hands mechanically scooping in and out of crisp packets, keeping their mouths busy. Daphne and Donnie talk about everything, constantly interrupting each other, finishing each other's sentences, gossiping, bickering, joking, laughing, even when they're arguing they laugh. They are best friends.

Donnie can be an extremely harsh critic, he says bluntly what he thinks but he is also very free with his compliments. Every day, several times a day, he will say something to show how much he appreciates her. He compliments her cooking, how clever she is, how fit she is. 'You're the best bird I've ever had,' he says. He calls her 'curvy girl' when she moans about the size of her bum. 'You really know how to fill a bra,' he says admiringly, staring at her breasts.

She knows he means it, he has an irrepressible sex drive that perfectly matches her own and he is always gentlemanly enough, after an impromptu fumble in her bra while she is cooking or watching TV, to do up her buttons for her.

Some nights Daphne wakes up and is frightened to touch his white moonlit shoulder. She knows that this kind of happiness can't last forever and she dreads the night she might find his shoulder cold and lifeless. She cries when she explains this to him and to cheer her up he says, 'don't worry about it, D, you'll die before I do.' Daphne can't imagine not touching his shoulder again and it is for this reason that she can't countenance this splitting up nonsense.

In the morning, after the night horrors have passed, she likes to watch him get dressed. She watches him put on shirt and tie and the boring anorak, disguising himself as a wee ordinary joe: unexceptional, unattractive to other women. As he bends to kiss her goodbye Daphne smears her juice on his face, marking him as her exclusive territory. Despite his metrosexual face lotions and hair gel and aftershave, he lets her do this. He enjoys her doing this.

The class come back all together in a noisy smoke-smelling crowd. They are keen to get on with the game and flick through their dictionaries, hooting when they find a particularly good word.

'Oh ya dancer! Nane ay yeez'll get this wan!'

'Aw man, ah'v fun a total beazer!'

Daphne crumples the sheet of paper and throws it in the bin.

*

She phones before she goes round. For the first time ever she can't just pop round. Already their relationship has changed, but, she has to remind herself, it hasn't changed, it has potentially ended.

He's a bit cagey on the phone.

'What for, Daphne?'

'Just to talk.'

She forces herself to ignore the reluctance in his voice and after a few minutes he says she can come round. As soon as she walks into the room she understands his reluctance. This is not the time to talk.

'Oh sorry Donnie, I didn't realise Rangers were playing tonight. We can do this another time.'

'No no,' he says, and he crosses to the telly. But he doesn't turn it off or even put in a tape to video it, he merely turns the sound down.

'Cup Winners' Cup,' he says.

'What, finals?'

'Well, no. Qualifying round ...'

'Yeah yeah,' Daphne says quickly, not wanting to see him squirm.

'Cup of tea?'

'Cheers.'

He turns the volume up again, louder so he can hear it from the kitchen, and twice while making the tea, he rushes through when it seems like Rangers will score. They don't and this vaguely satisfies Daphne. He gives her a giant mug, her hands are shaking and she's scared she'll spill it. Donnie brings from the fridge a bar of fruit and nut chocolate the size of an A4 envelope. Daphne jumps when he smashes it off the table to break it up. She lifts a piece but it is cold and sharp edged and she can't eat it. She hasn't eaten a thing all day.

'I haven't eaten a thing all day,' says Donnie, popping a piece of chocolate in his mouth. He turns the TV volume down again and sits opposite her, smiling. He is waiting for her to say something.

'Donnie, I don't understand what this is about. We're happy together, aren't we? We have good times, good laughs, there's no problem with sex or anything, is there?'

'Yes, yes, yes and no.'

Hearing the word 'no' panics her and it is a second before she realises that this is actually the right answer, the answer she was looking for.

'Well what is it then?'

'Daphne I thought I explained all this to you last night.'

'You haven't explained anything! What the hell is going on, Donnie, is there someone else, is that it?'

'Calm down. Please don't shout at me.'

'Sorry.'

Donnie is taking deep breaths, a sure sign that he's stressed. He lowers his head and breathes deeply before he begins to speak.

'You're right.'

Daphne quickly puts down the massive cup before she drops it. Her hands don't feel strong enough to hold it. She leans forward, desperate, terrified, to hear what he has to say.

'It is the antidepressant. Coming off it has made me realise I'm not able to hold down a relationship. You deserve better and I have to be alone. There's no one else, it's not about that. My nerves are shattered, my blood pressure's through the roof, I'm a mess.'

'I know, baby, I'm sorry.'

His face is red, almost as red as his hair and he looks as if he might explode. Daphne wants to sit beside him, to hold him but it's probably better just to let him get it all out.

'I've come to a point where I realise that for my own health, my sanity, I have to be on my own. I have to save myself. Believe it or not I think I'm worth saving.'

'What's going to happen to you? I'm frightened of what you might do.'

'Well, *que sera*. What's for you won't go by you, I'm a great believer in that. I'm fine, I'll be fine if I'm left to myself.'

A wave of impotence overwhelms Daphne. Her spine is sagging trying to shore up the dead weight of her body. Her hands are limp, her arms dangle uselessly at her side, even the muscles that hold up her head are struggling. This must be what it feels like to have a stroke, she thinks. At least she still has the power of speech. And her tear ducts maintain normal function.

'Donnie, you are the biggest and best part of my life. I don't know what I'll do without you. You're my ginger baby, remember? I can't be without you.'

Donnie makes no reply. Daphne forces her head into an upright position. The new Rangers striker, their most expensive player ever, is about to take a penalty and Donnie's eyes are glued to the screen. He shoots, he misses, and Daphne is glad.

'This is no use, you're not even listening.'

Daphne gathers her bag.

'I am listening, I heard what you said.'

She zips up her fleece and leans forward, about to stand.

'I'm the biggest and best part of your life. I'm your ginger baby, of course I remember. You can't be without me. But Daphne, you have to be. It's for the best.'

'Who's best?'

'Your best. I'm no good for you, you can do a lot better than me.'

'Please Donnie, don't do this, please.'

Daphne's tear ducts are working at full capacity now, punctuating her speech with sobs.

'No Daphne, it's over.'

'But Donnie, I'm fri-fri-frightened.'

'Please don't make this any harder for me. And don't contact me; don't pressure me. The way I'm feeling, anything could happen.'

They sit in silence for a while, both watching the football until it is half time.

'I've made up a box of your stuff, your pants and perfume and that. It's in the hall, I'll just get it.'

Chapter 3

Daphne is still awake at three am. When she looks at the clock again it's twenty past four, then ten past six, then it's time to get up. She considers phoning in sick but she has a class assessment today. Even though she's doused them in milk her cornflakes still look razor sharp, they'll cut her mouth to ribbons. The thought makes her taste blood at the back of her throat so she pours them down the toilet. The cornflakes separate and appear to swim through the cloudy milky water like sperm in semen. It turns her stomach. She can only take tea. She's living on tea and pints of water; she needs it to replace the tears and hot sweats.

The phone rings while Daphne is in the shower. He will have woken up alone and realised in the cold light of day, the mistake he's making. He'll want to speak to her before she goes to work, no doubt he'll be all clingy and insecure. Daphne puts one soapy foot on the floor and curls her toes to stop from slipping on the tiles. Her feet make loud frantic slapping noises as she rushes out of the bathroom. She has to reach it before the machine kicks in. He won't speak to the machine.

It's too late the machine has started. Daphne's recorded voice, unaware of the urgency of the situation, goes through its usual spiel with a careless audacity that now sounds rude. Dripping shampoo is giving her white sideburns and she grabs a tea towel and wipes them in a smooth movement while striding naked up the hall.

It's her mum. Not Donnie. He hasn't changed his mind, Daphne remains chucked.

Her mum is prattling: how hot Australia is, what a nightmare the flight was, how she's settling in, how grown up Albert's children have become, how disappointed she is to have missed Daphne, how much this call is costing, inconsequentialities. Daphne, soap sliding down her leg, doesn't pick up.

At work she avoids her colleagues by taking tea breaks when she knows they'll be in class. In the afternoon the assessment goes well. All the students receive remediation but that's normal. One lad, Gerry argues because she has marked him down for his spelling.

'Gerry, *their* is possessive, belonging to them: the stadium belongs to Glasgow Celtic. It is their stadium. *There* is location, a place: that place there. The way to remember it is it's spelt like where.'

An old song pops into her head, a song her mum used to sing when she and Albert were kids, before Dad died, before the rest of the family left for Australia without her, before she was chucked. Daphne, suddenly a bit light-headed, is finding it difficult to concentrate, and somehow it doesn't really matter. She begins to sing the old song.

'I saw a mouse,
Where?
There on the stair.
Where on the stair?
Right there.
A little mouse with clogs on
Well I declare
Going clip clippity clop on the stair
Right there.'

The class beg her to sing it again. She refuses. One or two of the older students know the words and begin to sing, those who don't, wanting in on the action, hum along. Gerry goes out on to the stairwell and sings as loud as he can. The whole college must be able to hear him; the Head of Department must be able to hear him, the Principal too, probably. He is laughing madly and Daphne wonders if she hasn't let it go too far.

'It's his methadone,' explains Thomas, 'he gets his script at twelve o'clock, it makes him mental for a while.'

Daphne wonders: she isn't on methadone; she isn't on antidepressants, why does she feel mental?

*

The mental feeling dissipates on the way home; Daphne is so exhausted she can't be bothered with Asda tonight. She's too tired for food anyway. She's expecting Donnie to be at the door of her building on the front steps waiting for her with a sheepish smile that says, 'what was I thinking?'

He's not.

Now she's hoping for a letter through her door, or a message on the answering machine and she's fumbling for her keys as she approaches. As she rummages in her bag a flying mouse narrowly misses entering her handbag and lands on the step beside her. This has no immediate effect on Daphne. She continues groping for her keys and only when she has them does she bend down to examine what the flying thing really is.

It really is a mouse, a flying mouse that appears to be critically injured. It is lying on its back with its legs jerking forward as though it might jump to its feet like a breakdancer. On its left side there is blood and some innards. Daphne screams.

A head pokes out of a window above.

There is a whispered shout of, 'Sorry!' Identifying the head as Daphne's downstairs neighbour Pierce, Daphne screams and screams.

'Shhh, I'm coming down. '

When the door opens Daphne lashes out and catches Pierce squarely on the jaw with her fist. The shock runs up her arm like electricity and the pain in her knuckles is excruciating. She is too weak to put up much resistance when Pierce grabs her arms and pins them at her side. Daphne is relieved she is unable to land another punch but she is no calmer.

21

'Oh my God. Daphne, I'm so sorry.'

'You sick bastard!' she screams into his face, spittle flying. 'What the fuck are you doing? What have you done to this mouse? It's only a wee defenceless thing. Look at it! Why are you torturing it?'

Daphne's crying is loud and uncontrollable. She cries so hard she begins to hiccup and she finds she's unable to stop crying and hiccupping. For the first time since she was a child, she has worked herself into a frenzy of crying.

The world has gone mad, her crazy boyfriend has chucked her; her crazy neighbour has chucked a mouse out of his window. She sang a song today about a mouse and now there is a mouse on the stair. She has a quick squint at the mouse's feet to see if it has clogs on but it doesn't, thank God. The mouse is writhing in agony, with its insides out, clearly dying, slowly, in hideous pain, there on the stair right there.

'Come in off the street, Daphne, please, I can explain. C'mon up the stairs.'

Pierce tries to haul Daphne into the tenement building but she resists by collapsing; now he has to hold her up or she'll fall.

Pierce is a big man, broad-chested, wide-faced. Daphne knows he fancies himself as a handsome man but she has always considered him to be just beyond handsome. Only just; perhaps a centimetre. It hardly matters in his big broad body but it is in the fine detail that she notices it: his nose is about a centimetre too wide, his hands a centimetre too pudgy. As she sags in his arms she notices that he stinks into the bargain, a sour smell of stale roll-up cigarettes and cabbage and lager and sex and hashish. It's teatime but he's unshaven and looks as though he's just got out of bed. He's trying to pull her away from the mouse.

'I can't leave him. I have to help him.'

She's wailing now.

'Okay, we won't leave him, I'll bring him in, but let's get upstairs.'

Pierce slowly lets go of his grip on Daphne, still with his arms around her in case she falls. He bends down and gently picks up the mouse. Blood is dripping between his fingers.

'Don't hurt him, please.'

'It's okay,' Pierce is whispering, 'he's all right.'

Daphne tries not to look as he lifts the mouse. She wishes she hadn't seen Pierce, with his too fat fingers, trying to discreetly tuck the mouse's entrails back in.

Daphne follows Pierce into his flat, this is an emergency, his flat is nearest and the door is open. Pierce lifts a green woolly jumper off the back of the couch and wraps the mouse in it. She is surprised to find that despite his hashhead lifestyle and body odour, his flat is beautiful.

'That'll keep him nice and warm, it's the best thing for shock. We'll see if he'll maybe take a wee saucer of milk. He'll be right as rain, wait and see, he'll be skiddling about the place in no time.'

'Why did you throw a mouse out of the window, Pierce, why? What goes on in that sick head of yours? You are scary man, fucking scary.'

'I didn't throw it out the window, it must have jumped!'

'Oh please!'

'I'm telling you, look!'

Pierce lays the mouse down on top of the coffee table wrapped in the jumper like a baby in swaddling clothes and drags Daphne to the open window. There on the outside ledge is a Perspex box.

'It's a humane mousetrap. I got it at the hardware shop. It was bloody expensive, I could have just got the old wooden type of mousetrap but I didn't want the mouse breaking its back or its leg or whatever. You bait the trap and when the mouse goes in the door comes down behind it without harming it, see? Like that.'

'Why is it on the window ledge?'

'Because the fucking stupid mouse ...'

Daphne pulls her head back as though she's been assaulted.

'Sorry, sorry, I'm sorry, right? The poor wee mouse walked into the trap the minute I baited it. It usually just comes out at night. You're supposed to take it at least three miles away to release it, otherwise it finds its way back, but I was knackered, I'd been out all night.'

'Yes, out all night,' says Daphne. She leaves Pierce at the window and turns to nursing the mouse. He has stopped kicking his legs. She can feel his wee heartbeat in her hand.

'Well, I was tired. Too tired to get up and walk three miles. But that box is small, I was worried the mouse would run out of air in that wee confined space. I didn't want it to suffocate. But I couldn't let it out again, could I? He might wise up and not go near the trap again. Mice learn fast, that's why they use them in behavioural science.'

'You are so full of shit.'

'So I put it on the window ledge. I thought if I opened the hatch it would let the mouse breathe and I would know where to get it when I was ready. How was I to know it would fucking jump!'

'You're so incompetent you can't even be trusted with a wee mouse.'

'Well, Doctor Fucking Doolittle, what would you have done then, eh?'

'I would have got off my arse and took it three miles away instead of forcing it into a suicide attempt!'

The good thing about the shouting is that at least Daphne has stopped crying. 'Right, okay, you didn't mean it, there's no point in arguing. We need to get him to a vet, right now,' she says.

'Where is the nearest vet?' says Pierce, scrabbling around under the phone table, 'I'll look it up. Vending machines, vermin control, should have phoned them in the first place, veterinary supplies, right, here is it, veterinary surgeons. Looks like the nearest one is Partick.'

But the mouse's breakdancing days are over. Daphne has already gently placed the green woolly jumper on the coffee table and once more started to cry. It's no longer loud hysterical howling. It is a quiet submissive weeping that lasts a very long time.

*

Donnie hasn't put a letter through her door and there are no messages on her answering machine. But she must keep her distance, play it cool, let him come out of it in his own time.

He's coming off the pills too quickly. His noradrenaline and dopamine levels are probably all messed up, she's been reading up on it, he probably isn't producing enough serotonin yet. The important thing is not to upset him, he said it himself and Daphne thinks about it constantly: *anything could happen.* Daphne doesn't want anything to happen. She emails him every day, jokes off the Internet, to keep his pecker up. What harm can it do?

A man walks into a theatrical agency.

'I'm a talented actor, singer, dancer and comedian and I'd like a career in show business.'

'Certainly sir,' says the agent, 'and what's your name?'

'It's Penis Van Lesbian,' says the man.

'I'm sorry, sir, but you'll never make it in show business with a name like that. The best advice I can give you is to change your name.'

A year late the agent receives a cheque for fifty thousand dollars and a letter which reads: Dear Bob, here is your commission on my latest hit TV show. By the way, thanks for all your advice. Yours sincerely, Dick Van Dyke.

She can't sleep. The T-shirt she wears in bed is Donnie's and smells of him. The sheets smell of him. From his pillows stuffed with a hot water bottle she makes a Donnie stand-in and cuddles it tight. She spends her night staring at the ceiling, wondering what he's doing right now. How is he coping without her to wash his hair? And what about his twizzley bits? He can't shave them himself.

Never employ a dwarf with learning difficulties – it's not big and it's not clever.

No one at college suspects a thing. She laughs and jokes with her colleagues whenever she can't avoid them; she marks essays, arguing with her students and her boss over the grades. Except to work and to Asda, she stops going out. She wanders round Asda on her way home, not buying anything. She lets the machine take her calls and doesn't return them.

The smell of Donnie eventually fades. Now the bed only smells of Daphne's nights alone; of sweat and oily hair and toe jam and lady juice and unwashed bum. It's so pungent that sometimes she emerges from under the covers gasping for breath. But it's comforting.

It'll blow over, she thinks. He's never gone as far as chucking her before, that's a shocker, but she knows it's only the medication, or lack of it. Four years ago, before he started the antidepressants, Donnie sometimes spent the entire weekend in bed, sad and nervous, saying she should leave him, that he was no good for her. Daphne's response was not to leave but to climb in beside him until he relaxed and fell asleep. He always recovered. This chucking her and having to be alone carry-on is just a new variation on his old black weekends.

A man goes into the doctor.

'Doctor doctor, I can't stop deep-frying things. Last night I was going to have a nice salad when I had this overwhelming urge to batter and then deep-fry it. Before I knew what I was doing I had rustled up a beer batter and was dipping everything in it: the lollo russo, vine-ripened cherry tomatoes, radicchio, Parmesan shavings, the lot. It tasted disgusting but this morning I found myself battering my Rice Krispies and throwing them in the chip pan, I'm obsessed, doctor, I even tried to deep-fry my mobile phone! You've got to help me, please.'

'I know exactly what's wrong with you.'

'Oh thank God, doctor, what is it?'

'You're frittering your life away.'

Daphne doesn't know whether he gets the emails, he never replies.

She wonders if she's frittering her life away.

Chapter 4

Daphne sits alone in the canteen at lunchtime but she has no appetite. She's bought a caramel custard but doesn't fancy it, she swirls the yellow goo around the ribbon of caramel until the two colours merge to a shade of taupe that makes her feel sick. Magda, Jo and Carol all come in together, Carol in her signature brown. She wears tan spiky-heeled boots, chocolate velvet trousers and a chestnut-coloured low-cut top. She looks like a multi-hued jobby.

Not for the first time, Daphne wonders what age Carol is. She could be in her thirties but it's hard to tell. Sometimes, when they've run out of students to slate and sit staring into their empty mugs, bracing themselves for returning to their classes, Daphne wants to ask. Instead she fishes. She initiates nostalgia chats, reminiscing about pop star heartthrobs of their youth. Magda, the oldest, talks Robbie Williams, Jo remembers Westlife but Carol keeps her own counsel on her teenage tastes. Daphne tries landmark events like the Twin Towers or the Arab Spring or, in desperation, surely she couldn't be that old, Charles and Diana's wedding, but Carol doesn't bite.

Going by her figure, Carol could be a teenager. Her long legs connect effortlessly with her tight bum, her tiny waist a perfect plinth for a top shelf of big sticky-out breasts. Her hair is long and fabulous, too. Her shaped eyebrows are dark but Carol boasts that the hair on her head is not less than eight shades of blonde: Baby, Ash, Honey, Californian, Ice, Strawberry, Scandinavian and Sandy. She spends one hundred and seventy pounds every six weeks on her 'T-bar': about two square inches around the crown of her head and her parting. But six weeks isn't long enough for grey to emerge, if there is any there, and this annoys Daphne.

Carol is single but very sniffy about men. She declines politely, even flirtatiously, when bald or fat or ugly men try to chat her up. But at break time, in the company of Jo and Magda and Daphne, Carol scoffs imperiously at the losers who imagined they had a chance with her. This confuses Daphne because, despite her figure and hair and clothes, Carol has a face like a bulldog licking sick off a thistle. Underneath the expensive brown patina of Clinique make-up, Carol's skin is lined and saggy. Perhaps she *is* thirty but just not wearing well, she smokes and virtually never eats. Perhaps she's fifty.

Based on a foolproof system, Daphne believes herself to be an excellent judge of character. On being introduced to new people she encounters one of four responses: fellow lecturers, usually of the left wing socialist type, pretend that it's perfectly all right to be called Daphne and demonstrate this by going out of their way to use her name at every available opportunity.

'So you teach English, Daphne? And how do you find it, Daphne? Daphne, don't you find the students are woefully ig-norant and immensely stupid, Daphne? Of course it's not their fault, Daphne, it's their background, Daphne, and lack of fund-ing, and poor housing, Daphne.'

Others say nothing but with a widening of the eyes, a tilt of the head and a sad smile they communicate their sympathy, no one deserves to be named Daphne. Students are the most honest. Some of them laugh out loud. The fourth response is, 'Oh, how unusual!/ quaint!/ pretty!/ charming!' Carol is one of these.

Please God don't let Carol have a date this weekend, Daphne prays. She doesn't know if she can stop from blurting the truth if Carol asks her what she and Donnie are up to this weekend. But God isn't listening.

'What are you and Donnie up to this weekend?' Carol enquires.

It's not even as if she's actually interested. She only asks so that she can bum about what she's up to. She can't ask Jo or Magda, they're married so they only cook, clean and get school uniforms ready. This is why she picks on Daphne.

'Staying in. We're just going to have a quiet weekend.'

The lie comes easily. Daphne doesn't go red or cry. It's not a lie, she thinks, we are going to have a quiet weekend; me in my house alone and crying and Donnie in his house alone and off his head.

'Again? Phew, your social life is a whirl.'

'Donnie's tired, he's got a big project at work, he's been working late, he…'

Daphne is beginning to make things up, her face is getting red, she can feel her throat get tight.

'You know Daphne, you're as bad as us,' says Jo, 'you might as well be married with kids.'

'I've got to go to a dinner party,' moans Carol. 'No way out of it, Cynthia's rescheduled twice already to accommodate everyone, I have to go.'

'It can't be that bad, getting your dinner made for you, sitting getting drunk, don't have to wash the dishes or anything,' says Magda. 'I bet the food'll be good too.'

'Oh yes, I suppose so,' says Carol in the bored voice she uses when she's bumming. 'She's doing salmon. Caught it herself on one of these corporate days out with clients, she's a manager with the Royal Bank. It weighs eighteen pounds apparently, some kind of company record. She's an excellent cook but she's had it in the freezer three weeks now. If she doesn't cook it this weekend it'll go off. I've no choice, I have to go.'

'You don't have to do anything you don't want to do Carol,' says Jo kindly. They all know that Carol never does anything she doesn't want to do.

'Oh no but I have to, Cynthia's got a bad leg.'

'Sorry?'

'One leg shorter than the other,' Carol lowers her voice and patiently explains, 'she was born that way, she's handicapped. I couldn't possibly refuse her invitation.'

'Carol, she's a bank manager with the strength to land an eighteen-pound salmon, she'll take it on the chin if you cancel. Don't be so bloody patronising, I thought you said she was a friend?' says Daphne.

'Oh! No doubt you'd tell her to stop bothering you with her gimpy leg and her rotten stinking fish but I'm not like you, Daphne.

And besides, it wouldn't just be Cynthia I was letting down, she's set me up with one of her friends.'

'Aha! So now we come to the real reason why you're going!' says Magda, jumping in to the fray.

'He's a vet. Gerald, his name is.'

'Where does he practice? Daphne could bring him her flying mice.'

'Cynthia says he's based in an abattoir.'

'Oh, so he doesn't do dogs and stuff, then?' asks Jo, slightly disappointed.

'No, not in an abattoir,' explains Magda, who is a vegetarian, 'he won't do puppies or fluffy kittens. It's a manky slaughterhouse where the animals are pissing and shitting themselves, knowing they're about to be murdered.'

'Magda, stop,' says Daphne, 'I'm feeling a bit rough.'

'Where they queue to be murdered by a bolt through the brain and have their guts ripped out.'

'Please,' begs Daphne, 'I'm going to heave.'

'Don't be ridiculous,' counters Carol, laughing, 'he's not a murderer, he's a vet. Vets look after animals, he's in Disease Control.'

'Carol,' says Magda, 'wise up. Gerald's job is to separate the terrified pissing shitting *healthy* animals from the terrified pissing shitting *diseased* ones.'

'Still and all,' says Jo, obviously impressed, 'a vet.'

*

Another early morning phone call, another slippery dash from the shower, but this time Daphne gets there before the machine and something makes her hold back. It's her mother; she was right to hesitate. Once again Mum is bright and breezy, chattering about her new home with Daphne's big brother, Albee, and his wife and kids. Albert has converted his basement into her granny flat. She has her own kitchen and bathroom, her own air conditioning, which is just as well because she wouldn't last ten minutes without it, her own television although God knows she hasn't had a chance to watch it she's so busy with the kids and anyway Australian TV is so full of swearing, even the adverts, can Daphne believe that they actually allow swearing on the adverts?

Daphne smiles, she's been so busy missing Donnie she hasn't thought about missing Mum. She's going to have to speak to her, but not now. She'll wait until Donnie is well again, until they're back together. Then she can laugh and gossip with Mum.

Daphne wakes the next morning in a hurry. It's only quarter past four but she braces herself and puts the light on. Now she knows what she must do. She can't believe it hasn't occurred to her before now. While she was half dozing, running over and over again in her mind everything that has happened, something Donnie said hit her like an anvil. *You deserve better.*

The significance of these words stir in Daphne a wave of pity for Donnie. He has spent his life unloved. He once told her that at school he was small, freckly, specky, smelly, bugsy, but worst of all, red-haired. A ginger nut, a carrot heid, a Bunsen burner, a ginguy. Nobody loves a ginger baby, he said, that's why she gave him the nickname.

It's so obvious to her now. The antidepressants have, for years, masked Donnie's total lack of self-worth. You deserve better, that's what he said.

She begins a letter.

Chapter 5

Dear Donnie,

How are you? I hope you're feeling better. Please try to remember baby, the bad times always blow over, always, and life is always sweet again.

Think back to when you used to have your black weekends. It's the same kind of thing and no wonder: you're coming off four years of medication. Please Donnie, don't shut me out. You say that nobody loves a ginger baby, but I love you. You deserve to be loved. I think about you all the time and worry. I send you love rockets that explode above your head and fall like kisses on your face while you're sleeping.

Please phone me Donnie, if only to let me know that you're okay and that you haven't forgotten me. My love for you is unconditional.

I will always be your
Daphne.

At twenty past eight the letter is finally finished. She's going to be late for work but it'll be worth it. In the departmental office she smiles at the secretaries. She sets exercises for her class to do and while they're busy she re-reads it. She's not one hundred per cent sure about the last line, is it too possessive? Perhaps she should go with something a bit chirpier: *Catch yae Versace!* Or *See yah, wouldn't want to be yah!*

At the postbox, after she has kissed the envelope, her heart is pumping and her spine feels like jelly as her fingers enter the mouth of the box and then, no going back, lets it drop inside. Immediately she feels better, a stout sense of having done the right thing. In years to come they'll laugh about this. All she can do now is wait.

The next day she skips the Asda run in case he phones. It was a first class stamp so he should have received it. The day after that she also comes straight home, he'll definitely have got it by now. The day after that she does just quickly nip into Asda because she's run out of milk but she's home in no time. The day after that is Saturday so if he doesn't phone by lunchtime he's not going to phone. On Sunday afternoon she phones him.

She can picture him lying in the bedroom with the blinds down. As she listens to the impotent *bring bring* of the unanswered phone, in her imagination she is in bed beside him, running her hand across his brow, brushing his hair from his face.

On Sunday night he phones her back.

'Daphne, you phoned me.'

'Yes, I…'

'I know it was you. Don't try and deny it. I checked 1471.'

'What d'you mean, Donnie?'

'Why did you phone me? What's wrong?'

'Nothing's wrong, well, other than the fact that we're apart. Did you get my letter?'

'What letter?'

'I sent you a letter. I posted it a couple of days ago. You should have got it by now.'

'I haven't opened any mail. Those neds found out it was me who squirted them with piss. They put a lit newspaper through my letter box.'

'Oh my God Donnie, that's terrible! Are you okay?'

'Well it's doing nothing for my nerves. But it'll take more than a couple of neds to torch me. I've fitted a metal box on this side of the letter box. They can't do any damage, the paper just burns itself out.'

Daphne had warned him there would be repercussions from the Super Soaker incident. She told him it would make him a target but now is not the time to say so. This kind of behaviour is all part of his illness, classic Donnie siege mentality.

'Well, the letter is probably in there.'

'You promised me you wouldn't contact me.'

'But Donnie, it doesn't …'

'Daphne, don't pressure me. I've told you, I don't know what could happen.'

'I won't pressure you, baby.'

'You'd better not come round here, stalking me or becoming some sort of bunny boiler. I'll get the police to you, don't make me have to do that.'

'Donnie. Calm down, pet. Just read the letter, eh? That's all I wanted to say, just read it. And phone me when you're feeling better. I miss you.'

'Daphne, I'm not going to read it, you can't make me.'

'I'm not trying to make you, I just wanted to…'

'And anyway, if they haven't burnt it by now, I'm going to shred it. You think you know it all Daphne but you don't, you just don't know.'

'I know, baby, I mean that I don't know, of course I don't, but it's okay Donnie honestly, take your time. I won't come round and I won't phone you I promise.'

'No, because I'll get the police! I mean it.'

Daphne knows she can't cry or respond to the threat; it will only intensify his hysteria.

'Just get well, Donnie. I love you.'

But he has already hung up.

No matter how she looks at it, whatever spin she puts on it, the phone call did not go well. The thing about getting the police was shocking and under normal circumstances would be a horrible wounding thing to say but it's the mention of the shredder which is the most upsetting. He'll shred everything, shredding till his fingers bleed, feverishly shoving through her handmade valentine cards with the glued-on stars and tissue paper, the funny rhymes she made up, the photos, all their photos. He'll slice their life into thin strips of rubbish for vermin to nest in.

*

Daphne is very good. Of course she worries constantly, but there really is nothing she can do. She's angry and frustrated and frightened but mostly she's lonely without him. It's hard but she often reminds herself that if it's this hard for her, how tough must it be for him? Paranoid, miserable, suffering alone. But if he can hack it so can she. At least in their separate pain they're sharing the experience. Daphne doesn't care how long it takes for him to get better, she'll wait. At least when he gets better he'll realise how much she loves him. She'll have proved without a doubt her love and loyalty even unto letter-shredding and police-calling. He'll see that despite everything she has waited for him, she hasn't taken up with other men. Although she worries that he might have topped himself she resists the impulse to phone or call round; for two weeks she is really good. Then she sees him in Asda.

Her first instinct is to hide because he'll think that she's stalking him, that she's become a bunny boiler after all. But then, this is the Partick Asda, the Asda he refuses to set foot inside for fear for bumping into his ex-wife, there's no way he can accuse her of stalking him in here. He is coming towards her. He looks a changed man, the separation really has done him the world of good, he looks relaxed and he's smiling as he walks towards her. And now he's laughing, he hasn't seen Daphne yet so who is he laughing with? Oh yes, now Daphne sees, he's laughing with his ex-wife. He's shopping and laughing with the woman he supposedly hasn't spoken to in six years.

Chapter 6

Daphne is squeezing a pineapple, feeling its bottom for ripeness, when she hears his voice. It's not so much that she hears his voice, more that she feels it, cutting through the supermarket sounds: the mumsy music of Radio Asda, a squeaky-wheeled trolley, the hum of the refrigeration cabinets, a wheedling child, a frazzled mother. Though he's not speaking loudly, his voice blares at her like a factory hooter. She can't pick out the words but she can tell from the tone he's in a good mood. Bertha, his ex-wife, his shopping partner, is responding to what he's saying, she's cracking jokes too and Donnie is laughing.

Trapped here in the fruit aisle with Donnie and Bertha advancing on her, like in a bad dream, Daphne wants to move but is paralysed. This is too much information, too contradictory, it doesn't make sense and if it did, its meaning would be dreadful. They haven't seen her so they're not avoiding her but they don't make it as far as pineapples. Donnie turns left into dairy goods. Bertha had headed back to tomatoes. They have split up, working as a team, buying dinner together, in exactly the same way Daphne and Donnie buy dinner. Daphne knows his next stop will be the beer aisle.

She gets there before him, her mind working faster than she can properly think through. San Miguel is on a buy-one-get-one-free, he'll go for that. She's waiting for him when he turns into the aisle. His face lights with automatic polite recognition, as if he has unexpectedly bumped into a colleague or a distant cousin but realisation makes an ugly mask of his face. He shakes his head sadly, disappointed, Daphne has somehow let him down. She tries to speak but her brain is not working in words, it's trying to process what she's seeing, trying to find some interpretation that will makes this acceptable.

Bertha walks up the aisle as, Daphne remembers, she has done once before. Donnie, staring hard at Daphne, puts out a hand to curb Bertha's progress, to protect her from Daphne. From Daphne? Then he turns and walks briskly, resisting breaking into a run, out of the shop. Bertha, bemused but apparently understanding that something is wrong, takes a passive look at Daphne and follows him.

Daphne's knees buckle. She falls on the floor below a pyramid of Asda own brand lager. A woman stops and looks at her.

'Are you okay, hen?'

Daphne can't answer, the power of speech has not returned. She tries to get to her feet but the shop is revolving around her. This is embarrassing, she thinks, people will think I'm an alcoholic.

'Just stay where you are, hen, don't try to stand up, I'll get somebody.'

But she does try to stand up. She's not making it and then she feels an arm around her ribs lifting her from behind. She is scooped up effortlessly. It is not entirely an unpleasant feeling. This fainting sensation is infinitely preferable to the sick panic she felt a moment ago.

A spotty youth with an Asda badge that identifies him as 'Dale' has returned with the woman. The person who has pulled her from the floor comes round in front of her and is dusting down her jacket. It's Pierce. This strikes Daphne as funny, funny ha ha as well as funny peculiar that he should be in the shop at this time and see this.

'It's okay, I know her, she's my neighbour, I'll get her home.'

'Are you sure?' says Dale, more to Daphne than Pierce.

She nods weakly. Dale obviously thinks she's mentally deficient. Daphne doesn't mind being mentally deficient. She allows herself to be led outside by Pierce and marched to the front of the taxi queue. Calmly and authoritatively Pierce calls through the people standing patiently, their kiddy buggies dangerously top heavy with loaded plastic bags, saying, 'Emergency! Coming through!' The crowd appear to take him for an undercover store detective who has arrested a mentally deficient shoplifter. This impression is strengthened when he puts his hand on her head and firmly ducks it as she enters the cab. Apart from Pierce giving the driver the address, neither of them speaks.

Pierce herds Daphne into the building and upstairs to her flat. She lets him take her handbag, dangling like a vestigial limb from her arm, and unlock the door. He guides her in then leaves. She stands in the middle of the room with her jacket on, not knowing what to do. Pierce has left the front door open but Daphne hasn't the power to go and close it. Pierce returns with a bottle of Glenfarclas malt whisky and goes to the kitchen, returning with two glasses. He pours large ones for both of them. They sit. He doesn't tell her to sit or to drink but she knows this is what she is supposed to do. After a few hesitant sips she gulps the whisky. As soon as her glass is empty he pours her another, another big one. She takes her time a bit more with this one. Pierce has still not said a word.

Daphne is getting used to the whisky. She knocks back the remains of her glass, ready for another. But Pierce doesn't give her anymore. He takes the bottle under his arm, like a dockworker with a tabloid newspaper or a farmer with a pig, but Pierce is neither of these. Pierce is voluntarily unemployed, a work-shy lazy dole scrounger, a hash head, a mouse murderer, a cheat. Pierce takes his bottle of whisky and says,

'That'll give a you good sleep.'

He walks out, closing the front door softly behind him.

Oh yeah, thinks Daphne, a few slugs of whisky, a few miserable slugs, let me get a taste for it, let me know how sweet it can be, and then take it away from me. It's the story of her life.

The phone rings. It's Donnie. She can't answer it; she won't speak to him. There's no way he can explain this away.

It isn't him.

It's her mum, again.

Mum's voice is burbling down the Australian phone wire, right now it's being beamed through the hot dusty Australian atmosphere, through Australian air space, dodging Australian planes or maybe beaming right through them, maybe beaming right through the passengers as they pass, and into space, hitting the target, a giant saucer which bounces Mum's burbly voice to other saucers in an interstellar game of rounders till it reaches the Scottish saucer, a big tartan one, which changes the trajectory and pitches Mum down, from the dark zero gravity of the cosmos through cold damp Scottish air space and Scottish planes and Scottish passengers and streets and wires and up through the building, past Pierce's flat, and in through the wire in the hall through to the living room into the answering machine.

'Hello Mum.'

'Oh, you're there. I was beginning to think you'd fled the country. Why d'you not answer your phone, Daphne?'

'I do. I've answered.'

'Anyway, everything okay at your end?'

'Aye. Never better.'

'Daphne, are you drunk?'

'No, I'm just tired.'

'You are so, I can hear it in your voice.'

'Yeah, I've had a drink but I'm tired as well, I've been working really hard, that's why I wasn't here when you phoned. It's the end of term; you know what it's like.

'Well get to your bed then, hen. Just so long as you're okay. I worry about you. You're so far away.'

'No, *you're* so far away.'

'Och well, you know what I mean. Email me Daphne, I'm on hotmail, Albert set up an account for me. I'll send you some pictures of the kids tomorrow, they're a couple of wee smashers. Albert's here, do you want a word? '

'No Mum, actually I'm on my way out the door, going out tonight.'

It's another five minutes before Daphne gets her mum off the phone. She holds the empty whisky glass over her face, like an oxygen mask, breathing in the fumes.

Chapter 7

He quite literally bumped into her. On the Underground he had been strap-hanging but stood freestyle, legs wide for balance, just for a second, to put his ticket in his pocket. In that second the train jolted and launched him into her arms.

He didn't even have to see her face to know it was her. Her fleeting embrace, more to protect herself than to catch him, was so sweetly familiar it made him want to cry. Her perfume, no, it wasn't even perfume, it was her smell, the smell that no other woman had, smelled like home. The atmosphere around her seemed to be vibrating, like jungle drums beating out a message that only he could understand: *yes, this is right, yes, this is right.*

Up until that moment he hadn't even seen her on the train. They were only a few feet from each other but on the Underground in the morning rush hour no one looked at anyone else. Not even their ex-wives. He wouldn't have spotted the woman that he'd worked with and dated, and slept with, and fallen in love with, and married, and bought his first car with, and developed a drinking problem with, and fought with and whose CDs he'd smashed and photos he'd ripped, the woman he'd divorced.

If he hadn't put his ticket in his pocket at just that moment, or if he'd fallen to the left on to the fat man on the other side of the carriage, his life, and her life, and Daphne's life, would have gone on exactly the same.

The train was so noisy it was pointless trying to speak. He mouthed the word 'sorry' and she nodded her acceptance. It was just as easy as that. Sorry for all the shit, the tantrums and paranoia, sorry for the ugly angry stuff, sorry for divorcing you, sorry I was ever stupid enough to walk away, sorry.

Okay, forget it, she nodded.

She looked so much older. Fifteen years ago, on their honeymoon, lying in bed chatting, too tired for sex, she'd asked if he would still love her when she developed jowls like her mother and a sagging turkey neck like her TV star aunty. He said he could hardly wait, that he'd probably love her best when she was old. Then she couldn't leave him for someone handsome; she'd have to depend on him not leaving her. Looking at her now, at 8.15am without the benefit of soft lighting or make up, there was no disguising the gravitational pull and weight of the years. And it was true; he loved her. What must she see when she looked at him?

Though he was eight years younger than Bertha, the clock was running at the same rate for everyone. He was not ageing well; he knew it. It wasn't his fault; it wasn't as though he didn't try. He didn't smoke, he tried to eat healthily and played football twice a week, but he couldn't fight his genes. Donnie came from a long line of wasters: puny disease-prone alcoholic smokers, generations who had abused their lungs and livers and hearts. When members of his family died, from their heart attack/ stroke/ cancer – one or two of his bad boy uncles had the hat-trick – nobody paid inheritance tax. There was no estate to be fought over. They bestowed the only thing they had: their sorry DNA. His dad was barely fifty and fucked with the fags and drink. They were a family neither blessed with good health nor longevity. As far back as they could tell no male member had made it past their 63rd birthday. That's why Donnie so resented the compulsory pension scheme at work; he would never live to see it.

He was mortified to be caught wearing this jacket. It was functional: wind and waterproof, but it was nothing to look at. Daphne hated it and called it his Postman Pat anorak. He resolved to bin it as soon as he got home that night.

Bertha wished she had written down what the spey wife said, the exact words. It was something along the lines of *I see falling, a man, the man who left your life is falling.* Bertha had thought at the time, had fervently hoped, that she was talking about Charlie, her boyfriend of the last three years who'd left for a job in Dublin. Charlie couldn't get to Dublin quick enough. He'd only phoned twice in three months although she phoned him all the time. Bertha would have given up calling him after the first month but for what the spey wife had said. Charlie didn't ask Bertha to come with him or invite her to visit, not even for the weekend. He seemed to like it when she called but talked less and less about what he was doing. As if it wasn't any of her business. If Charlie ever did fall for her he quickly recovered his feet. He was not in love with her now, and Bertha doubted that he ever had been. If he didn't already have another girlfriend he was working on it. Bertha's hopes and memories of Charlie were dimming. As things stood, there was no way he was coming back.

But maybe the spey wife had been right after all. This, seeing Donnie like this, was pure destiny. She'd lost her purse the day before and ended up staying the night at her friend Bunty's. If she hadn't lost her purse, her ex-husband, a man who had left her life, would not have fallen, just as the spey wife predicted, into her arms. And his timing was perfect.

After a few glasses of wine with Bunty last night they had discussed it and Bertha had made up her mind that she wasn't going to call Charlie again. She wasn't going to call Charlie and she wasn't going to invest any more time in men. Coming from an accounting background, Bertha realised sadly that the three years she'd spent on Charlie, at this time in her life, had a high opportunity cost.

Three years ago she could, just, get away with going out looking for men. They'd called it 'sharking expeditions' and Bunty and Bertha had made an effective team. Not terribly successful, Bunty had yet to land a catch that didn't wriggle off the hook after three or four dates, but they were an effective team nonetheless.

They entered a bar and swept through, checking out the talent. Where there was none, they moved on. Where there was potential, they positioned themselves downstream of the gents' toilet. They drank diet alcopops with their thumbs as stoppers to avoid getting spiked. They drank too much, which helped embolden their dancing, they giggled when lads chatted them up or made jokes they didn't get. They didn't need to go to the toilet to discuss things, they had a code for when they wanted to escape losers, when they wanted to swap men, when one or both had pulled. But at the end of the day, after three dates or three years, they all wriggled off the hook.

Last night Bertha had decided that she was too old and too tired to resume sharking. Now, in a bar, standing shoulder to shoulder amongst girls of twenty with flawless naked legs and faces, she'd feel like a pensioner. Bunty and Bertha agreed it was time to grow old gracefully. There had been no shame in their sharking, nature dictated that men and women should find a mate and drove them to it, but nature no longer had such a hold on them.

If Bertha was honest, she'd never really liked sex anyway. She did it though, she had to, and she tried to enter into the spirit of the thing but she found all the huffing and puffing faintly preposterous. She often felt cheered up after sex, not because it had been so great, but because it would be at least a week or so until she'd have to do it again. And anyway, there were too many diseases out there, too many men who wanted it without a condom, too many with weird ideas, who wanted it more than once a week, who grabbed on to her all through the night, who snored or smelled or farted in bed.

It was time to settle down, to accept that married life was not going to be her lot. She had a career and a few good friends; she'd take up a hobby, go to night classes, make friends with her neighbours. Bunty and Bertha even discussed getting a pup, one between them, one they could share the costs and responsibilities of. Puppies were ideal for exercising and companionship and home security if you got a big one. They were tremendous icebreakers with strangers. The more wine they consumed, the more Bertha relished the idea of taking up voluntary work, something green.

They giggled as they went through the relative merits of joining a local Crimestoppers vigilante squad, or a church. Last night Bertha made up her mind that if she couldn't get a husband she'd get community, and a dog. And then Donnie fell into her lap.

*

Pierce pours a beer, gets comfy on the couch, sparks up a joint and then dials the number. This is his one extravagance of the week, an expensive long-distance call to the island.

Ever since he can remember he has spent his summers with Aunt Bernie and Uncle Sean at their cottage on a remote island. They don't have kids of their own. Pierce's parents, aware of Sean and Bernie's painful situation, used to rent him out to them as a summer holiday surrogate son. No money changed hands but the boy always came back with a new school uniform and lots and lots of clean white pants and socks. And every August when Sean reluctantly returned him to his parents, Pierce seethed for weeks. Why did he have to come back to Glasgow? Why couldn't he stay on the island with Uncle Sean and Auntie Bernie? Even now he could never understand why Bernie made him go back when she cried so hard each time he left.

'Bernie? How you doing?'

'Aye, I'm fine, son, I'm fine.'

Bernie and Sean always call him son. Since he was a child, and now, as a fully grown man, whenever he visits, Bernie shows him off around the village saying, 'ah look, I have my big boy back again,' and Pierce pretends to be embarrassed.

'And yourself, son, how's the writing going?'

Bernie always tries this diversionary tactic but it never works.

'Aye, I'm grand too, Bernie, but what did the doctor say?'

Pierce knows she doesn't want to talk about it, she never does. He doesn't want to talk about it either but her visit to the specialist on the mainland was this week's big event and must be acknowledged. It seems callous to phone and not ask.

'Och, the usual, a lot of gobbledegook. He's increased my medication, as if I've not got enough bloody medicine to take. Honest to God, Pierce, I'm on more pills than Elvis!'

This makes both of them laugh. As usual she's kept it light but it's what she's not saying that quickly sobers Pierce. If there were any good news she would have told him.

'I tell you what though; getting a hurl in that air ambulance was brilliant. The whole pub turned out to see the helicopter landing on the beach.'

'Did they let Sean go with you?'

'Oh aye, there's no show without Punch. Your Uncle Sean won't let me off the island without him, he's scared I'll run away with a big black man!'

'Well, I can understand that, I wouldn't put it past you, Bernadette.'

'Oh you, you cheeky monkey, you're not too big for a slap, you know.'

Aye, but I'm too far away, you'll need to scramble your helicopter to get me. Unless you want me to come over,' Pierce says. He says it ever week, always dressed up in a jokey way.

'Och, don't be silly, I've told you, wait till I'm better and come over in the good weather.'

He knows why she won't let him come: Sean has told him that she's embarrassed by her illness, her weight loss, her lack of energy. She's bad tempered and doesn't want him to see her like this, she's irritated by her incapacity, annoyed about everyone fretting, angry in the face of their sympathy, guilty that Sean and Pierce feel so helpless. He's promised Sean that he won't put any pressure on her; he'll let her deal with it her own way. Pierce knows all this but it still stings, and he just wants to see her.

'You just stay there and get on with the writing.'

'I am, I'm getting on great with it, Bernie.'

'Good for you, son. Don't let that guy in the job centre, what do you call him again?'

'Eh, I don't know Bernie, Employment Advisor?'

'No, I mean his name. What was it again?'

She addresses the question to Pierce but Sean also likes to take part in these weekly conference calls. Pierce can hear him behind her, probably in his chair facing away from her: eyes glued to the telly, ears glued to their conversation. He's mumbling something.

'That's it, Hugh Jorgen. Where did he get a name like that, is he a foreigner?'

'I'm not sure.'

Pierce can't hear but he can visualise Sean sniggering at his little prank.

'Anyway, don't let that Mr Jorgen push you into some dead-end job, you're an artist, Pierce, sooner or later they'll recognise that, your time is coming, I can see that from your work.'

A flush of pride and gratitude suffuses Pierce when he hears this. Bernie and Sean are the only people in his family, the only people he knows, who refer to his *work*.

'But I'm still waiting for the rest of that book you were writing, what happened? And don't bother telling me it's in the post.'

'No, no, I'm cracking on with that now. I'll send it over the minute it's finished. I've been a bit busy this week. Some people have been talking to me about a new magazine, they want me as the editor.'

'See? What did I tell you? Sean, they've asked him to be an editor on a magazine!'

'Bloody brilliant,' says a voice strained through the telly noise.

'That's bloody brilliant your uncle says,' Bernie tells him unnecessarily. 'Now, let's get down to business, young man, have you got yourself a nice girlfriend yet?'

Tactical error, thinks Pierce, shouldn't have mentioned the editor job.

'I've a lot of nice girlfriends, Bernie.'

'I'm not talking about those women you pick up, what d'you call them?'

Pierce hears Sean make a muffled contribution.

'Slappers. I'm not talking about them, surely you've had your fill of them by now Pierce, have you not?'

'Aye, thanks, I can't complain. I had fifteen slappers up here last night. Well, to tell you the truth, two of them weren't fully qualified, they were just wee slapperettes.'

'I don't want to know what goes on!' Bernie squeals in mock disgust.

'Ripping my clothes off they were, they couldn't get enough of me.'

'Well I hope they formed an orderly queue. And was any of them wife material?'

'Whoa tiger! You're going a bit fast for me. What do I want with a wife? Who needs a car when there's plenty of taxis?'

'C'mon Pierce, you know what I mean.'

Bernie's tone has changed to serious. She still likes a joke, she can take a joke better than anyone else Pierce knows but these days she quickly tires of banter.

'I'm not saying you shouldn't sow your wild oats. It's only natural, you're a fine looking big fella.'

'Thanks very much, you're not too bad yourself.'

With this Pierce hopes that she'll follow him back into the more comfortable repartee zone but she doesn't.

'It's none of my business I know, son, but we'd just like to see you settled, that's all. Would you not like that, Pierce? '

Oh, illegal manoeuvre, thinks Pierce, unfair: she can bat away enquiries and make jokes about her illness but she demands of him deep and meaningful answers to impossible questions. She's teased him for years about his love life, even taken vicarious pride in her stud muffin nephew but she's never said anything like this before.

His resentment is momentary, she's not well, that's why she's talking like this. Given the difficulty of the situation Pierce feels justified in doing what he does best. He improvises.

'Actually, I *am* seeing a nice girl at the minute.'

Chapter 8

Daphne wonders if there is special rehab for people like her; if there is, she doesn't want it. Daphne loves Asda, can't get enough of it. It began a few years ago when she popped in on her way to work. There for the shop opening, the first and only customer, when Radio Asda started up and the familiar theme tune kicked in:

Doo doo doo doo doo
Doo doo doo doo doo
That's Asda price!

It was then, while the checkout girls fed through their till rolls and the shelf stackers placed a final can of spinach here, a bottle of sauce there, happily, rhythmically, like characters in a Disney film, everyone excitedly preparing for the big event, the big shopping event, that Daphne realised she had a problem. As she walked through the store she had a strong sensation of being a Disneyesque General inspecting the troops. But her Asda addiction is innocuous. Yes, she probably spends too much money there and she definitely spends far too much time, but she's harming nobody.

She enjoys the whole Asda experience. She enjoys the Greeters and recognises all of them in the stores within a twenty-mile radius around the city. The chirpy old guys on the front door who refuse to retire and are paid simply to engage in petty gossip with anyone who stops: usually other not-so-chirpy oldsters who wish they had a job.

She likes the bag-packers, the local Scout company who are stationed, smart in their uniforms and kilts, at each checkout, packing bags for a small donation. Meanies who won't donate find that the next time their bag is packed tins are slammed on to eggs and peaches and they carry home a bag of mush.

Daphne is so familiar with Asda she has picked up the lexicon. The vocabulary is tactile and respectful. People who work there are not *staff* but *colleagues*. Colleagues do not have a *meeting* they have a *huddle*. Money-off stickers are marked *whoops!* And even more money off is a *smile voucher.*

A visit to Asda is, for Daphne, a sensual delight. She loves the soapy perfumes of the toiletries, the rich backlit colours of the bubble bath: shelf after shelf of bright rubies, emeralds and sapphires. She loves the feel of the fruit, the rubbery texture of green bananas, the scrape of the yeast on the grapes and the satisfyingly taut skin. Colleagues not only approve, they encourage sampling, and Daphne swallows a juicy grape or slither of ham or sip of cocktail and smiles: *mmmm.*

The smell from the bakery is irresistible. Daphne has read in the paper that all supermarkets pump the smell of fresh bread into their shops but Daphne sees it not as a cynical marketing ploy but as another complementary service. The smell of fresh bread and doughnuts and cheese scones is a pleasure that cannot, and should not, be denied.

Daphne spends an hour or more in garden furniture, checking and comparing prices and she doesn't even have a garden. She can lose herself for hours in Asda; it is her hobby, an escape from the college canteen and Carol's boasting, from her demanding students, from the problem of Donnie.

*

It is the middle of the day; Donnie and Bertha will be at work. There is absolutely no danger that she'll bump into them; this Asda is on the other side of town. Yet she is terrified.

Daphne never makes a shopping list. She despises people who charge purposefully round the shop crossing off items on their list. Daphne prefers to patrol each and every aisle in order, letting her memory be jogged and her imagination be fired by the goods on display.

She is halfway round the shop and has put nothing in her trolley. She can't think what she wants; she doesn't want anything. The light is all wrong. It's too bright and false. There are no windows, it was overcast when she came into the shop but maybe the weather has changed, maybe it's sunny or raining now. She doesn't know; she's not in control. She's in the queue at the cold meat counter but the man behind her is standing too close, she can't move or she'll lose her place but now she can't remember what she wanted at this counter anyway.

There is a gridlock of trolleys in the personal hygiene aisle and usually when this happens she waits and lets people pass or reverses if she can, but there is a woman behind her who won't back up. Daphne is taking big breaths, trying to slow down her breathing. Her back feels damp and she can feel sweat making rings round the leg holes of her pants. She leans over her trolley, frightened that her legs will buckle again and she'll fall. The trolley is still empty when she parks it in the biscuit aisle and walks out of the shop.

*

Some days later, very early in the morning, when Daphne's supplies have all but run out and she's down to half a jar of gluey sweetcorn chutney and a parsnip, she realises she'll have to shop elsewhere. No more Asda but there's an all-night deli just across the park. At quarter past four on a Saturday morning Daphne is enjoying having the park to herself. It's big and wide and densely wooded, a forest in the middle of the city, even more so at this time when there is not the usual background drone of traffic, just the wind whooshing high in the trees. A good place to get lost.

Daphne is the only customer in the all-night deli. The only member of staff is a skater boy who correctly identifies her as a low shoplifting risk. He nods as she comes in then disappears down into the basement. Every so often he climbs the stairs carrying boxes and fills the shelves.

The shelves are made of dark expensive-looking wood. These right-on, new-age places sicken Daphne. They charge a fortune for save-the-planet, wholegrain, organic, recyclable crap and then use hardwoods for their shelving.

The shop sells white asparagus, artichoke hearts, dried ham, queen-size olives and buffalo mozzarella. It doesn't do practical stuff like Heinz beans or Tetley tea bags. But at least she won't bump into Donnie. And the bread looks really nice.

Daphne has no appetite for anything other than bread and butter. She has spent the day snoozing and dreaming of thick slabs of crusty bread with butter so thick that a dentist could render a perfect set of dentures from the impression she leaves. Asda bread is fantastic and their butter reasonably priced but it's become for her a no-fly zone and she quietly accepts that if she wants to eat she'll have to settle for this mahogany emporium of pretentiousness.

*

'Daphne, is it okay if ah keep my phone on today? Ah'm waitin fur a call fae ma lawyer,' says Mark.

'Och Daphne, he's at it!' Thomas remonstrates. 'He tried that wan in George Simpson's class as well.'

Daphne isn't sure what to make of this. This class, her adult returners, are very strict about phones in the classroom. With her other classes Daphne makes her standard mobile phone speech at the start of each lesson. They listen politely, nod and pretend to switch their phones off. Daphne knows they're on silent. Students take calls from behind and under the desks, even sometimes texting each other while sitting five yards apart. But not this class.

This class are self-policing. She doesn't bother with the speech with them, they've already turned them off. The odd time a phone rings, the disapproving whistles and tuts are enough to ensure it doesn't happen again.

'Daphne, ah'm sorry aboot this. If it's a problem, ah understand,' Mark says. She can see how uncomfortable he is with this. 'I'll leave noo if ye waant but ah need to speak tae him when he phones.'

'Oooooow! ah need tae speak tae him!' echoes Billy, followed by various cynical quips.

'He thinks he's the President of the fucking United States!'

'Aw Mark, geez a shout when we go to Def Con One, will yae?'

'Aye me tae, I'll need to get hame. Ah've left a waashin oot.'

They run a tight ship, thinks Daphne.

'Oh come on, give the guy a break! Mark, we'll make an exception today because of your circumstances. You can leave your phone on *discreet* and take the call outside when your lawyer calls, how's that?'

'Brilliant. Thanks Daphne.'

He is obviously relieved, today is another assessment and nobody wants to miss it.

'Right: assessment,' says Daphne, smiling gleefully as though an exam were something to be relished. 'Great to see you've all turned up and after today that's another one under your belt. Remember: bit by bit. We'll do it together.

'Since you started you've all sat and successfully passed four assessments. We're definitely getting there; we're halfway there already. And you're going to pass this next one. Some of you might not pass the first time and get remediation, so, big deal, you'll pass the next time or the time after that. The important thing to remember is to not panic; we can do it, a wee bit at a time. You're going to leave this course with your qualification; all you have to do is keep going, keep the faith.'

Daphne always gives them a pep talk before any assessment but they really need it today. Assessment five is public speaking. They each have to prepare and deliver a five-minute speech. The topic was supposed to be *My Hobby* but nobody has a hobby so Daphne has changed it to *The Person I Most Admire*. Daphne arranges herself at the back of the class with her stopwatch and evaluation sheets before the talks commence.

June is highly organised with flash cards and props and she opens well.

'She wis a Land Girl in the war and as yae can see fae the photaes she wis a crackin lookin wummin in her day.'

June's talk is well paced and interesting with many facts and quirky details about the Land Girl. The photos take a few minutes to reach Daphne and it is not until she sees them that she realises the woman June is talking about is her grandmother.

'She's ninety-two and she's still a brilliant laugh. She loves it when I bring her in a magazine, *Cosmopolitan* or something. She's gettin a wee bit incontinent noo but it's only a matter ay changing the cushion oan hur cher, they're machine-waashable.'

Several other of the students talk about their grandmother as the person they most admire. It is so prevalent that Daphne begins to understand that this is not due to having come from a tightly-knit extended family. They are paying tribute to the woman who brought them up. Usually single-handed.

Dan's talk is about dogs, Rottweilers.

'The Rottweiler breed comes from Germany.'

Dan seems to have done his homework but Daphne is not sure which topic he has chosen because as he begins to talk about his pet Rottweiler, Perla, it sounds like the person he most admires.

'The guy that hud the pups owed ma brother a favour, a big favour, know what I'm sayin? I got Perla when she wis only a week auld. Ah could hod her in ma two hons she was that wee, ah hud to feed her milk through a sock.'

'Did yae waash it first?' shouts Billy to some laughter.

'Naw, ah didnae, actually,' counters Mark, 'she prefers the cheesier flavour.'

The girls cry 'euww!' The lads snigger.

'The first night she gret the whole night. ah hud to take her in beside me. You waant to see her noo: fourteen stone ay solid muscle and she still sleeps in beside me. She could rip yer throat oot in a minute. It's in her nature, it's no' the dug's fault, it's been bred intae her and she'll never lose the killer instinct.'

Dan could talk for hours on the subject but after eight and a half minutes, and several 'time's up' gestures, Daphne is forced to stop him.

Next up is Michael who has composed a rap to his mother.

'Ah wis aff ma heid, Ah wis fuckin nearly died
Wi' ma habit shoutin 'FEED me'.
Ah stole your telly, your rings, aw yer wee things
Anythin ah could sell, ah took the wean's XBox as well.
But it was never enough, ah wis feeling bad and mad and sad and rough
but ah needed mair STUFF.
I'm sorry Maw
and ah'll
no
dae
it again.'

Michael uses his mobile phone as though it were a mic. He postures; crouching and squatting, moving around the class gesturing with outstretched arms and fingers in what Daphne recognises as a gangsta stylee.

'Yae loacked me in ma room wipin' up spit, and sick and piss and shit, even when I HIT yae yae widnae gee up.
Yae brushed mah teeth that went black, yae kept me and fed me and led me back
fae the CRACK. The crack in ma life, that caused aw the strife that made me come it yae wi a knife,
the crack ah fell through, that cut me in two, but it wis YOU that put me back on track.
Ah'm sorry Maw
And ah'll
no

54

dae
it again.'

It's unconventional but it fulfils the requirements for the assessment so Daphne ticks all the boxes. She just hopes the external examiner never asks for a demonstration.

'The cunts sellin the stuff are sellin yae death, they're thugs,
Drugs is for mugs, drugs is for mugs, hear me now.
Ah'm sorry Maw
And ah'll
never
dae
it again.'

Michael finishes to tumultuous applause.

'Fantastic Michael,' says Daphne, taking her time, letting the atmosphere, which is close to revivalist meeting fervour, settle down again. This will be a hard act to follow.

'Let's see, it's you, Jamie. You're the last. Ladies and gentlemen, I give you our last speaker of the day: Jamie.'

Jamie slowly stands and moves to the front of the class, tilting his head to see over his almost opaque glasses, resting his clasped hands gently on his soft round paunch in a relaxed professorial manner. He is a big man, red-faced but quietly spoken, a placid, self-contained man.

'Ah've done terrible things. You don't want tae know the things ah've done. But that's aw in the past. And the thing that ah've goat oot ay it, the wan maist important thing in ma life is: friendship. Honest open friendship wi' the maist important people in ma life: ma faimily and ma pals. Billie for wan.'

Jamie gives a slow nod towards Billy, which is just as solemnly reciprocated.

'Ah'd say Billie wis ma best mate. Me and Billy came through rehab thegither and when ah wisnae able tae hondle it he kept me gaun, and when he wisnae able for it, ah kept him gaun. Mind you, it wisnae aw tears and snotters, we've hud some great laughs as well. Me and Billie are lucky, we're at a stage in wur lives where there's nay need for aw the shite that we used tae dae, there's nae need for any mair lies. Ah'm telling yae, honesty is the best thing. Honesty sets yae free.

'The day ah start lyin tae Billie is the day ah start lyin tae ma case worker, lyin tae mysel, the day ah start back oan the smack. And ah don't want that day ever tae come, so: honesty. Billie knows me, he knows whit ah've done, he knows who ah wis and who ah um noo and that's okay wi'him. *Ah'm* okay wi' him.

'Ah know you're a Rangers supporter, Billie, but naebody's perfect. And ah just want tae say, thanks wee man. Your okay wi' me. Thanks for aw the hard things yae telt me: the honesty yae gave me, the friendship yae gave me. Cheers Billie.'

Jamie makes a dignified return to his seat, slapping a high-five with Billy as he passes without breaking step.

Daphne roots around in her folder, pretending to be collating marks. Don't cry, she tells herself, do not fucking cry.

'Well, I did say earlier that not all of you would pass this assessment and…'

Daphne looks around as the faces change from expectant to crushed.

'I have to tell you that you have all …'

She loves these people. She wants them to take her home with them to the rehab centre and infuse her cold lonely bones with their warm acceptance of their lot in life, their honesty.

'Every one of you has passed.'

*

Sunday lunchtime and Daphne is silently sliding down the wall. She wants to go back to the bedroom and hide under the duvet but she's frightened that they'll hear her if she moves. Her friends are at the door. She's been ignoring their phone calls for weeks and now Lucy, Colette, Mark and Joe are standing waiting for her to open the door and let them in. But she can't do that, she's not dressed, not ready, not able to explain.

She hears the outside door slam, they've given up, at last.

On the front step there is a jokey card signed by everyone. There's also a cake in a box. It's a *Star Trek* cake with a picture of Captain James T Kirk and the crew of the *Starship Enterprise* on the front. It's funny, a reference to her party piece. Once, drunk at a party she challenged them to sing the theme tune to the original *Star Trek* series. She knew she'd be the only one who could do it properly. They all tried, some more successfully than others and none without laughing, to hit the high note at the end.

'Aah ahh,
ahh ahh ahh ahh ahhh,
Ahh ahhh,
ahh ahh ah ahh ahh ahhh,
Ahh ahh ahh ahh ahh ahh ahh ah ahh
Ahhh ahh ahh ahh
Ahhh ahh ahh aahhhhhh!'

Daphne keeks out from behind the curtain and sees them at the bottom of the street. She considers opening the window and calling them back, she can pretend she was asleep or in the shower but she knows they'll ask questions. They'll ask where Donnie is and she can't tell them.

As they disappear out of view she wishes she had opened the door, brought them in, gave them a cup of tea and a slice of cake. They could have had a laugh about who got the bit with Captain Kirk's face on it.

She cuts herself a slice, taking care not to chop Mr Spock's ear off. Underneath the vivid icing, the cake is a jam sponge. She wants to, but she can't eat it. It's making her gag. She opens the kitchen window and sits at the table breaking pieces off and throwing them into the backcourt for the birds, although there are no birds at the moment. The big lime tree, which in the limited space has had to bend and twist it's way up as far as Daphne's window, isn't dressed yet either. Its naked branches offer no cover for small vulnerable city birds. But spring is coming, only another few weeks. Then the hard knobbly buds will relax. They are bashful, they won't do it while she's looking, but eventually, while Daphne is sleeping or making tea, while she's doing anything other than watching for them, the leaves, tightly folded and concentrate, like green seahorses, will unfurl. Daphne has the feeling that something is going to change, all she has to do, all she *can* do, is wait. Bit by bit she crumbles the cake with her fingers and throws it out the window, each piece she breaks off getting smaller and smaller until she's only throwing crumbs.

Chapter 9

'Yeah okay, I'll come back with you but I'm not doing anything.'

'Sure, that's fine, whatever you want.'

'Just for a cuddle, okay?'

'Whatever you want, baby.'

How many times has he heard that? *Just for a cuddle.* Pierce is not so cynical as to think that ladies are lying when they say it. But he knows that after two spliffs, *The Best Of Marvin Gaye* and a half-hour of snogging, fondling, licking, nibbling, sucking and dry riding it's often a different story.

'Great flat, you've got it lovely.'

'Thanks.'

Pierce smiles as he remembers one of his precoital preparations: tidying the flat. In determining the likelihood of getting one's hole an important factor was location, location, location. The flat with its understated furnishings and tasteful décor was a leg-opener for most ladies.

'I'm sorry, I've forgotten your name.'

'It's Pierce.'

'I'm really sorry, I'm a bit drunk.'

She is half sitting, half lying on Pierce's couch with her bra flipped up and her tights round her ankles.

'It's okay.'

'Do you remember mine?'

'Of course I do. It's Marianne.'

'Martha.'

'Sorry. Martha. That's what I meant to say.'

'Pierce?'

'Mmmm?'

'Will you fuck me?'

Result.

Pierce prefers a slower more seductive undressing but as they move to the bedroom Martha is whipping her kit off. She steps out of her pants and leaves them, sunny side up, where they fall.

She smells fantastic and her skin is soft and warm. He considers himself a gentleman and is old-fashioned enough to believe in Ladies First. He always gives it a good twenty minutes, longer if it looks like they're going to come, before he takes the reins and goes for gold.

She is pushing his head down and her hand explores his balding crown. Recently Pierce has taken to picking up the shorter lady. But now that she's found it he must acknowledge it.

'It's not a bald patch. It's a solar panel for a sex machine.'

Martha laughs and he is relieved. He's still got it. When all his hair falls out and his belly hangs over his trousers and his teeth turn yellow he'll still be able to laugh them into bed. Except that the balder he gets the shorter the women will have to be. The older and fatter he is the uglier the ladies will be. He'll have to start taking Viagra, not because he can't get it up but because the only ladies he'll be able to pull will be decrepit disfigured midgets.

These thoughts are having a deflating effect. Pierce returns to thinking about how great Marianne smells and how nice her tits are. This is going to be a quality shag, he can sense it. He hasn't had sex in three weeks but compared to married guys he knows, Pierce gets plenty. If he could find a nice lady who offered quality sex and was willing to put out on a regular basis, he might even think of going steady. Maybe it's time. Two weeks ago when the barber showed him it in the mirror, the bald patch definitely looked bigger.

Pierce is unaware that she has been moaning until she suddenly stops.

'What's that noise?'

She sits up, alarmed.

'Somebody's crying, upstairs, can't you hear it?'

Pierce considers pretending he can't hear it but the sound-proofing in the building is non-existent and he'd have to be deaf as well as bald.

'Yeah, it's Daphne. She cries all the time, she's mental, don't worry about it.'

'Oh God, the poor soul, what's she crying for?'

'I don't know, I told you, she's mental.'

The way this comes out sounds ratty and less sympathetic than Pierce meant and instantly changes the atmosphere. Backpedalling is required.

'I'm sorry; it's just that I find it upsetting. Poor Daphne crying every night like that. It's the usual story. Dumped by a man. Bastard. She's so depressed, you hear of people dying of a broken heart and I think that poor kid might. I've talked to her of course, tried to help but, oh I don't know, what can I do? All I can do is be a friend, I just feel useless.'

Martha throws her lovely warm fragrant arms around him and holds him tight. The New Man thing is quite effective, and it isn't entirely bullshit, he does feel rotten for Daphne. But it's backfiring; Marianne's sobbing in his arms now. At this rate he's never going to get his hole.

Struggling to catch her breath after every word, she blurts, 'I've been there. Damian left me three months ago. For the guy who sold us the new patio doors. We didn't even need new patio doors, the old ones were fine.'

Now he throws his arms around her. How many times has he heard this? *Damian or Michael or John left me.* It's always Pierce who has to pick up the pieces, to hold them, stroke their hair, assure them they're desirable, fuck them, when he knows that what they really want is to be in the arms of Damian or Michael or John. Pierce is their substitute.

'Shh!'

They listen intently to the silence.

'She's stopped!' she whispers.

'Good,' Pierce whispers back, 'she's at peace now.'

'Oh my God! What d'you mean?'

'Nothing! I don't mean she's ...'

It is at this point that Martha actually kicks him out of his own bed.

'Quick, go and see she's alright. She could be doing anything up there.'

'It's twenty past two!'

'Please Pierce!' Martha sobs; she's becoming hysterical.

'Okay.'

Throwing on his trousers he tiptoes upstairs and lightly taps his neighbour's door. No doubt Daphne is sound asleep and completely unaware that she's destroying his love life. He intends to wait a few minutes and nip back downstairs again but to his surprise she opens the door.

'What's wrong, Pierce? Come in.'

'Eh, no, nothing's wrong, it's just, eh, just a social call.'

The fact that it's after two doesn't seem to bother her. She leads him into her living room, pours two large malt whiskies and hands him one. She's wearing a thick fleecy dressing gown but Pierce's eagle eye detects that Daphne is piling on the beef. Her face has filled out but it quite suits her.

'I just came to see if you were all right.'

'Me? Aye, I'm fine. Rinky dinky, never better.'

'It's just that sometimes I hear you, you know, the walls are paper thin in this building. Sometimes I can hear that you're upset.'

'Well I'm sorry if I'm disturbing you!'

'Don't take it like that Daphne. I'm just trying to be neighbourly.'

'Yeah well, sometimes I hear you. You and your lady friends. Mind you, you've hit a bit of a dry spell, haven't you, Pierce? I haven't heard anything for about a month now.'

'Three weeks.'

'Oh excuse me!'

They are both smiling.

'At least all you hear is me girning. I've got to put up with a full-on sex show,' she says, and then shouts, 'Pierce me baby, Pierce me!'

'Shh!'

Daphne's hand flies to her mouth. She's whispering and pointing downwards.

'You've got a woman there just now?'

Pierce nods.

'D'you think she heard?'

He nods again and now they're giggling.

'Well, what are you doing up here?'

'I'm just checking you're okay.'

Though this is the perfect opportunity Pierce doesn't have the heart to ask Daphne to keep the noise down.

'Thanks Pierce, I'm fine. Don't worry, I'll ask for your help putting the noose up when I'm ready. And maybe you can read one of your poems.'

Twenty minutes later Pierce is heading back down the stairs when Daphne calls him back.

'Pierce?'

'Yeah?'

'I'm developing a new method of silent weeping, look, what d'you think?'

Daphne screws her face up and mimes vigorous crying.

'No, you're alright, Daphne, you bawl away. It's better out than in.'

Marianne has fallen asleep. Pierce climbs in behind her and makes spoons. She responds and throws an arm behind, hugging him to her. Just for a cuddle. She mumbles something but it isn't real words. Just don't say Damien, Pierce thinks as he tries to fall asleep.

Chapter 10

Donnie is having a bit of a clear-out. He starts at half past eight, just until the football comes on but after the football he's still at it at quarter to three in the morning. I can't stop, he laughs. Donnie laughs a lot now. He's cleared three black poly bags full, mostly Daphne's or Daphne-related stuff. He's already given her the personal stuff back and that was difficult enough, he won't give her this; he can't bear to see how hard she's taking this. Even thinking about seeing her makes his heart beat too fast.

She's been phoning him. Usually when he's out, probably checking if he's there or not. He knows because when he comes in he always dials 1471. She never leaves a message, probably too scared to after the bollocking he gave her last time. He cringes when he remembers the harsh way he spoke but his nerves were in tatters, she knows that. The machine says *we do not have the caller's number to return the call.* It's Daphne. She's masking her number so he won't know it's her but who else would it be? Sometimes she calls when he is in but she doesn't speak. Donnie doesn't speak either. He doesn't know what to say.

He hadn't realised how much junk had accumulated in his flat, in his life. Well, he thinks, a new broom sweeps clean. It feels good to get rid of all Daphne's shit: all her arty-farty books. Donnie shakes his head in wonder now to think that under her influence he actually bought a book of poetry. Not even proper poetry that rhymed and had verses and had some sort of point to it. No, he bought a book of *concrete* poetry; fair enough, it had been at some charity fundraising do, but for fuck's sake, it didn't make any sense at all. It was just a bunch of words that had been shaken

64

and thrown on to the page like dice on a table. He had paid good money for that.

Then there were the videos: total mince, there wasn't one that was worth keeping. Most of them were French or Croatian or some such shit and either really boring or total porn or both. He can't have that kind of filth in the house anymore, not with Bertha around.

And as for the CDs, hoighty-toighty classical music, it was nice enough to fall asleep to, but it had no beat, no words, nothing you could remember about it. Daphne always seemed to be able to recognise that kind of music, she knew the composer and the name. Sometimes just to test her he'd put on a CD and say, 'Yeah, I really like that Mozart one'. And Daphne would say, 'Oh, I thought that was Beethoven'. She knew it was Beethoven. But Daphne never knew how he'd tried to swot up her favourite pieces and composers just to get it wrong and fall flat on his arse again the minute he heard it. Donnie breathes a big sigh of relief. It feels so good he breathes another one, then he laughs. Never again will he have to pretend to know the difference between Mozart and Beethoven.

There is a helluva lot of Daphne-related paperwork. There are birthday cards, Christmas cards, Valentines cards, there are the letters, the notes she left on his pillow when she went out early to work, *remember to leave the bin shed unlocked for the bin men.* Why had he kept all this crap? *PS if you are a good boy you'll get steak for dinner and a smoked sausage for supper – I love you, your very own Sweet Pea.* He'd kept it as a receipt, a promissory note.

Donnie doesn't suppose anyone would know what 'smoked sausage' means, a cryptic code only he and Daphne are privy to, but you can't be too careful and something like that, if Bertha ever found it, would be embarrassing. The note is going in the shredder too.

Donnie is laughing until, out of nowhere, a cold shiver runs down his back. He's remembering when he and Bertha told everyone they were back together again. Now *that* was embarrassing. His family at least had the good grace to pretend to be pleased but each of them, mum, dad and both his sisters, had privately asked him, 'Are you sure this is really what you want, Donnie?' It was a bit sudden, they said, he shouldn't just jump back into this. He knew why.

His face flushed hot when he thought of all the nasty ugly things he'd said about Bertha six years ago when she left him, the dreadful, embarrassing, private husband and wife stuff he'd told them. Worse than that, he remembered the nastier, uglier things they'd contributed. And he saw it in their faces now, he might forgive Bertha, but his family would never forget.

He felt it coming when Dad decided to *have a word*. Donnie did his best to avoid it, trying not to get stuck alone with him but Dad wouldn't be put off: Mum was worried, what had gone wrong with Daphne? He had seemed so happy with her. Donnie had changed so much recently, was he on drugs?

Donnie had to laugh at that. Little did they know that, for the first time in years, he wasn't on drugs. And it felt great.

But if his family was sticky, hers was a nightmare. The worst was Bertha's mother. He had never liked the old cow and she knew it. Within the first few months of Bertha and Donnie's marriage, Gerty had tried to put her oar in. It had caused trouble between them, Bertha was loyal to her mother though even she realised what a controlling old bitch she was. With neither Gerty nor Donnie prepared to meet in the middle, their relationship deteriorated until it became a power struggle, a fight for the territory that was Bertha. Donnie, in the honeymoon period of the first year and still confident of his new wife's love, forced Bertha to make a choice between them. Quite correctly, Donnie thought, she chose her husband and Gerty, ignominious in defeat, no longer held sway.

But Donnie's triumph came at a price. Bertha, temporarily at least, lost her ally, Gerty lost control and Donnie only won a vengeful enemy. In the long run it was to prove a hollow victory. Later, when things got worse between the couple, when the ugliness crept in and then became commonplace, Gerty re-established herself as Bertha's collaborator and worked tirelessly to make the marriage fail.

And she hadn't changed. He was now summoned once a week to Gerty's for a cold supper of humble pie where she routinely treated him with barely disguised scorn. She took every opportunity to remind him of her daughter's earning power and affluence. It had always been an unspoken sore point that before they split Bertha was earning twice his salary, now it was even more. Donnie lost everything their double salary upwardly mobile lifestyle had financed: the house in the best part of town, the latest model car, the luxury holidays. Gerty didn't bother to hide her smirks each time she interrogated him now on where he was living, what he was driving. How the mighty had fallen. And he had to smile and agree, to genuflect at the altar of the great big fat ugly stupid bitch, Goddess Mother-in-Law. It wasn't enough that he had paid heavily in the shame of a failed marriage and the humiliation of divorce. From her position of strength Gerty made it clear she would insist on him paying obeisance and keeping up the payments.

*

Pierce is having a quiet one tonight, a couple of cans in front of the telly. He was out at a party last night but it all went a bit tit-shaped.

Used to be Pierce went to parties every weekend. Used to be he'd get asked. Girls he didn't know would approach him in the pub and demand his attendance. Failing that, him and a few mates would crash whatever party they could hear from the street. A couple of handsome lads with a carry-out, they were welcome. Used to be.

He fucking blew it last night. That wee burd, Angela, she was up for it. He could have fired in, nae bother. No, but he had to be Bertie Bigbaws, didn't he? He had to pull more burds than the other guys, drink more beer, do more lines than the other guys. The other younger guys. Came with the territory, the old geezer out with the young blades, he had to earn his place. And the thing is, the thing he's kicking himself for is: he knew he shouldn't have touched the coke.

Pierce had realised years ago that he didn't need cocaine. They could all be coked out their nut and he was always more lively than everybody else. Apart from which, it did nothing for him.

Well, no, actually it did. It loosened his bowels, replaced his libido with that of an amoeba's and shrivelled his cock to the size, shape and texture of a peeled prawn. It also gave him a sleepless night and a stinking cold the next day, hence the quiet night tonight. He shouldn't have touched the fucking coke. He should have walked away, politely declined. Used to be he had the confidence to do that.

If it had been one line he might have got away with it but Bertie Bigbaws had to do three. Angela was leaning her heavy tits against him, giggling – she was fucking gagging for it – as he snorted the long thin lines.

The coke was cut with laxative and the effect was immediate. He had to get out of the flat. He was touching cloth.

Pierce briefly considered using the toilet in the party flat but he'd been on the Guinness all night and, without the benefit of a splatterguard, he knew the effect that would have in the toilet. There were people standing in the hallway, they'd know it was him. He knew his precarious social standing would never survive the ignominy so, with quivering sphincter, he bolted. Never mind that he was on a sure thing with Angela or wasted the money he'd had to chip in for the coke, it was better to squirt in the privacy of his own home.

A wee Saturday night in the house, how long has it been since he's done this? He should do it more often, although it would be more fun if he had a wee burd to do it with. They could get in a curry and a bottle of wine, watch *Casualty*, have a leisurely shag then off to bed and fresh as a daisy the next morning.

'Sean? It's me.'

'Oh hello son, everything okay?'

'Aye, why wouldn't it be?'

'No, it's just that you don't usually phone on a Saturday, I thought there was maybe something wrong.'

'No I'm just having a night in the house and I though I'd give you and Bernie a phone. Is she there?'

'Eh… aye.'

A second's hesitation, if that. But it's enough to chill Pierce.

'Is she okay?'

'Aye, fine son, she's just having a wee lie down, I'll go and give her a shout.'

'Don't disturb her, Sean…'

'No, it's no bother, she told me to get her up for the lottery anyway. So, how

comes you're not out tonight? It's not like you.'

'Well I had a big night last night. Thought I'd take it easy tonight. Two nights out in a row, I can't do it anymore.'

'Aye, it catches up with you eventually.'

Pierce doesn't want to dwell on how his social life is killing him.

'And how's the refrigeration plant doing then, Sean, is it up and running?'

'Oh aye, we've had it on-stream for over a month now.'

It amuses Pierce that his Uncle Sean, the woolly-jumpered island fisherman, uses the expression 'on-stream.'

'A couple of wee technical hitches at first but it's going fine now. Aye, here's your Auntie Bernie now, I'll just put her on.'

'Oh son, thanks very much for the lovely book you sent me, *The Big Apple*,'

is the first thing Bernie says.

'The photos in it were smashing, especially the Manhattan ones.'

Years ago Bernie had purchased a Hoover vacuum cleaner as a surprise for her husband. What was most surprising was that the Hoover entitled them to two free flights to destinations throughout the world, but there was no need to consult the atlas. Bernie knew exactly where she wanted to go: New York.

It still occasionally rankled with Pierce that Bernie and Sean had abandoned him that summer, leaving him three weeks in Glasgow with his parents. The longest three weeks of his life. And when they got back and Pierce finally joined them, all Bernie could do was talk about Manhattan.

'You know it just took me back there. I was looking at the pages and there I was, walking the streets again.'

Pierce has heard her New York stories a million times but he never tires of them, not because they are so riveting but because, even now, despite her illness, her pleasure in telling them makes her shine. He can hear it in her voice.

New York had been by no means a luxury trip. Money was tight and the exchange rate hadn't been in their favour. They found a cheap hotel, which didn't seem too dirty or dangerous and spun out their spending money by walking or taking the subway around the city. Bernie seems almost proud to tell him that they walked past the swanky restaurants and lived on hot dogs and coffee from street vendors. They preferred hot dogs, she always says. But they didn't really need money. There were plenty of things to do, walking only cost shoe leather, the views were free and so were Central Park and some of the museums.

Although they couldn't afford it, Bernie insisted on bringing home gifts for friends in the village to prove that they had actually been there, the only people from this small island, she is fond of saying, ever to have visited that one. She skipped hot dog dinners to buy plastic models of the Empire State building and snow domes of the Statue of Liberty.

'Oh, the picture of the statue is fantastic, Pierce, I haven't got one of it from that angle.'

It was the Statue of Liberty that had the greatest impact on Bernie. Its majesty and beauty had a profound effect on her. Sean says it was the first and only time in her life that she shut up talking. Bernie herself confirms that she was very quiet during their long visit to the statue. While they queued to go up, and all the way on the ferry back, she never said a word.

Back home she told everybody that up close it was actually *a pale green colour,* made of copper, the biggest copper sculpture in all of America. She insisted that Sean rename his boat, scraping off the faded white paint inscribed *The Lady Bernadette* and replacing it with much bigger fancier lettering *The Statue of Liberty*.

On their return the living room in their tiny croft house became a shrine to all things New York. Pride of place above the fireplace was given to the big poster of the statue she had bought in the gift shop and carried it as hand luggage rolled in a towel on the plane and train and boat home.

Pierce remembers his dismay when, as soon as she came back, she began talking about their next trip as though it would be happening soon. She tried to buy another Hoover but the special offer had finished and was never repeated. Her kitchen cupboards became filled with unlabelled tins and cut up breakfast cereal packets as she enthusiastically entered competition after competition to win another trip to New York. It never happened. And then she became ill.

'You shouldn't have done it, Pierce son,' she berates him. 'That book must have cost a fortune; you can't afford stuff like that. It's not even my birthday or anything.'

'Och, it was nothing, Bernie.'

It was an expensive book, even for Oxfam, and in pristine condition.

'Well, that was very kind of you son, greatly appreciated, wasn't it, Sean? Sean says greatly appreciated too. But anyway, what's going on? Why are you phoning on a Saturday night?'

Chapter 11

For some strange reason Daphne wakes up in a good mood. She's had a lovely dream and lies enjoying the rare sensation of joy for a few moments before reality must inevitably kick her in the teeth. The dream reminds her of a day when she and Donnie went to the beach and she manages to extend the pleasurable sensation by re-running in her mind that perfect day.

It was that deliciously uncommon luxury, a hot day in the Highlands, and they had the green-blue of the water and the vast expanse of virgin sand all to themselves. Donnie was agitated because Daphne wanted to strip off there and then. Someone, somewhere, with a long-range lens, perhaps hiding in the marshy clumps of heather that stretched for miles behind them, might try to take photos of Daphne's big white naked arse.

But he couldn't stop her once she was in the water. Squealing like a teenager, she pulled the wet sticky costume off and swung it above her head. She jumped and dived, white arse up and over, imagining herself a mermaid. The chill of the air and the water on her naked skin excited her and excited Donnie too. The salty water didn't inhibit her lady juice, it made it thicker, more slippery. Daphne tugged at his shorts and, reasoning that the photographer's lens – high-powered though it may be – couldn't record their underwater shenanigans, Donnie let her. As the shorts floated at his side Daphne fumbled between his legs and, just to scare him, pushed him from behind.

'Up periscope!' she laughed as his cock and belly broke the surface. As they discovered, the water supported any number of positions, some romantic, some erotic and some just plain silly. It was a wonderful day. Daphne will never do sea sex again, she'll never do any kind of sex again. She is old now. And her brief joy melts away.

The first leaf on the tree has opened. Actually at least six of them are open but only one is within reach of her window. The spring sunshine lights their new green like traffic lights, green for go.

Daphne loves spring. Every year she celebrates the end of winter by taking part in every spring ritual she can think of and makes up some of her own. She vigorously cleans the house and packs away her cheery red and green winter cushion covers, replacing them with lilac and pale yellow ones. On Pancake Tuesday she makes pancakes, getting the ready-mixed stuff at Asda and ambitiously flipping large floppy undercooked dods of batter around the kitchen. She buys daffodils and hyacinths and plants them in bright yellow plastic pots. She paints boiled eggs and gives them out to her students; she bakes hot cross buns for the staff. And every year for the past five years, she has made a ceremonial present of the first new leaf off the tree for Donnie.

This year she has done none of these things. It's half past three in the afternoon and Daphne isn't dressed yet. Unwashed and unconcerned for personal hygiene, she slobs around in her nightie and purple dressing gown. Spring has sprung and she's missed it. The season has started without her.

*

Now he's living the dream. Now Pierce McCormack is a bona fide editor. *Pierce McCormack*, it'll say on the inside cover, *Editor*. He and Tam, at a business meeting over several pints, have just settled on the title *Poyumtree*. Pierce thinks this name indicates the edgy, experimental unpretentious nature of their publishing policy. Tam is to be production manager, advertising exec, circulation manager and assistant ed.

Pierce is sick of knockbacks from wanks who graduated from posh English universities and don't get what he's about. Or they do get what he's about and it scares them. Either way, he isn't one of their clique and they refuse to publish him. But *Poyumtree* will. No more email submissions to slush piles that never get read, no more expensive photocopying, mailing and fruitlessly waiting, no more sipping vinegar wine at shitey readings, pretending to laugh at the obscure literary jokes made by hairy-faced, elbow-patched, Arts Council-funded wanks. They'll schmooze *him* now.

Except he's not sure how he's going to fit it all in. Pierce McCormack is a busy man. He's not one for lying in bed wasting the day, usually he's up for at least nine or half nine but by the time he faffs about the house it's time to go to the gym. He freely acknowledges himself to be a man of poetry, intellect, dreams, ideas and philosophy but this shouldn't and doesn't, preclude the corporeal. In the gym he loves the feeling of circumspectly, successfully, returning the weight to the bar, the sweet, relaxing, muscle tiredness. Through all the sweating and grunting he knows the tears in the muscles will repair and get bigger, make him stronger. And anyway, he enjoys sweating and grunting. It's a good way to work up a thirst.

He likes all kinds of sweat, for instance the sweat that breaks out on his top lip and forehead with a good vindaloo contrasting with the freezing fizz of the lager in his throat. He loves the gulab jamin and ice cream and coffee and After Eight mints. Pierce's dad has retired and, for the price of his company, the old man often meets him and treats him to a businessman's lunch at the Indian.

Sometimes, as Pierce rarely cooks, he just buys a big healthy bag of fruit, but more often than not he'll be so hungry by the time he leaves the pub that he'll need a Big Mac or a sausage supper. That's why he has to go to the gym. What with the curries and the big Macs and the pints, if he didn't train, he'd have to cart his belly around in a wheelbarrow.

The other kind of sweat Pierce likes is the kind to be had from a right good sex sesh. Because he has such a hairy chest he sweats a lot in the act of making love to a lady. But it's not only on his head that he's losing hair. With a bit of energetic *up and down* he sheds hair like nobody's business. The girl he shagged the other night ended up with almost as much chest hair as he had. She looked like Tarzan by the time they were finished. She was nice, she said she liked muscles on a man and a hairy chest and she never mentioned the bald patch. It's a pity she was married. Pierce started a piece about her. He's working on a collection of romantic poems, writing one for every girl he humps. It's called *For all the Girls I've Loved Before.* He thinks it's a pretty good title but he can't help thinking that he's heard it somewhere else. It could be *Poyumtree*'s inaugural publication. But he needs time to write.

Pierce has always to guard his RAT time, his reading and thinking time; so many demands are made upon him. He's always scooshing about like a burst hose. He feels duty bound to attend readings and book launches, even where there are few networking opportunities there is usually free drink and ladies to be pulled. If it's not business meetings with Tam or lunch with his dad, it's Wednesday night Poets and Pints, or Thursday afternoon reading group or the gym or the fucking buroo.

The buroo is getting to be real nuisance. Not content with him signing on every bloody week, now they want him to attend some stupid Restart interview. They're threatening to stop his money and he's running out of strategies. It was okay when Miss McLaren was in charge of his case. She'd haul him in at some ungodly hour in the morning for one of her wee chats but he'd show her some phoney job applications along with a haiku he'd written for her and she was quite happy. And quite fit for a woman of fifty. He would have given her one but Pierce feared it would spoil their professional relationship. As it turned out, he missed his chance because Miss McLaren was transferred. Now he has some hairy-arsed hot shot with the unshakeable belief that everyone is employable. The guy actually had the cheek to ask Pierce if he was embarrassed to be living off the state. Pierce replied that the state would have no problem living off him when the time came; taking fifty per cent of his income in taxes once his book was published.

As he turns the corner into the street Pierce is preoccupied with how he can get this guy off his case and get on with the work of being a poet. He has a Restart appointment with him tomorrow morning. It's not going to be easy, the guy is a fucking terrier. Then he sees Daphne, her purple goonie cracking in the sharp spring wind. At first he thinks she must be washing the windows, she always does mad things at this time of year. He stops and watches her for a moment. She's just sitting there. There's no sign of cleaning; she hasn't got a cloth or water or anything. Then it dawns on him. Oh no, the stupid depressive cow is trying to top herself.

Chapter 12

'Daphne!'

She looks up but only gives him one of her 'you're-shit-on-my-shoe' stares.

'Daphne, stop!'

She doesn't even look at him this time. Ah fuck her, he thinks, but it only lasts a second. He can't bear the idea of Daphne, of anyone, splattered all over the pavement.

He takes the stairs two at a time. His heart is pumping, he's buzzing with excitement. Pierce has been waiting all his life for this moment, the moment when he saves someone's life. She's not really going to kill herself. He's going to talk her down. Pierce is the best man for the job. He, better than anyone, can explain to her how beautiful life is. As a poet he does it every day.

This is going to be all over the papers. POET RESCUES SUI-CIDE. 'Pierce's poetry saved my life' says local woman. They'll be queuing up to offer him a publishing deal. He'll need an agent, a London agent. It's a pity Daphne doesn't smoke because he could give her a fag and when she leans in for a light he could grab her and pull her to safety.

He rattles her letter box and immediately sees that this is stupid, she's on the window ledge, she's hardly likely to answer the door. He'll have to break it down. He rams his shoulder into the door. It's fucking sore and the door doesn't give an inch. The hot flush of excitement is quickly cooling to fear. What if he's too late? That selfish cow better wait. He steps back along the corridor and takes a run at it, bracing himself for the pain. He rushes at the door with all the energy and life force that Daphne is about to squander.

The door opens. But Pierce's energy and life force is irresistible. It carries him on, past Daphne, along the hall until it meets an immoveable object, the inside wall. The pain in his shoulder makes him shake from the inside out. Pierce slides down the wall whimpering as Daphne stands over him.

'Pierce, what the hell are you doing? Are you drunk?'

Pierce can't reply. He'd like to reply, he's like to tell the fucking bitch ... but he can't, the pain in his shoulder is demanding all of his attention.

'Are you okay?'

Obviously he's not fucking okay. He's lying in her hallway in excruciating agony but it's just like Daphne to ask a question like that.

'Can you stand? Here, let me help you.'

Help from Daphne is the last thing Pierce wants. Not only has she spoiled his chances of a publishing deal, now she's made him break his shoulder.

'Have you hurt yourself?'

Duh! He thinks.

'Hmmm,' he nods.

'You need to sit down, your face is chalk white. Come into the living room.'

Stand up, sit down, the bitch is torturing him, but he lets her lead him into the living room. When he goes to sit down a new even sorer pain starts up. He has to go to the hospital.

'Daphne, phone an ambulance,' he whispers hoarsely, he can't feel or move his right arm.

'Pierce ...'

'I've broken my fucking shoulder. Would you please just phone an ambulance?'

'Really? You've broken your shoulder?'

Pierce means to just say 'yeah' manfully, but he's nodding his head and it's coming out like a baby's cry.

'Oh for God's sake! What the hell were you playing at, running in here like a madman?'

This is too much. Indignation gives Pierce his voice back.

'What the hell was *I* playing at? What the fucking hell were *you* playing at, Miss Hanging Off The Windowsill? Miss Melodrama? Miss I've Been Chucked And Life's Not Worth Living? Miss, Miss … !'

'I *was not* hanging off the windowsill! I was sitting on it. And I most certainly *was not* trying to kill myself; I can't believe you thought that.'

They sit in silence for a moment, Pierce wanting only that she'll make the call. He doesn't give a shit anymore what she was doing.

'No, actually, sorry. I can. Yes, I suppose someone who's been a bit fed up, sitting on a window ledge, it might look bad, but honestly, I was only trying to get a leaf from the tree, that's all I was doing.'

'A leaf from the tree?'

'Yeah, I do it every year, I pick the first leaf and give … er, I … That's why you were banging the door, you were trying to save me.'

Pierce nods. Now she gets it, now she'll phone.

'Oh God, I'm so sorry, Pierce.'

Daphne comes towards him and takes his head in her hands. Pierce has never noticed before what nice bouncy tits Daphne has. He's sure she never had them before, he would have noticed. Despite her purple goonie he has a great view from this angle.

'Just phone, Daphne, please? And get me the strongest painkillers you've got.'

'Pierce, I feel really awful about this. That was a wonderful thing you tried to do, even if you did get the wrong end of the stick. I'm so sorry you're hurt and I really, really, appreciate you trying to help.'

Pierce nods, accepting her thanks graciously. She really does have a lovely pair.

'But they're not going to send an ambulance, not for a broken shoulder. That's classed as a non-emergency.'

'I've broken my shoulder! I'm in pain here!'

'I know you are Pierce and I'm really sorry.'

'This *is* an emergency, I need pain relief and I need it now.'

'The hospital won't see it like that. Look, I'll phone a taxi, I'll pay for it. I'm very grateful for what you tried to do. You can't take anything, not even an aspirin, they might have to operate if the fracture is complicated. They have to see you first. And …

'And? And what?'

Pierce gives an involuntary shiver.

'I think you should brush you teeth.'

'Eh?'

'If they smell the drink off you they'll assume the worst and leave you waiting. I know, I've heard this story a hundred times from my students, trust me.'

Pierce has gone quiet. Really he would like to cry. They might have to operate. And they're going to make him wait just because he's had a few pints. They'll treat him like he's a jakey and have no respect and do a shoddy job or let students practise on him. They might put metal pins in him. If things go wrong anything could happen. He can't move it now, what if he loses the use of it? He'll be left with a useless withered thing. Disability might raise his poetry profile but for fuck's sake! Really he would like to cry.

'Will you come with me, Daphne?'

*

Daphne is at the window every time she hears a car pull up. Pierce has been gone four hours. She feels guilty about not going with him but she wasn't dressed. Dressed or not, it was the least she could have done for the poor guy. In between running to the window she makes a pot of camomile tea. Normally this relaxes her but with every sip a wave of self-loathing breaks over her and makes her back sticky with sweat.

The leaf is too far out of reach anyway. But even if she could reach it, what would she do with it? Take it to Donnie? And that would make everything alright? She should have gone with Pierce to the hospital; she owes him. Pierce, stupid and irritating as he is, rescued her in Asda and broke his shoulder thinking he was saving her from suicide.

On the windowsill she *had* thought about suicide. But only for a moment, less than a moment, a fraction of a millisecond. From a sitting position it would be easy just to slide forward a bit, lift her bum, until her weight carried her off the ledge and down, flying through the air. It would be a short flight. Three seconds max, she reckoned, before impact.

It would be a messy business, her body burst like a melon. She wouldn't make a pretty corpse but this appealed to Daphne's sense of the dramatic: all the more sickening for Donnie to look upon. She wouldn't oblige as a beautiful Ophelia, she'd make for him an ugly distorted thing, a pile of slimy cartilaginous muck, no longer recognisably human.

With such extensive damage putrefaction would be all the quicker, but this wasn't a bad thing. Apart from a bit of theatre at the funeral Daphne didn't want to hang around in earthly form. Compared with her constant exhausting state of anxiety the Big Sleep was an attractive option.

But then there was no guarantee that he would show up at the funeral. And if he did, would he bring the wife? Surely not, that would be the final insult. Apart from in Asda she had never even met the woman, never been introduced. And anyway, even if he didn't bring her she'd certainly comfort him when he came home. It might bring them closer together. She'd kiss him and reassure him that he mustn't blame himself. Once he'd shed a few tears and she'd made him a nice cup of tea they'd realise that perhaps it was for the best. Poor Daphne was obviously crazy.

And Mum would have to come back from Australia. She couldn't afford that kind of expense, she'd only just gone. And Albee, he'd probably come with her, he'd want to support Mum. She'd be gutted; she'd blame herself. Mum would think that because she went to live in Australia with Albee's young family that Daphne's suicide was her fault. And the death of a child, an only daughter, especially by suicide, would be a terrible thing to live with.

Daphne might not have anything to live for but she had something to live with. Something keeping her wrath warm. She just had to wait. If it meant she had to be alone and miserable, then she could do it; Daphne was tough. Some of her students, members of Alcoholics Anonymous, had a saying for when things weren't going well: *this too shall pass.* This was going to pass; nature would have to run its course. And then anything could happen, life was full of opportunities. That's why when Daphne heard Pierce banging and demanding to be let in she got off the windowsill and opened the door.

*

Daphne can't believe how chirpy he is. When he got out of the taxi he looked up and waved, gave her the thumbs up with his good arm. The other one was in plaster. He really had broken his shoulder.

She stood at her front door and called to him and, happy as a sandboy, he passed his own door and came up to meet her.

'Right, get the kettle on, Daffers, wounded man in need of a cuppa. Not unless you've any of that quality whisky left?'

'I think you're better off with tea, Pierce. You were an awful long time, what happened?'

'Well as you can see, I'm up to my neck in plaster.'

'Is it sore?'

'What d'you think? Fractured humerus, nasty. '

'What did you tell them? I hope you didn't say you were rescuing me from suicide.'

'Well I had to tell them something. I wasn't going to be treated like a jakey. Don't worry, I didn't mention your name.'

'Cheers.'

'Actually the nurses were really nice, and dead chuffed that I managed to talk you down. I'm a hero. No wonder they call them angels, they couldn't do enough for me. There's something about a handsome man in plaster that seems to bring out the mother in them.'

Pierce gingerly eases himself into a chair and puts his feet on the coffee table. Daphne says nothing but goes to the kitchen and makes tea. By the time she comes back he has worked out the remote control for the telly and is watching a re-run of *The Sweeney*.

'Be a love and stick two sugars in that for me, would you?'

Daphne is putting the sugars in while Pierce leans over awkwardly to reach the biscuits. She gave him a twenty for the taxi, the only money she had in her purse. There and back would have cost him eight quid tops but he hasn't mentioned giving her change.

'Unfit for work, I'm afraid. All I can do is rest it.'

'Well, that'll be a wee change for you.'

'Now Daphne, no need for sarcasm. I'm quite looking forward to seeing that git's face at the Restart interview tomorrow.'

'How long will you be in plaster?'

'Who knows? Months anyway. I've to go back in three weeks and they'll look at it.'

Daphne has the sinking feeling that she is going to be lumbered with him, that he'll milk this for as long as he possibly can.

'Totally starving, man. Being a hero gives a man an appetite. Any scran in the house?'

'By scran I take it you mean food?'

'You've got it Daphne, food, sustenance. A wee steak or maybe a chop, my body needs protein and calcium and stuff to repair, I need fed.'

'All I've got is soup.'

'Homemade or tinned?'

'Homemade.'

'Mmmm, lovely. Haven't had real soup for ages, bring it on, Daffers. Oh but, see before you do, I've got to pee, I don't know how I'll manage, you wouldn't mind…'

Pierce levers himself out of the chair and stands in front of her, his crotch at Daphne's eye level. He seems to be waiting for her to unfasten his zip.

'What's wrong with your other hand?'

'It's just that it's a bit awkward.'

'Take a flying fuck to yourself, Pierce. I'll give you soup but there's no way I'm touching your fly.'

Pierce shrugs and turns towards the toilet. 'Worth a try.'

Chapter 13

The silent calls from Daphne have stopped. Donnie's glad she's stopped calling, apart from the nuisance factor, he's relieved that she's through that phase. That stupid girly thing of phoning and not speaking was freaking him out. Maybe he should have spoken, maybe if he had spoken, acknowledged that he knew it was her… But there are too many maybes.

He's shredding again. And when he thinks of Daphne, silent at the other end of the line, it makes it all the harder. He's having difficulty shredding one particular photo. It was taken on a holiday in Spain with Daphne; taken without their knowledge or consent in a tourist trap nightclub.

Towards the end of the holiday, with a few bob left in the kitty, they had splurged on an expensive excursion to a nightclub advertised as exclusive. It was a chance to dress up and a change from the shorts and T-shirts they had worn every day for the last two weeks. Daphne was desperate for a chance to wear her new dress and Donnie had not humphed his good suit across Europe for nothing.

On the day of the big event, while he had his usual siesta, Daphne spent the afternoon shopping. She woke him to show what she'd bought: a sexy underwear and stocking set and some nail polish. She was so excited because the nail polish was the exact shade of her dress. Daphne was always enthusiastic about such simple things, like an untrained puppy, she was enthusiastic about everything. It was something that he had loved about her. Donnie didn't do enthusiasm, considering it showy and vulgar although he quietly and vicariously enjoyed Daphne's. But it was a constant balancing act. Unchecked, Daphne would reach intolerable levels of keenness and he would instinctively close her down. They were both sorry when this happened and both vigilant against extremes of high or low.

They took ages getting ready that night; taking turns in the bathroom, playing Spanish radio and pouring liberal measures of the duty-free Bacardi. Daphne lay on the bed with one foot in the air and wads of toilet roll between her toes applying the polish, giggling when she missed the nail. When she finished her foot she waggled it above her head in her usual indecorous fashion. With only one eye made up she couldn't wait to get into her new undies. Daphne favoured bright colours, yellow, pink, orange, the outfit was a gaudy but not unsophisticated mix of all three. She leaned into the mirror adjusting her bra straps as Donnie watched her. One side of her face an innocent goofy schoolgirl, the other a painted seductress. He couldn't resist either.

They had spent the holiday as they spent every holiday: shagging. They had shagged so much that two days earlier they had run out of condoms. Donnie refused to enter the *farmacia* with her. She was the one who claimed to speak a bit of Spanish, she could ask. Daphne returned giggling but condomless. Though she had tried, with various unseemly gestures, thank God he hadn't gone in, either her Spanish wasn't up to it or the shop girl was taking the piss. Two days without sex, the stockings and the Bacardi combined to make Donnie horny.

But it was a different kind of horny. He didn't just want to take his pleasure, to empty the tubes; he wanted to adore his beautiful silly Daphne. Sex was slow and tentative; Daphne making her little mewing noises that he found so humbling. This woman knew him, all of him, and still loved him.

When they first had sex without protection Daphne used to constantly remind him not to come inside her. This annoyed him. He wasn't some teenager who, unable to control himself, would go off like a two bob rocket. Eventually she trusted him and stopped saying it.

That night she didn't say it and that night, swept away on a romantic notion, Donnie came inside her. She came too, at the same moment, a feat they had not often accomplished.

He apologised profusely, pretending it had been an accident. Daphne hurriedly ran a bath. Although he said nothing, Donnie was vaguely insulted. Why was she so keen to flush him away? But he knew the answer. It lay in his response the last time her period was late. He ranted and sulked and behaved as though it was all her fault.

He followed her into the bathroom and saw her: the goofy schoolgirl hunched crying in the bath, hugging her knees to her chest, scooshing the showerhead inside herself. She looked so alone. This was his fault; he had caused her to feel like this. He tried to do something to help. Daphne allowed him to gently push her back, to open her legs. He filled his mouth with water, took a deep breath and dived. He found her cunt, clamped his mouth to it and blew. Daphne was laughing as the tears dried on her cheeks.

She cheered up before he did. There was nothing more to be done that night. Tomorrow she would get a morning after pill but the *farmacia* would be closed now. It would still be okay to take it tomorrow so long as she got up early. And anyway they had spent all that money on the nightclub excursion. Why not just enjoy themselves tonight and sort it out tomorrow? She was taking this all on herself and letting him off the hook. Daphne referred to it as the accident, not his accident; she apportioned no blame. She had never been so precious to him.

She looked stunning in her dress but his eyes were constantly drawn to her little round tummy wondering what was growing there. Cells dividing and separating, half her, half him. On the coach he put his arm around her, protecting what was his, and kissed her hair and stroked her belly. It was the closest he could come to telling her.

As their bus pulled up they had an appreciation of just how exclusive the place was. The coach park was the size of several football pitches, the club held thousands of fleeced and befuddled tourists. They were rounded up and prodded like prisoners of war towards the entrance and once inside, a bright flash exploded in their faces as their photo was taken.

The next day, hung-over and sunburnt, dehydrated and without protection from the tremendous heat, they walked the streets of

Alcudia looking for a *farmacia*. It was Sunday and most shops were closed. When they final found the one duty pharmacists the man explained in halting English that they needed a prescription. There was a doctor who would give them one but he was on the other side of town and charged 50 euros for a two-sentence note. The doctor, gleeful of their predicament, issued the note and they trudged, too broke to take a taxi, back to the *farmacia*. On the flight home and for the next two days Daphne was sick with the effects of the pill. Her head hurt and she cried all the time reassuring him that it was just the hormones. But in the photo that was taken in the club, there was no sign of that.

In the photo they are looking not at the camera but at each other. Caught unawares, Donnie is smiling. Not his usual lips pulled tight photographic smile. He is relaxed, mellow, handsome in his suit. His face has caught the sun and his eyes are shining. In Daphne there is no hint of the tearful kid hunched in the bath of a few hours ago. Donnie's hand rests on her tummy and her hand on top of his. In that moment, caught forever by a Spanish tout, they are happy.

Chapter 14

As she walks along the corridor Daphne senses an atmosphere of excitement. The students are louder and more boisterous than usual. Her own students are usually hanging around the door waiting for her to open but today they are clustered at the opposite end of the corridor, something is going on. Then she sees it on the door handle. She looks back along the corridor but the students have disappeared. Her arms are sore with the weight of the exercise books she has humphed up two flights of stairs and now she has to go all the way down again to get the janitor.

'Bloody condoms everywhere,' grumps the Andy the Janny, twanging on his rubber gloves for the fifteenth time that day, 'happens every bloody year.'

The college is hosting its annual Sexual Health Awareness Day to encourage responsible attitudes in the student population, the chief element of which seems to be an unending supply of free condoms that the students blow up like balloons, fill with water and throw at each other, stretch over their heads, or pull over classroom door handles. She hasn't looked too closely at the contents of the condom, just seeing it makes her feel queasy, but it appears to contain organic matter in a semi-liquid form.

With the protection of his rubber gloves it's easy for Andy to slide the condom off. The handle is slimy with it and a glutinous strand dangles but at least he has unlocked the door and Daphne need not come into contact with it.

'Yeesh,' she says, 'what the hell is that? Ectoplasm?'

'It's egg white,'

'How do you know?'

'Och, that's an old trick. We did it to a guy in the TA.'

'Did what?'

Daphne instantly regrets the question. Andy is always full of ugly macho tales about what they get up to in the TA. He has no shame and relishes telling anyone who is prepared to listen.

'Big Arthur, he was blind drunk one night. We were away on manoeuvres and he passed out in the tent. Terrified of poofs he was, a total phobia. A couple of the lads had the idea to shove a condom up his arse. Let him think he'd been assaulted.'

'Let him think? He *was* assaulted!'

'Oh no, there's none of that in our company, no poofery on my watch. It was just a bit of fun. He was that drunk we knew he wouldn't feel a thing. Obviously we had to make it look good. Egg white's the very dab,' says Andy, holding the condom up to the light for her inspection. 'You can't tell the difference, see?'

Daphne can hear her students whispering and giggling around the corner of the corridor and worries that they can hear Andy.

'Funny, y'know, he never said a word about it the next day, never a dickie bird. Poor bugger still thinks he was poofed,' Andy says, shaking his head in wonderment. 'He gets called Martha now, no to his face right enough, he's a big guy.'

'Right, class, c'mon, let's get in and get started,' Daphne calls up the corridor to the students. She places herself as a human shield between the innocent young people in her care and the sick weirdo employed as the janitor.

Daphne knows she should attempt to discover the condom culprit but it'll be the usual accusations and denials and after Andy's flippant homosexual rape story the door handle prank seems innocuous. To the class's disappointment, the matter is dropped until Omar, the class clown, leaves the room and, on his return, touches the offending handle. Everyone laughs heartily, terror and disgust are all over his face as he frantically tries to find something to wipe the smeg from his hand.

'Miss, miss! I've got it on me, the dirty bastards!'

Up until now Daphne thought the likeliest suspect was Omar himself but his distress seems genuine.

'Omar, calm down, go to the toilet and wash it off.'

'Miss, could I get Aids from that?'

Omar's voice is cracking and he's not playing it for laughs.

'No. It's only egg white. Don't worry, wash it off and on your way back get the leaflets from the Sexual Awareness stall, enough for everybody, that's what we'll work on for the rest of the class. '

A communal groan surfaces above the tittering.

'Okay, the lesson today will be '*everything you need to know about sexually transmitted diseases but were too busy playing with condoms to find out*'.'

'Miss?' says Gary.

'Yes, Gary.'

'How did you know it was egg white?'

Daphne has found her culprit.

'Andy the janitor told me, how did *you* know?'

The class whistle and bang their desks at her implied accusation, confirming her suspicions.

'The janny told me,' Gary replies.

Chapter 15

Daphne doubts if she'll ever set eyes on the lovely shelves of Asda again. She can't get to sleep at night and she can't get out of bed in the morning. It's like her jammies are made of Velcro. Her life is an exhausting whirl of getting up and going to work, walking straight home, not sleeping, making soup and sneaking out to the deli in the dead of night. Every night she buys increasingly exotic ingredients for the soup. Yesterday she made a pot of spinach and coconut.

Pierce loves the soup. Every night when he comes back he lifts his hoover with his good arm and uses it to bang on the ceiling. This is his signal that he's ready for his soup. Daphne hates being summoned like this but she heats the soup and pours a huge bowl for him and a smaller plate for herself and takes it down to him on a tray.

The first few days he expressed gratitude but now he just expects it. He even complained when she brought lentil soup for three days running. He demonstrated to her the effect it was having on his bowels by squeezing out long squeaky noises that sounded more like a cat trapped in a washing machine than a proper fart.

For the purposes of nutritional balance, because she suspects that this is the only decent meal Pierce gets all day, she has started to vary the soup and has become increasingly ambitious. He seems to enjoy her experiments, and her company. He tells her about his pathetic pie-in-the-sky *Poyumtree* plans and the women he cops off with and reads her his latest oeuvres. If she's honest she too looks forward to soup time. After weeks of Daphne not answering the phone or texts or Facebook messages her friends have given up on her and stopped.

Now Pierce is banging up through Daphne's floor. Usually he bangs twice. Thump, pause, thump. The building is old and it can't be doing the plasterwork any good but he's too lazy to walk up one flight of stairs and tell her that he's home now and would she please bring him down some soup.

But Daphne's thinks it's not really laziness, he's embarrassed to come and ask. She has also suggested that if he must bang then can he not use something lighter than the vacuum cleaner? Lifting it above his head with his one good arm can't be easy. The pause between the thumps is evidence of this. Daphne has suggested a brush or mop handle but he claims to have neither of these.

Pierce is far from housebound, although he freely roams the pubs and parks of Glasgow; he likes to imagine himself as the writer character in Steven King's *Misery*.

When Daphne laughs at this he tries to make her feel guilty by saying that with this stookie, this plaster cast up his arm, he's not allowed in the weights room at the gym. It's all her fault his training programme has gone to hell, he implies.

Thump, thump, thump, big long pause, thump, thump, thump. These three new thumps mean something different. Could it be an S.O.S? She turns the gas off on the soup and goes downstairs to investigate.

Pierce's friend Tam answers the door.

'Hi Daphne.'

'Hi Tam, where is he?'

'I'm here!' shouts Pierce from the living room. 'Clever girl, I knew you would get it.' He bursts into song: '*Knock three times on the ceiling if you want me*, Didn't I tell you, Tam?'

'Three thumps?'

'Aye, you, Tam and me. Tam'll take a wee plate of soup if there's enough in the pot.

Pierce returns to his one-handed joint rolling and an earlier conversation with Tam.

'Listen,' Pierce says, 'I'm not kidding. Every young guy gets a guitar or a drum set and joins a band, we've all done it.'

Tam is quiet but he's nodding his head.

'And being able to sing, so what? Everybody can sing, we're born with it, it's no big deal.'

Pierce breaks off to lick the cigarette paper. He is concentrating so intently on the joint that it is a few seconds before he begins to speak again.

'And,' Pierce continues sagely, 'I've no doubt that some of them, many of them in fact, have some talent. But talent's not enough.'

Although Tam is still in agreement Daphne thinks Pierce is being a bit harsh. Tam is the guitarist and singer with a local band. She's about to stick up for Tam when Pierce says something quite unexpected.

'It's stamina that's required. Staying power, sticking at it, believing in yourself enough to keep going. You *don't* have to be a pretty boy, you're wrong if you think that, Tam. Look at some of the ugly fuckers you see on the telly. And anyway, you're no movie star but you're not the ugliest.'

Tam begins to protest but Pierce cuts him short.

'Look, I'm telling you, you've got it. Fuck's sake, I hardly saw you the first year you got the guitar, you practised non-stop. How many other guitarists put in the hours that you do, eh? How many? And how many songs have you written now?

'Don't know, more than fifty anyway,' says Tam.

'Good songs, some of them. All you need is the break, but it'll come, Tam, it'll come. The cream always rises to the top. Once the record companies hear you they'll want you. They need talent.'

Daphne is surprised to hear this. This is the wrong way round. She had always assumed that Pierce kept Tam as his sidekick to flatter *his* ego. Probably, she thinks, they take turns at bumming each other up. She has stumbled into their cosy little back slapping club. Of course there is always an outside chance that Pierce actually means it.

'I'm telling you, Tam, I've seen more than my fair share of chancers, a lot of wannabees. I don't see many like you,' says Pierce, handing the joint to Tam, allowing him first dibs.

'Cheers Pierce,' says Tam, blushing.

Daphne thinks she's going to be sick. With arms folded she goes and looks out of the window until the feeling of panic goes away.

With things as they are, people saying nice things about other people make her nervous. She prefers it when Pierce is a smartarse, that she can handle. By the time she rejoins the conversation she is relieved to discover that Pierce has returned to more familiar ground, being the Voice of Authority. He has on his loud patient instructing voice, talking to Tam as though he's an idiot.

'Pretty much everything in the house, except the mattress on the bed, I wouldn't have a used mattress.'

'Man, that's amazing! Did you hear that Daphne? See everything in this flat? Pierce got it out of a skip.'

'*Objets trouvés* I prefer to call them, Tam.'

Daphne, looking round and appraising the furniture is forced to admit, at least to herself if not to Pierce, that he has some lovely furniture.

'You'd be surprised the difference a tin of varnish or a packet of fabric dye can make. Or even just giving something a good clean. D'you never watch these makeover programmes on the telly? I've had some good ideas from them.'

There is a lot of dark polished wood in the bookcases and the roll top writing desk. None of the chairs match and the sofa is different again. There are many different identifiable styles and eras but rather than look like a mishmash it looks deliberate; stylish and well thought out. The overall effect is a witty take on the reading room of a gentleman's club.

'Yeah but you have to find the stuff in the first place, man,' says Tam. 'You've been unbelievably lucky finding all this stuff in the street. Typical Pierce, always lands on his feet. '

'Luck is only a part of it, Tam, it's having an eye for it, for the potential it might have. See that chest of drawers?'

Both Tam and Daphne twist their necks to see a tall elegant tower of drawers which bow out, like an hourglass, wider at the top and the bottom. It looks like the kind of thing that costs a fortune in the designer shops.

'That's just two sides of an old desk stacked one on top of the other. And the lamp? That's the fitting from a seventies lamp from Oxfam and a fancy box, a sewing box I think it was originally.'

'I didn't know you could buy electrical stuff at Oxfam,' says Daphne.

'You can't. That's the beauty of it. People take stuff into Oxfam, Oxfam have to refuse it, health and safety or something, and then they can't be bothered to humph it home again. You know the wee lane down the side of the Oxfam shop? I've found tons of good electrical stuff down there.'

'You'd better watch out, Pierce, telling Tam and me all your trade secrets. We might get there before you.'

'Listen Daphne, this city is replete with good stuff that people throw out, there's plenty for all of us. If you're interested I'll tell you exactly how to go about finding it.'

'I'm interested,' says Tam.

'I'm not,' says Daphne, but she listens anyway.

'It's all about timing,' Pierce tells them as he receives the spliff from Tam and inhales. 'Timing your run. Tuesday nights for this area for example, people want rid of their old stuff and phone the council to have it uplifted. They're told to put it out for a Wednesday morning uplift so mostly they put it out on Tuesday night. Best times are the first Tuesday of any school holidays.'

'School holidays, why is that?'

'Think about it. Mum and/or Dad have to take time off work to look after the kiddies. The kids are driving them crazy so, to while away an afternoon, they take them out to Ikea or wherever. More often than not, they come home with a few self-assembly boxes.'

'Therefore, they have to chuck out their old stuff to make way for the new,' says Daphne.

'Spot on, Daphne. More often than not there's nothing wrong with their old stuff.'

'Pierce, see the broken chairs you have out in the hall, what are you going to make with them?'

'Nothing, they're bait.'

'Bait?' asks Daphne.

'Yeah. Some people would never take the initiative and chuck stuff out by themselves; sometimes they need a little encouragement. I bait the trap with a few bust-up old chairs or whatever, strategically placing them for easy access but low visibility and sit back and wait.'

'Oh nice one!' says Tam, slapping his thigh in appreciation.

'Aye, it's a laugh to watch them sneak out of their posh houses and dump the stuff. They skulk about like criminals. I've had some great stuff that way, good enough to sell on to the dealers, it's always a bit of pocket money.'

'Aye, I suppose it beats earning a living,' mutters Daphne.

'Oooooow!' Pierce cries in mock anguish. 'Anyway, it'll not be long now till I'm earning a good living, eh Tam?'

'Too right, Pierce.'

'Tam's band have sacked that dickhead manager,' he says by way of explanation. 'They've got themselves a new one, a real manager, someone that knows what he's doing, someone that'll take them the whole road: gigs, record deal, tours, stardom.'

'And who is that then? Asks Daphne, although, recalling the pep talk Pierce gave Tam, she thinks she knows the answer.

'Yours truly.'

Daphne smiles. Tam's band has been going for two years with a different manager every few months. They are yet to play a properly paid gig, but Daphne feels bad about having a go at Pierce. In an attempt to restore the bonhomie between them she exaggerates her disdain and banters, 'The only thing you can manage is a left-handed wank.'

'Aye well,' says Pierce laughing, 'you won't help me out so what's a boy to do? A man has needs you know.'

'Pierce has already got us a gig,' says Tam, full of indignation. 'In that new pub Moda, the trendy place, he knows the manager.'

Daphne accepts the reprimand from Pierce's faithful acolyte and nods solemnly. Pierce knows quite a few pub managers. Throughout the years he has invested many hours drinking with them when they were mere bar stewards and chargehands. Now that they have reached the exalted position of pub manager maybe Pierce can call in a few favours. Good for Tam, thinks Daphne, she's heard demos of Tam's band and they're really not that bad.

'We're playing next Friday, you should come, we've got a whole new set.'

'Aye, why don't you, Daff? Get your glad rags on and come with me, I'll put you on the guest list,' says big-hearted Pierce.

'Love to, Tam. But I'm a bit busy.'

'Busy doing what?' says Pierce, 'Making soup?'

'D'you not want any then? I've got it ready upstairs.'

'Too right I want it and so does Tam. Get your arse up those stairs and get me my soup, woman. And a plate for Tam too. He's got to keep his strength up, this boy's going to be a star.'

'Right you are, Sir.'

'Don't go to any bother, Daphne,' says Tam. 'Are you sure there's enough?'

'Tam, there's enough,' says Pierce. 'She always makes tons. A superfluity of soup.'

Daphne doesn't know what superfluity means but it annoys her anyway. Pierce is taking advantage of her good nature.

'Mi casa, su casa,' says Pierce.

'Cheers,' says Tam, 'Olé.'

But your casa hasn't got any soup, thinks Daphne. Your casa is a soup-free zone.

'Daphne is the Soupmeister. If there's a name for it, Daphne'll make soup with it.'

Pierce is talking about Daphne as though she wasn't there, as though she were the hired help. She has half a mind to tell them soup is off today, and she would but she's quite keen to get feedback on her new recipe. Pierce, although he's an arrogant git, is very constructive about what he thinks of the soup but it is, after all, only one man's opinion. It might be interesting to have another perspective.

'Yeah, Tam,' she reassures him, 'there's enough but I don't know if you'll like it.'

'Aye well, you see, he's a man of simple tastes. Meat and two veg, that's Tam. The soup might be a bit rich for your peasant blood. What is the soup du jour, Daphne? Something with pumpkin and rosemary?'

'Aye, I know why you're saying Rosemary,' says Tam, with a sly glance towards Daphne. 'That's the bird you were telling me about, isn't it? The one you got off with on Monday?'

This is a game Tam plays. He tries to dub Pierce in, to tell on him, mentioning other women as a way of trying to spoil Pierce's chances with Daphne. What Tam doesn't realise, and what Pierce and Daphne realise very well, is that Pierce has no chance with Daphne. Never has had, never will.

'Aye, sweet Rosemary, out spending her income support benefit. Monday night in Clatty's, Tam, lots of lovely ladies, you should come, it's rich pickings.'

Nicely deflected by Pierce, thinks Daphne in grudging admiration. Tam is thwarted in his attempt to thwart a Daphne/Pierce liaison; he has been out-thwarted. Tam changes the subject back to soup, which he pronounces *syup*.

'My Ma does a lovely syup, scotch broth, nothing to beat it.'

'Your loyalty to your Ma is touching Tam but what Daphne creates is more than that. 'Soup' is an insufficient word to describe it, 'consommé' doesn't cover it either.'

'Bisque,' counters Tam.

'Chowder,' says Pierce after a few moments' thought.

Things go quiet while the two men, and Daphne too, try to think of another soup word. Daphne thinks of potage but she's embarrassed to say it.

'But it's the fertility of her imagination that's so breathtaking,' says Pierce finally, changing the subject. 'The variety of ingredients, where do you get that stuff, Daphne? Hey Tam! This is a good one: It's *pure potage poetry*.'

Pierce sticks his good left arm in the air for Tam to give him a high-five in recognition of his superior wordplay.

'I'll get the soup,' says Daphne turning to leave.

'D'you need a hand? There's Tam'll go with you, help you bring it up.'

Though Daphne doesn't reply, doesn't actually want Tam in her house, she hasn't cleaned up for a while, he dutifully follows her upstairs.

The soup has thickened and when she turns the heat on again it's bubbling so Daphne is keen to get it out and on to plates before it sticks to the bottom. Tam is all business, overeager to help; he opens cupboards randomly, leaving the doors open before eventually finding plates and laying them out on the table. Space in her wee kitchen is tight at the best of times but with two people and an obstacle course of the open cupboard doors to negotiate, the pot is becoming a lethal weapon. It's too heavy and too hot, she's about to drop it but somehow she makes it to the plates and pours. It is still boiling and some splashes onto the edge of her thumb. With the consistency of molten lava the bright orange soup sticks to her thumb. For a moment it feels cold on her skin, then it burns. Her thumb finds its way to her mouth but it feels even hotter in there.

'Stick it under the tap, Daphne, that's the best thing.'

Tam turns on the tap and Daphne tentatively puts her thumb under the flow. That hurts too and she pulls away but Tam takes her arm and guides her hand back under the tap. A blister is developing, Tam is tutting as he examines it but Daphne's attention is taken with the hair on Tam's arm. It is golden, each strawberry blonde strand brushed in a sideways sweep. Like Donnie's. Tam has the same red hair and skin colouring of Donnie. She stares at his arm. She doesn't look up, she doesn't want Tam to see how sad she feels but also she wants to pretend, just for a few moments that the arm that is holding hers is Donnie's.

'Hey!' says Tam with a soft laugh in his voice.

Daphne's face has crumpled to an unflattering girn. She's angry with Tam and with Pierce for placing Tam here in her kitchen, she's angry with Donnie for having golden arms, angry with herself for crying.

'C'mere.'

Tam pulls her towards him and Daphne lets him. The embrace is awkward, Tam has kept her hand under the flow of water, his other arm he uses to encircle her head.

'It's only a wee blister. We'll get a plaster on that and you'll be fine.'

Daphne tries to lift her head, she is being pathetic, but she is caught in the lasso of his arm and she rests her nose on it, sniffling amidst the gold.

The throb of pain in Daphne's thumb feels right. It is a focus for her nagging free-floating hurt. This is something she can pinpoint, a good reason to cry. And there is justice in it. Any woman who puts up with a nutcase boyfriend for years, too stupid to see his weakness, her own weakness, should expect all she gets. A woman vacuous enough to be an Asdaphile, shallow enough to become Asdaphobic, a woman, who despite getting her fingers burnt, still yearns for the heat of the fire.

'Sorry Tam, I just got a fright. I don't need a plaster.'

Tam's ginger arm hairs are tickling her nose, his skin smells of cigarette smoke and sweat; manly, familiar and strange. Her thumb pounds in time with her heart, hurting, burning; the righteous agony of an ecstatic flagellant. This is best time she's had in ages.

Tam releases her, she would like to stay there but feeling good is unmerited and confusing for Daphne and anyway, the soup will get cold.

'You sure?'

'Yeah, it's nothing. Better get the soup downstairs before he starts chapping up again. Can you carry the tray?'

'Nae bother, hen.'

Daphne smiles. She can see that Tam is chuffed with himself for taking charge of the situation, for being a shoulder for her to cry on. He is ten years younger than Daphne, a good twelve years younger than Pierce, but he's old-fashioned in his manners and seems as pleased as a pensioner to have served a useful role.

It occurs to Daphne that she has always found Tam attractive. With him being a friend of Pierce's, she has never even imagined fancying him but now she understands what the attraction is. He looks a bit like Donnie; not only do they share the same Celtic hair and skin tones, he has the same shape of nose, the same curve to his chin. They could be related, maybe distant cousins, it's not beyond the realms of possibility, but Daphne won't ask.

'I thought you two had eloped,' says Pierce in a childish whine when they go back downstairs.

'Daphne burnt her thumb on the soup.'

Pierce is not mollified.

'Ace beats a king; gammy arm beats a burnt thumb, no contest. I trust the thumb is no impediment to your soup duties, Daff?'

A few weeks ago Daphne would have told Pierce that there are no soup duties, that she brings it from the goodness of her heart and that he better be damned grateful or he'll find himself soupless and hungry. But the fight has gone out of her. She accepts her fate as his lackey, in a way she likes it, Pierce is Daphne's hair shirt.

'What is it today then, loganberry and turnip? Aardvark and liquorice? With maybe a few crispy croutons of armadillo?'

'Have you been thinking them up while we were upstairs? Is that the best you can do? We were away a good ten minutes, Pierce.'

'Shut it, wife, and serve.'

Tam is visibly surprised and alarmed at the way Pierce talks to her but it's water off a duck's back to Daphne.

'Carrot and orange,' Daphne says in a flat world-weary voice. 'No croutons. But there's nice bread.'

'You know, Daphne, you want to lay off that bread. You're piling it on, hen. I was planning on sending you out to sell your body and bring me back the money but nobody'll want you if you keep getting walloped into the bread like that.'

This is nothing Daphne has not heard before so there is no shock value for her, unlike for Tam, who is open-mouthed with the scale of Pierce's affront. But when Pierce mentions her increasing waistline Daphne instinctively tugs at her baggy jumper pulling it out to disguise the curve of her belly.

'And the amount of butter you put on it, it's not ladylike.'

'But prostituting myself with you as my pimp is?'

'Look Daphne, I've told you before; you're not a bad looking lassie even if you are a bit lardy. You could earn in a night, say, twenty-four quid?'

'Twenty-four is a lot of tricks, I'd be knackered.'

Tam is the only one who laughs. 'Aye, some men like a fat burd,' he says, warming to the subject, 'something to bounce on.'

Pierce has not yet tasted the soup. His spoon is halfway to his mouth but he stops to rebuke his foolish friend.

'Ho! Bit of respect, Tam. Daphne isn't fat, she knows I'm only kidding her on.'

'Oh sorry Daphne, no offence.'

Daphne smiles in sympathy for poor confused Tam.

'None taken, Tam. Try the soup.'

'Cheers Daphne. It looks brilliant.'

'Carrot and orange, eh?'

Pierce has cued a soup-appreciation moment and they all look down at their plates. Steam rises from the old-fashioned blue-patterned plates as the savoury smell perfumes the room. The bright orange colour seems solid but close up consists of pulp held in a thick glue. Daphne has already tasted it from her thumb and knows it's good, one of her best, though it could do with a bit more salt. Pierce gives a slow majestic nod; he closes his eyes and begins an incantation.

'Let us give thanks for this humble meal, that heart and soul and art and poetry, that spirit may be sustained and the muse, and our bowels, may move through Daphne's super-duper soup.'

Grace having been said, they take up their spoons.

'It's not the worst I've tasted,' Pierce pronounces.

This is of little help to Daphne. It probably means he doesn't like it but doesn't want to say in front of Tam. He's sparing her feelings, presenting a united front, overcompensating for Tam's earlier rudeness.

'Hey Tam, was Daphne telling you that her house got robbed last night?'

'No way! Really?'

Tam looks to Daphne for confirmation but her head is down in her plate.

'Aye well, she was a bit embarrassed about it, weren't you, Daphne?'

Daphne nods, there is little point in doing otherwise.

'The swines that broke in trashed the place, turned it upside down. Took her all night to clean up.'

'Well you've done a good job, Daphne, your house looked fine to me.'

'And when they couldn't find anything, God love her, she hasn't got anything worth blagging, they helped themselves to soup.'

Tam raises his voice, indignant on Daphne's behalf. 'Junkie bastards, these people have no respect!'

'So, not content with tearing up the house and eating the soup they actually shit in the pot.'

'In the pot of soup?'

'Aye. A big toaly floating about in it, wasn't there Daphne?'

'Aw man, that's disgusting.'

'She had to throw half of it out.'

Tam's lips are approaching his spoon and he stops to take in the significance of what Pierce has said.

'Mmmm,' says Pierce, 'I don't know, I think it gives it a certain piquancy.'

Daphne and Pierce share a smirk as Tam returns his spoon to his plate.

*

On her way into the consulting room Daphne catches sight of herself in the big gilt mirror in the passageway. She is white-faced and puffy-eyed and embarrassingly conscious that she probably smells. She's only met Dr Wilson once before but Dr Wilson doesn't seem aware of this and greets her like an old friend. Daphne hasn't quite made up her mind what she is going to say or what ailment she will come up with but as soon as the door closes, she starts to cry. This is a surprise to her but not to Dr Wilson. The doctor produces a large box of hankies from her desk, compliments of the manufacturers of Prozac, and hands them to Daphne. Without Daphne saying anything, Dr Wilson begins to question her.

'What seems to be the trouble?'

Daphne doesn't know what to say.

'Any pain or physical symptoms?'

Daphne can't think of any except for the constant sensation of having a big hole in the middle of her chest but it sounds such a stupid thing to say.

'How have you been sleeping?'

She knows the answer to this one.

'Okay, but I wake up early and can't get back to sleep.'

Dr Wilson nods.

'Tired all the time?'

Daphne nods.

'I can't think straight.'

'Eating?'

Daphne shrugs.

'Feelings of sadness, anxiety, hopelessness?'

Spot on. Daphne nods emphatically. She knows Dr Wilson is going through a checklist of the signs and symptoms of depression. It is another surprise that she can answer honestly to most of them.

'How long have you been feeling like this?'

'I'm not sure, months maybe.'

'Any particular reason? Anything significant happen recently?'

Daphne shakes her head; emphatically denies.

Daphne leaves Dr Wilson's surgery with a sick note for a month and a prescription for antidepressants. She can't believe how easy it was. She's heard of people throwing sickies when there was nothing wrong with them but she is amazed that she got away with it so easily. A free month-long holiday from work. Daphne is bona fide now, she's off her head and has a doctor's note to prove it.

She has brought an envelope addressed to the college and stops at the postbox, reading what the doctor has written and then sealing it in the envelope. Dr Wilson has said that she is suffering from *free-floating anxiety*. Daphne laughs. She tears the prescription into confetti-sized pieces and pushes them into the postbox.

Chapter 16

Pierce gets a phone call.

'Hello Pierce, is it yourself?'

'Aye, hello Sean, that's weird. I was just thinking about you. How're you and Bernie doing?'

'I'm fine, fine. Still working away up at the new refrigeration plant.'

'And Bernie? How is she?'

'Ah well, she's not too great just at the moment.'

'What have they said?'

'Och, you know, just the usual. They've given her one of these fancy things for the pain, a driver they call it. It's not a driver to drive a car, like,' Sean says with a chortle, 'it's a wee button she presses when it gets sore.'

Pierce responds to his uncle's wee laugh with one of his own but it's strangling his throat. He is as uncomfortable hearing this as Sean is having to tell him. Pierce thinks if you could hear pain down the phone, the wires would be screaming. Sean always underplays his wife's illness and Pierce, to help him out, keeps up the pretence.

'What are you up to at the minute, Pierce, are you awful busy?'

'No, no, not at all. Is there something…'

'I'm over on the mainland and I just thought if you fancied a wee jaunt over to see us…'

'Aye, sure Sean, I can come right away.'

'Now there's no great hurry, son. I'm here with a bit of business tomorrow and maybe the day after.'

'Is there someone with Bernie?'

'Don't you worry. Agnes McConnell will look in on her, she's only through the wall. I didn't want to leave her but, as I say: a bit of business, it couldn't be helped.'

'Oh no, I understand, Sean.'

Pierce feels bad; he hadn't meant to imply criticism.

'Aye, sure. I'll come and meet you, Sean. Have you brought the boat?'

'How else would I get here? I'm getting a bit old for the swimming,' says Sean, laughing his hearty nothing-gets-me-down laugh.

You're getting a bit old to be bringing a forty-five foot boat alone, thinks Pierce, but he would never say it. Instead he laughs.

*

Pierce meets Sean at their usual rendezvous, The Harbour Arms.

He has been coming here to meet him twenty-odd years. It was his mother who first brought him and left him standing outside with his poly bag. His parents felt it pretentious for a child to have personal luggage and anyway, the family only had one jumbo-sized suitcase. The poly bag, packed for all eventualities: shorts and T-shirts, plastic sandals, warm jumper, denims, anorak and wellies, was light enough for him to carry although he was only a little lad. Pierce used to lean against the wall of the pub close to the flue from where the sickly-sweet grown-up smell of beer and cigarette smoke came. Always, eventually, Sean came out. His mother was still inside, still enjoying her drink but Sean came out to make his ritual welcome. He whacked young Pierce over the head with a rolled-up newspaper, rubbed his rough whiskers in the child's face and brought him a packet of cheese and onion crisps.

As the years went by Pierce's poly bag became an adolescent's sports bag then a teenager's rucksack. It was still a rucksack, but he no longer waited outside.

'All right Sean? Same again?'

The conversation always began the same. Although they had

not seen each other from one year to the next, Sean and Pierce, on their first encounter, both behaved as though he had only popped out momentarily.

'Aye, same again will do me fine, son. What happened to you?' says Sean, pointing at Pierce's plastered arm.

'Och, it's nothing, I broke it,' he says rather obviously. 'Rescuing a damsel in distress.'

Pierce would like to tell his uncle the whole story, it's a good one but Sean's mind is apparently on other things.

'D'you know anything about cameras, Pierce? I'm in the market for a good one.'

'It depends on what you want, Sean. How much are you looking to spend?'

'As much as it takes.'

'Oh, splashing it around then? It's not like you.'

'I want one of those that you take the picture and then you peel the back off and you have it right there.'

'An instamatic? They're ancient technology, digital's the thing.'

'But I want the photos right away.'

'You can do that with digital. You just have to download it and print it off…'

As soon as he hears the word 'download' Sean's hand goes up.

'I'll get an instamatic.'

While they are in the photographic shop, after Sean has chosen the most expensive instamatic model and the shop assistant is wrapping it, Pierce asks Sean quietly what the camera is for. Sean winks. The exaggerated comedy of the wink is as eloquent as whale song. It tells Pierce that this is something to do with Bernie. It tells him that this is one of Sean's daring schemes, his cheeky manoeuvres and one that Bernie does not know about.

Back in the Harbour Arms Sean asks the barman to turn the telly over to the BBC. He takes a pencil out of his pocket and careful begins to take down the winning lottery numbers on the back of an envelope.

'Now that's a turn up for the books, you doing the lottery, Sean. Don't they say that lighting doesn't strike the same place twice?'

Sean smiles at Pierce, 'Ah, but I know a mighty woman with a torch, whose flame is the imprisoned lightning.'

'And her name Mother of Exiles,' Pierce responds automatically, nodding, as if to a priest during Mass.

They are quoting from 'The New Colossus,' written for the Statue of Liberty. It is a poem they both have good reason to be familiar with.

'Indeed you do, Sean.'

Sean is the only man Pierce knows who has ever won a big money prize. The reversal of fortune was not entirely a positive experience. It brought Sean to disaster but it also brought him to life.

*

Forty-odd years ago, Sean had won the pools. He was a nineteen-year-old recently qualified joiner, a grown man though he lived with his parents and was yet to have a steady girlfriend. He worked for Glasgow City Corporation, a feather in the cap of his unskilled Irish Catholic family. His work was in building the new houses in the schemes on the outskirts of Glasgow to house the overspill from the crumbling city slums. Sean was not handsome or any good at football and he was shy with girls but he had friends and it was a good life: working, drinking, gambling. Along with his father he filled in his pools coupon every Friday night, but he never really expected to win.

He had eight no-score draws but so did a lot of other people so there was no outright jackpot winner. For a nineteen-year-old lad, his share of the pot was plenty. His father and everyone around him counselled him to set up his own business; there was money to be made. The city was being rebuilt and a man with a trade and a bit of money behind him could make a comfortable life. His parents were keen that he should buy a house; lifelong council tenants, no one in the family had ever owned a home. But Sean had other ideas. He wanted a yacht.

At school Sean had been given a project on sailing. From the limited resources of the school library, the local library and the city library, he studied latitude, longitude, compass deviation, tide tables, tidal streams, tide curves, spring and neap curves. He retuned the family radio to BBC Radio Four and listened to the shipping forecasts. He cut pictures from magazines. He practised complicated knots with a piece of washing line. He learned the names and shapes and lengths of all sailing crafts, past and present, falling in love with the strange-sounding words for the techniques and equipment used in sailing.

The money was enough, just, to buy a luxury forty-five foot cruiser. Without telling anyone, he travelled to the coast on a Saturday morning and, after a turn around the harbour with the chandler, took it out alone. He could use the motor until he learned how to operate the sails properly. Then he would bring his mum and dad on board and show them his competency, his mastery, as a sailor.

She was beautiful, streamlined and sleek, and sat high in the water, built for speed sailing. Sean's yacht, too young yet to be named, was made of virgin plastic, so modern and clean and white that it hurt his eyes to look at her in the bright sunlight. Fresh from the factory, the immaculate upholstery was still wrapped in polythene and smelled like a newborn baby. There was nothing left of the pools money to pay for mooring or maintenance but Sean didn't care, it was a dream come true.

Using the motor was a little frustrating, too easy, and, new as the boat was, he could get no real speed with engine power alone. Sean was keen to unfurl the sails and catch the wind. He took her out to open waters leaving the coastline far behind. But he could find no wind. It was an unusually hot, still day. He was fast using up his petrol supply so as a precaution he cut the engine and waited for a breeze. Eager to see her in full trim he hoisted the sails, but without wind they sagged impotently. Sean was getting hungry and needed to pee.

In his excitement he had forgotten to bring a sandwich but he could get something to eat later. The boat was not so luxurious that it had on-board toilet facilities and Sean was reluctant to pee over the side. He worried that it would spill; he didn't want his lovely new white boat streaked with yellow. On the spur of the moment he decided on a swim.

He pulled his clothes off and jumped with a 'wahoo' from the deck. After the heat of the sun the water was shockingly cold and took his breath away but peeing was a sweet relief. To warm his muscles he swam hard and fast away from the yacht and then back towards her again. This was the life, a man alone in the elements. He floated on his back, letting the sea support him like a babe in arms, bobbing in the current of the water. He was relaxed but not so relaxed that he wasn't alert for the sound of approaching vessels. It would be extremely embarrassing to be caught swimming in his Y-fronted pants but more importantly, he didn't want to get his head stoved in on the prow of a boat that hadn't seen him. It was time to get out. There was always next weekend, and every weekend. Perhaps he should keep the boat a secret a bit longer. He had all the time in the world to learn to sail.

He turned on to his front and swam towards the boat. She was further off than he'd thought and he was tiring by the time he approached her. To his surprise she had started to drift, the sails were flapping and were beginning to fill. She had picked up a wee wind. Good girl, Sean thought, as he slapped her smooth bow, now he might get some sailing done. He circled the boat and came all the way around, back to where he'd started from, before he realised the shockingly simple stupid mistake he had made.

He couldn't get on board. He had dropped no anchor or line, nothing with which he could use to scale the sheer even sides of the boat. He felt all along the waterline as she glided slowly and gracefully but there were no ledges or toeholds that would give him access. He jumped and lunged, he threw himself at her, but though he was less than three feet below the deck, it was three feet too far.

He chased her for twenty minutes before he had to give up and watch her, his ghost ship, now splendid with white sails billowing, cruise away without him. He began conserving energy, treading water, hoping for a passing boat, his Y-fronts now the least of his worries. Where would she end up? America? How would he ever get her back? What if, without him to tend her, her mast cracked in heavy weather? Would she sink?

After another twenty minutes or so he had all but forgotten her. How much longer could he last in the water like this? Nothing came near him. He could see three boats in the distance and shouted till he was hoarse, choking on seawater in his panic, but it was useless, they were too far away to see or hear him. He was tired and cold and he wanted to go to sleep.

Suddenly his eyes were filled with colour. A bright orange had replaced the grey blue haze of the sun and the sea. It wasn't until they were nearly upon him that he heard and understood their instruction to grab the lifebuoy.

To this day Sean remembers nothing of his rescue. He remembers only Bernie, standing over him; walking him, bedraggled and rubber-legged, with her mighty arms around his shoulders, from the quayside to her house. And later, how she looked after him, fed him and gave him clothes, how she phoned his family and asked the fishermen to find his boat. He remembers how he fell in love with her.

He did not return that weekend to Glasgow, to his job as a joiner with the Corporation. He did not return to Glasgow ever again except to visit. He married Bernie and sold the cruiser for a fishing boat. He struggled hard to make a living on the island and considered himself a very lucky man.

And now he is apparently trying to win again. After forty-odd years of accepting his destiny he is gambling again. Not the football pools this time, but the National Lottery, a pound for a chance to change his life. In the noise of The Harbour Arms he is ducking around heads that obscure his view of the telly. He is licking his pencil and recording the winning numbers in large smudgy figures.

Then he asks Pierce to do him a favour. Pierce has a bad feeling about this but what can he do?

'Aye sure Sean, no bother, what is it?

Chapter 17

'Come with me to the phone box and we'll give her a tinkle. I'll say these are the numbers on my ticket and ask her to check it. She keeps the numbers for me every week now. I've been buying these bloody things for months. If you're there, she'll believe it, she won't think her big boy would get up to any jiggery pokery.'

The underlying jealousy in the way Sean says the words *big boy* does not escape Pierce. There is no rancour, but there has always been a rivalry for Bernie's love between the two men. Pierce doesn't yet understand the game plan but he understands his role: to add authenticity to the deception and, trusting that Sean's intentions are good, despite the bad feeling in his gut, he is willing, eager even, to play his part. Anything for Bernie.

'Agnes? Aye. Can you take the phone through to her? Ah there you are. You'll never believe who's standing here with me. How the hell did you guess? You're a witch, so you are, woman. He's right here. Just bumped into him. He's standing here with a stookie up to his shoulder. Aye, broke it, rescuing some damsel, he says. Well I'll ask him, okay okay, I'll put him on.'

In the cramped stinking space of the phone kiosk Sean hands Pierce the receiver. With desperate smiley gestures he is miming, trying to convey that he has accidentally run into Pierce but it's okay, Pierce is up to speed. The cord on the receiver is too short and he has to stand with his head cocked at an awkward angle.

'How's my best girl?'

His best girl, in a far away sleepy voice, probably something to do with the pain control drugs, assures him she is fine.

'Aye, I was here with a bit of business. It's nothing, Bernie, I'm fine, a couple of weeks and I'll have the plaster off.'

She takes a bit of persuading but is eventually satisfied. It is so like Bernie to be more worried about him than her own precarious health.

'I popped in to the Harbour Arms on the off-chance and who should be standing there but your old man. Well I wasn't planning to. Aye, I suppose I could for a few days if Sean will bring me back to the mainland. Sean, can you bring me back over in a few days' time?'

Sean is smiling, delighted, with his thumbs up signifying how well it's going but now his demeanour changes and he says in a loud gruff theatrical voice, 'Well, I suppose so, but I don't know who's going to pay for the bloody fuel.'

The moment his line is out of his mouth he clamps his hand over it, scared he'll laugh down the phone. His wide eyes demonstrate how much he is enjoying the schoolboy naughtiness of it.

Sean lets Pierce chat with Bernie for a few minutes and then makes impatient signs that he wants the receiver back. He is bursting to get on with the ruse.

'Bernie, have you the numbers in front of you? Wait, wait. No, don't read them to me. The best thing is if I tell you what I've got and you can tell me if any of them have come up. Okay? Okay.'

Sean fumbles around in each of his trouser pockets but he can't find the envelope. It is in the breast pocket of his shirt, Pierce can make out the outline of it through Sean's threadbare green woollen jumper and is pointing to with his stookie arm it but Sean, with panic building, misunderstands and slaps his hand away. Realisation dawns on Sean and he smiles an apology while keeping up a cheery banter with his wife. In the limited space he ties himself in knots trying to extricate it from his shirt. As Sean's face gets redder Pierce is forced to put his good arm up his uncle's jumper and grope at his breast. He has turned his head away, he doesn't want to feel the soft warmth of his uncle's belly, he doesn't want to smell the sea and the sweat off him.

'5, 9, 12, eh? Oh ho! Well that's us won a tenner at least, fish suppers for the tea tonight! 26, 37, you are kidding me on? Last one 44 …'

A worried look has come over Sean's face. The line has gone quiet. Pierce realises instantly how dangerous this is. Bernie's heart is probably weakened. This could kill her.

'Bernie? Oh, you're there.'

Sean screws his face up knowingly at Pierce but they both feel tremendous relief that Bernie has not keeled over with a heart attack.

'What? Are you sure? All of them?'

Sean nods and grunts into the phone for a good few minutes letting her get used to the idea.

'Now listen, Bernie. You keep this under your hat until I get it checked out. Don't tell a soul. I'll phone up the lottery people just now and find out what we have to do. I'll maybe have to stay here another night until they can get a cheque to me, can you wait another night to see him? Yes, I'll bring him first thing tomorrow as soon as I've sorted it all out. And I'll tell you another thing my girl. Me and you are going Stateside! I'm going straight from here to the travel agents to book two seats to the Big Apple.'

At this moment Sean winks again and effortlessly produces two airline tickets from his back pocket and waves them at Pierce.

Everything falls into place. Pierce never doubted Sean but now he sees why he needed the elaborate scam. This is no joke. Sean has somehow or other come by the money to take her to New York, something she has dreamed of for years, something she has talked of every summer for as far back as Pierce can remember. However Sean has come by the money, he is unable to tell her the truth.

Perhaps it's the drugs but, as unlikely as it seems that a penniless fisherman with a terminally ill wife should twice win a fortune, Bernie readily accepts it. She's asking her husband what clothes she should pack.

'No, forget that old thing, and anyway, it's too big for you now.'

Pierce cringes at this: Bernie's losing weight, diminishing, fading. He's frightened to see her, frightened of how she'll look. He doesn't know how he's going to hide his fear, she knows him so well. But he must hide it, the way Sean does, or she'll spot it before he's even off the boat.

'All you need is something comfy to travel in. We'll buy new stuff when we get there. We'll go to Macy's.'

Pierce never ceases to be amazed by Sean. On the outside he seems like a fat old codger in a green woolly jumper. But he is much, much more. The new refrigeration plant demonstrates just what a player he is. The woolly jumper and easy manner are a perfect disguise for his Machiavellian intrigues. By playing one government body against another, slowly, deftly, despite funding being repeatedly withdrawn, he secured almost half a million pounds to build the plant. But raising the money for this New York trip would not have been as easy. In the island's only pub, The Pibroch, there had been talk of a whip-round to send Bernie to America but Sean is not a man to accept charity. He must have got the money some other way. He must have sold the land.

A few times over the years when the fishing was particularly thin Bernie begged him to sell the fields. Sean always refused, he did not consider them his to sell. They were Bernie's, they came to her from her father when he died. Sean, more than forty years on the island, still an incomer, had no business selling them. He always found a way to keep going, to hold them in trust. The fact that Bernie and Sean had no children held no irony, the land must stay in the family. A few fields on a lonely island are all they have to pass to posterity.

The whole lottery scam, which had at first the feel of one of Sean's cheeky manoeuvres, is much sadder than that. It's desperation, a selfless act of love.

'When are you going to New York?' Pierce asks as soon as Sean comes off the phone.

'Next week.'

Now Pierce understands why the camera has to be instamatic. Sean and Bernie don't have enough time for anything else.

*

Next morning, after a cramped rocky night aboard *The Statue of Liberty,* Sean insists they wait a few hours. Pierce is impatient to get started; he wants to see Bernie. However ill she might look, he wants to see her face when Sean hands her the airline tickets.

'First class, all the way,' Sean shouts proudly above the roar of the engine. 'None of your rubbishy cockroach hotels this time: New York Hilton, best-of stuff.'

'How long are you staying?' Pierce bawls as spray crashes over the port side. After waiting till after lunch to strengthen the illusion of the arrival of the lottery cheque, Sean is now pushing the wee boat as fast as he can back to the island. The throttle screams as the boat rises and falls with the water slapping the sides. Black smoke is belching from the engine with a thick grease that lines Pierce's nose and throat and masks the comforting old-fish smell of the deck but Sean, usually carefully nursing his old boat, never lets up.

'The whole week.'

It's a long way to go for such a short time, thinks Pierce, but maybe that's all Sean can afford, or maybe that's all Bernie can manage.

'I've a full programme lined up and you can bet your life it doesn't include bloody hot dogs! That American bread is stale and the sausage tastes of nothing unless you put half a ton of sauce on it. I'm going to book dinner in one of these places where you can see the whole Manhattan skyline. It's a pity the towers are gone now but that's your bloody terrorists for you.'

It's typical of Sean's island mentality to think that the biggest, potentially the most cataclysmic event in modern history, has spoiled the view for Bernie's posh Manhattan dinner.

'And the best Broadway show, I'll need to get tickets. What is the best show on Broadway just now, Pierce?'

'Don't know, what is it?'

'I don't know either; I'm asking you. It doesn't matter. Whatever it is I'll get tickets.'

Pierce can make out the outline of the island on the horizon now. He loves this feeling: the anticipation of stepping on to the quayside, back on the island, back with Sean and Auntie Bernie.

'Night cruise as well, it's a bloody rip-off but she'll want to see the statue. She's too… she's not up to the ferry trip just at the moment.'

A look of anguish crosses Sean's face and Pierce turns away. The wee boat is too confined a space for such big grief. For the next five minutes Pierce busies himself preparing the mooring lines ready for landing.

'I'm getting a carriage,' Sean shouts, perky again, calling Pierce to join him at the wheel. 'One of those horse-drawn carriages to take her round Central Park. I hope there's going to be moonlight. And I'm keeping the best till last.'

Sean indicates that he wants Pierce to take the wheel and he nips below deck. On land Sean moves at a ponderous pace but aboard *The Statue of Liberty* he is as agile as a monkey. He's back in a jiffy and hands Pierce a small dark red-padded velvet box. There is a ring inside, gold with a row of tiny diamonds.

'It's beautiful, Sean.'

'She has my mother's wedding ring but it's worn away to nothing. I gave her scrambled eggs and toast the other night and she when she rubbed her hands to wipe the crumbs it flew right off her hand.' Sean is laughing. 'She's that skinny!'

Pierce would like to laugh but he can't.

'It's an eternity ring, son. When you find a woman like Bernie you want to be sure and keep her. '

Sean pulls back the throttle and the noise is now a gentle thrum. Pierce can see the quayside and watches it get bigger. The sea-swept weather-beaten harbour and the houses that huddle around it look like they always do; quiet, permanent, but the refrigeration plant, too new and alien to have yet been assimilated into Pierce's mental picture, spoils the view. It's not the same anymore. He's looking for Bernie but of course she won't be there to meet them.

'Now remember, Pierce, mum's the word. If she finds out we didn't win the lottery she'll skin me alive.'

But Pierce isn't listening. He's looking at the quay. Now he can make out a small group waiting at the moorings. He recognises some of Sean's friends, Bobby and Jim, and though they are still some distance from landing, he can clearly read their expressions. Agnes McConnell is with them. She is looking down at her feet and ringing her hands.

Chapter 18

Bertha books the Nile cruise as a lovely surprise for Donnie. If she *has* to have a reason then it's an anniversary present, wedding or divorce, they both happened around the same time. Now that they are back together it's the only way she's going to get a half decent holiday. Donnie freely admits it; he earns peanuts.

Bertha's sister and her friends who have kids can't afford interesting holidays. They go to camps in Skegness or take cottages in the Highlands. When they pull out pictures of the fruit of their loins, Bertha counters with photos of Machu Picchu or hot geysers in Iceland.

But the banks of the Nile aren't all that. The mud-brick houses are quite biblical and picturesque, she supposes, but the kids playing football spoil the overall effect by wearing Nike. The heat is like a giant hairdryer on full power. Day one, Bertha is overwhelmed by the bad smells; the rotting vegetation and petrol smells of the river, the embarrassingly obvious rank smell within fifteen yards of every toilet on board, the stomach-churning rancid stench from the kitchen area even when they're not cooking, but worst of all is the smell of the staff. Bertha and Donnie agree, without being racists about it, that Egyptians stink. They have no appetite and can only nibble at pre-packed crisps and biscuits.

Their cabin is not the best. Because she is paying for them both she has economised by taking second class. A frequent business flyer with all the perks, Bertha is unused to compromising quality. For Donnie's sake she's slumming it but rather than appreciate her gesture, Donnie is too busy being scared.

He's scared of everything. Donnie's fear of flying, with sweats and swearing and apoplexy at take-off and landing, makes the flight a nightmare but that is to be expected. She thought he might be a bit more relaxed on the coach but as they are finding their seats he yanks her down. She tries to remove his hand, it is a designer top and he is knocking it out of shape but he holds fast, gritting his teeth and staring ahead. Such is his terror that he can only communicate with nods. Bertha thinks this is getting out of hand and is about to remind him that they have left the plane now, they're only on a bus for God's sake when, following his manic stare, she glimpses what has so terrified him. Their tour guide, a plump young Egyptian woman, is packing a pistol. As she reaches into the overhead luggage rack her holster becomes momentarily visible.

Donnie will only converse in a whisper with his head between his knees. The woman is a suicide bomber. She and the driver plan to drive the bus at full speed into a target. What target? Donnie doesn't know for sure, some American interest, maybe an oil company depot or something. He begs Bertha not to think of any have-a-go- heroics, he weeps silently, tears channelling into the rigidly set folds of his mouth. He says he is crying because he can't remember the line after 'hallowed be his name' in the Lord's Prayer. Every time the driver changes gear Donnie moans through gritted teeth, 'This is it.'

Later, once they have found their tiny sweltering cabin, Bertha seriously wonders if she can ever have sex with Donnie again. The flying phobia she can just about handle; lots of men are afraid of flying, but that palaver on the bus, well. Obviously she feels sorry for him, who wouldn't? The poor guy was in a terrible state, but that was the whole point. He had made her feel sorry for him. How can she fancy someone she pities? She can kid herself only so far. She knew when she took him back that he was a bit mental, he always had been, but that was not insurmountable. The fact that he had shown himself a pitiable coward was selfish and damned inconvenient.

*

Friday night.

It isn't true that Daphne doesn't wash; she does, just not with the same frequency that she used to, that is to say, daily. But though her ablutions have taken on an infrequency that gives her clothes and her armpits a mushroomy honk, the lack of bathing quantity is made up for in quality. Sometimes the only place to be is the bath, a return to the warm watery womb.

She places tea lights in whisky glasses all around the bathroom and pours bubble bath, which leaves the bottle in thick reluctant pulses, under the rushing hot tap. She carries the iPod player out into the hall and drags it as close to the bathroom door as the socket will allow. She puts on gentle piano music – Einaudi.

She no longer listens to the radio, which is just a constant stream of smug gits who are in love or sad gits who have been chucked. When she plays Einaudi she thinks of … nothing. She lies back, up to her chin, not caring if her hair gets wet. The bubbles provide a safe haven, a cosy hiding place where no one, not even Daphne, can see her blubber body. She takes the time to wrap one foot in bubbles, layering bubbles on bubbles in time to the music as they sparkle in the candlelight until the bubble ball slides down her leg, fragrant and slippery.

Clean skin means clean underwear and, what the hell, a clean jumper. One good thing about the sickie is that Daphne has dramatically cut down on laundry. With her new more relaxed system, one jumper, even with the odd soup slurp down the front, which nobody sees anyway, can last weeks before it needs washed.

Dressed all in clean clothes Daphne feels a sense of occasion but there is none. She can't even pop in and visit Pierce. He has unaccountably bolted. No word, no soup cancelling, no nothing. Daphne has had to eat spinach and coconut soup for the last three days to use it up. He'll be back. He's probably shacked up with some woman.

Daphne is preparing for the three a.m. deli run, standing in the hallway buttoning her coat. She doesn't need a coat in this weather but that's what she's comfortable with. She has a peek in the full-length mirror. Her face has filled out a bit recently giving her a softer more girly look and she still has not a bad pair of pins on her, not a bad pair at all, it's just the bit in between her face and her legs that she's not so keen on. Now then, she thinks, where's my stick with which to beat the men off? Where *did* I leave that shitty stick?

Just then a rowdy drunk knocks and bangs her door. Pierce. She knew he'd be back. She keeks through the spyhole but it isn't Pierce.

'Tam, are you okay?'

Tam's face breaks into a wide infectious smile as she opens the door.

'Daphne!'

Tam throws his arms open wide and pulls her towards him into a clumsy bear hug. Daphne has, in an instinctive protective gesture, brought her arms to her chest and now Tam in his exuberance locks his arms behind her back. She is trapped inside his enthusiastic embrace. His cold outdoor ear is touching her warm indoor one.

'Oh Daphne, Daphne, lovely lovely Daphne.'

'Tam, how many Es have you had?'

'Two.' Tam pulls away enough to let her see his unrepentant smile and then returns to the ear-on-ear clinch. He rocks from side to side and Daphne has no option but to rock with him. The rocking gains momentum until it has become a heavy swaying dance, a dance that neither of them know the steps to.

'Is he here?'

'Who, Pierce? No, I don't know where he is.'

'He missed our fucking gig, man.'

Tam nods his head in a sad knowing way. Daphne takes this opportunity to break free. They are standing just inside her hallway and, sensing that this is going to be a long story, Daphne brings Tam into living room.

'He's the one who got us the gig and contacted the record companies. And then he doesn't even bother his arse to turn up! I mean, the rest of the band didn't want Pierce after he gave us the big speech about us all having to be *a hundred and ten per cent committed,* all that shite. The rest of them thought he was an arse but I stuck my neck out for him and anyway, we couldn't find anyone else who would do it. But still and all, I stuck my neck out for him and he doesn't even show up on the night.'

'Aye, he's a useless git,' Daphne confirms. 'You should know better than to rely on him, Tam.'

'Man, it was a brilliant gig. We were on fire. My wee sister came with a big crowd of her pals from school and they were right into it. The A and R man stayed until half time.'

'The what man?'

'A and R: Artistes and Repertoire. From the record company, a talent scout.'

'A record company scout was there?'

'Yeah, he came over and asked who wrote the songs.'

'It's you, isn't it?'

'Too right it's me, I'm making sure none of those shitheads get the credit, they're my songs.'

'What record company was it?'

'I don't know, I didn't like to ask.'

'Then how do you know he was a scout?'

'Well, I don't know for sure, but he looked like one. He had really trendy clothes, looked dead wanky and he had a London accent.'

Daphne and Tam are now in the living room and Daphne, still with her coat on, locates the whisky bottle and two glasses. She plunks herself down on the couch and Tam follows. Daphne pours while Tam describes in detail each song that the band played and his sister's pals' fervent appreciation. By the time he has finished Daphne has drunk two large whiskies and is feeling warm and relaxed. She stopped listening about ten minutes ago. She is wondering where Pierce is.

'Wouldn't it be great if the record company want to sign us?'

Daphne is nodding. Tam says something else and Daphne nods. A look of surprised delight comes over Tam's face and he takes Daphne's head in his hands and gently kisses her mouth.

Daphne has always liked snogging; it is her favourite thing, but this snogging is confusing. It's not that Tam is a bad kisser. In fact he is pretty good, his basic equipment is sound: above-average size of orifice, superior lip girth, sturdy teeth, no obvious presence of halitosis. Whisky on the breath is always a bonus. And his technique cannot be faulted. There is none of the jaw-grinding or teeth-clashing she remembers from her dating days. There is no weirdness like teeth licking or forceful sucking. Kisses remain within acceptable limits for saliva production and exchange. But still she is uncomfortable with it. It's too much.

Tam is ideal boyfriend material. Isn't he? He has golden hair on his arms, on his head, in his genes. But he's a few years too young and a few months too late. Whichever way she looks at it, the arithmetic won't add up.

*

The first sign is when she doesn't open her mouth properly for a kiss. She doesn't entirely lock her teeth but they are closed enough to be her drawbridge, denying him access to the inner sanctum, and he is forced to slurp from the saliva moat around her lower gums. With an involuntary moan he opens his mouth wider but she has not followed, their lips are out of synch. Now he's kissing chin instead of lips and it's a bit embarrassing. It's a bad sign. His suspicions are confirmed when, later that night, after he has pushed the twin beds of their small cabin together, Bertha ignores the signal.

When they were married Donnie slept tucked into Bertha's chunky back and when they got back together again it came naturally, her arse parked on his warm groin, his legs folded inside hers, his instep against the sole of her foot. More often than not Donnie will wiggle his toes tickling the underside of hers. Once or twice a week Bertha's toes wiggle back, saying hello, pleased to meet y ou. That is the signal, when that happens they wordlessly turn to each other and fuck. If her toes don't wiggle they don't fuck. This is not something they have ever talked about.

Bertha's toes are still. She seems to have curled them in tight. Okay, thinks Donnie. The holiday might have got off to a rocky start but I'm determined to enjoy it, after all, Bertha paid good money for this. It's our first night, on holiday, not working, sunshine, Egypt,

Cleopatra, the Nile, Pharaohs, what better opportunity for a blow job can a man have? So he wiggles again.

'It's too hot!' Bertha snarls as she throws his arm off.

It is too hot.

The next morning Donnie gets an upgrade to a room with air conditioning. It's the least he can do. He feels a bit guilty about how much Bertha spent on this holiday. She always was a spend-thrift, now that they're together they could have used the money for something practical but, God love her, she was trying to please him. And he's trying hard to please her but it's not his fault he doesn't like it here; she knows he can't take the hot weather. It's not as if she doesn't get to go abroad, Bertha is always jetting off to exotic locations with her job but she says that's work; it's not the same without your partner. He didn't sleep a wink all night in that sweatbox of a cabin. It was like being in that Steve McQueen movie. There's no way he can spend another night in *the cooler*.

'Oh Donnie, it's fantastic!' she says as they both stand beneath the wall-mounted air conditioning unit. She turns to face it, splays her legs and lifts her skirt letting the cooling air waft around her knickers. Yesterday, Bertha made the mistake of packing her sun cream in her big case and it was several hours before she had access to it. He had warned her to cover up and offered her his cream but she scoffed at it. Not surprisingly she ended up burnt. On the way from the airport to the cruiser she has caught the sun on her face and her shoulders giving her the appearance of a ruddy peasant. She has a red stripe of quite severe sunburn down the length of each leg.

'Hang on, that's it only at half-power. Wait till you see what this baby can do,' says Donnie. 'Hand me the remote control, see? Impressive, eh?'

The machine, which was almost noiseless, moves up a couple of gears and now drones. The steward who demonstrated the controls told Donnie not to turn it beyond this point but he's paid for it and he's going to bloody well make full use of it. Within minutes the temperature has noticeably dropped. The cooler air rejuvenates them both, Bertha's earlier mood of stoically enduring her sunburn and the heat has lifted and she seems much chirpier. This is more like it, thinks Donnie, he has to try hard to enjoy this cruise, it's the only way she's going to enjoy it. Now she is jiggling and dancing around the room. Donnie can't help but notice that through her blouse, Bertha's nipples are stiff.

He paid for the room upgrade with his Visa card that he always takes on holiday for emergencies and has never, until now, used. He can't believe how expensive it is, it's going to take at least a year and half to pay off, but in this heat these bastards can charge what they like.

'It's pretty cool though, isn't it, Bertha?'

'It's brilliant, it's absolutely freezing.'

*

Donnie is not keen on the excursion but he goes anyway. If he's honest, he doesn't really like Egypt. He would rather go on holiday to the Highlands like he used to with Daphne. Apart from the odd outbreak of foot-and-mouth or E. coli, it was a much healthier place to be. Donnie is already sick of crisps and biscuits but there's no way he's going to eat anything in this Third World country. He's seen too many guys from his football team go on backpacking holidays to Africa and the like and come home three stone lighter with a suppurating ulcer on their leg. These guys are out of the team for weeks. The first thing he's going to do when he gets back, apart from watch the Rangers matches that he's taped, is get a fish supper.

As soon as they arrive at the pharaoh's temple Donnie seeks the shade. The only reason he agreed to come was because it was to a temple, he thought they would be inside, out of the sun. But this pharaoh's temple is just a bunch of ruins. To avoid the powerful sun he has to stand in the shade of a huge and quite dodgy-looking column. If the column has been standing here since the pharaohs then hopefully it'll last a wee while longer and not fall on top of me, he tells himself, how unlucky would that be?

Donnie's luck has not been great on this holiday with the embarrassing bus incident and terrible heat in the cooler all night long and Bertha pushing him away. What else could go wrong? At least the cabin is sorted, and hopefully that should cure the Bertha problem, too. They are on holiday, they are supposed to be having sex, that's what holidays are for, not schlepping round looking at piles of rubble.

With Donnie's Celtic skin he has to watch he doesn't get burned. He carries a large bottle of factor sixty- five sun block and applies it often. This gives him a ghostly blue-white colour. He is the only person here, maybe the only person in this country, who is blue-white and it makes him feel weird, lonely. He is an alien in this environment. He knows the Egyptians are laughing at him; he sees the shadow of a smirk on their weaselly faces when the stewards talk to him. Though he rubs and rubs the sun block is not absorbed and lies on his skin like a thick coating of lard. He longs for the sensation of dryness, for his face and hands not to be greasy and his groin not to be damp.

He has noticed that he's stopped noticing how smelly the crew are, and this is not good. When he first came on board he was overwhelmed by the smell of BO from all of them. Now he has stopped noticing it, does that mean he smells as bad as they do? He showered four times yesterday but even then the feeling of freshness only lasted a few minutes until he began to sweat and had to reapply the grease again. But being greasy is better than being burnt. He can't understand why Bertha goes on deck to sun herself, her skin already looks wrinkled, does she not realise the damage she's doing? But it would be stupid to tell her this, she's already pissed off with him because he won't come and look at the hieroglyphics.

While Donnie lurks in the shadows he suddenly feels a sharp pain in his nether regions. Something has crawled up his shorts. Halfway between his arsehole and his cock something has bitten him. In horror he puts his hand in his pocket and shakes as hard as he can, trying to dislodge it. Nothing drops out, whatever it is it is hanging on. Panic is mounting, it's a snake, no maybe a beetle, fuck, no, it's probably a scorpion. Nearby, the guide is marshalling people to return to the boat but Donnie can't think of that right now. He thrusts his hand down the back of his shorts and scoops between his buttocks opening his legs as wide as possible. He is about to grasp the invader when his nerve goes. He could be attacked again. One bite or sting might be survivable; two might not. But he has to get it out of his pants.

In blind panic he looks around for toilets or even a dark doorway but there's nothing. The best he can do is go round the other side of the pillar into the deep shade and hope no one sees him. As quickly as he can he pulls the shorts down.

His right leg steps out easily enough but the material is bunched round his other ankle. He can't see very well in this darkness and he's scared to use his hand to pull his shorts off in case it bites him so he lifts his left leg and shakes. It's no use; he can't get them off. Holding the shorts in place with his right foot, he tries to tug his other leg out. He's tugging so hard he begins to lose his balance and cries out in terror. He's hopping backwards to keep from falling over. Hopping takes him out of the shadows, out into the bright sun where at last his leg pulls free. He's puffed out with the effort and as he sighs his relief he looks up to see a crowd of tourists from the boat scrutinising him.

He is not wearing pants he now remembers. This morning he decided it was too hot for pants and anyway the elastic chaffed his groin yesterday and gave him an angry rash. Panic and dilemma throw Donnie's mind into a series of bullet points:

- I can feel air on my arse but no scorpion.
- It's still in my shorts.
- These people can see my cock.

In a frenzy he stamps all over the shorts, his pale cock jiggling, unprotected from the scorching sun. Then he stamps on them again, this time methodically working from top to bottom, right to left, making sure every inch of the khaki safari shorts are well trampled. At the very edges of the pockets he takes the shorts within two fingers and, bowing his body out, gingerly shakes them. He doesn't want it landing on him. In the midst of this he becomes aware that someone is calling his name.

'Donnie, Donnie!'

It's Bertha. She is hurrying towards him, bustling through the bemused tourists. From the tone of her voice Donnie understands that Bertha is angry but she doesn't know about the scorpion.

'Donnie, what are you doing?'

Bertha seems distraught.

'There's a scorpion…'

'Put your shorts on, please!'

'Bertha it was in my shorts!'

Bertha comes and stands beside him with a hand on his shoulder, shielding his nakedness from the assembled audience. She whispers gently, 'Get your fucking clothes on, Donnie.'

The thing that Donnie is now most aware of is that he is standing in front of Egyptians and a large party of his shipmates, with his shorts ground into the dust and his penis dangling.

Gritting his teeth he checks the inside of the shorts before carefully pulling them up. His fellow travellers don't even try to hide their laughter. They titter openly at the strange looking blue-white man who has his cock out.

Chapter 19

Donnie would like to walk away with his head held high but the pain of the bite on his undercarriage is such that he is forced to walk with his legs open, as if he has just soiled himself.

On the bus back to the boat Bertha isn't speaking to him. Donnie continues to speak to her, he has to; this is an emergency.

'I'm telling you, the thing crawled up my shorts and bit me, how is that my fault?'

Bertha is not inclined to comment, she turns her head and squints out of the window into the blinding sun.

'The thing is, I'm in need of medical attention. Is there a doctor on the boat? Coz if there isn't they'll have to send for one, are we insured for this?'

'Insured against mosquito bites? I don't think so,' says Bertha evenly.

'I've told you it wasn't a mosquito. I've got to see a doctor, I need to know what's going on with my arse, it's nipping like fuck.'

Back on board Donnie quickly establishes that there is no doctor. However, an officer, who is qualified to administer first aid and has experience of dealing with scorpion bites, will take a look at it. It is the best they can do and Donnie must accept this treatment or none at all. The officer is very professional and ensures that the proprieties are observed. Donnie is given a white gown and instructed to make himself comfortable on the consulting table of the tiny first aid room. He lies firstly on his back then on his belly but it's no use. To accommodate the officer examining the affected area, he has to kneel doggie fashion on the table with his bare arse in the air. Never before has Donnie felt so vulnerable.

On sight of the wound the officer is quick to reassure Donnie that he believes it to be a mosquito bite.

'How can you tell?'

'Ah, this is a very common complaint sir; we see this all the time. I can assure you that there is no danger. It is true that the location, at the perineum, is a little unusual ...'

'Are you absolutely sure?'

'Absolutely.'

Donnie has already told the officer how sore it is, surely the guy can see the pain he's in by the way he jumped when his bum cheeks were probed? Does he imagine Donnie is enjoying this? Never in his life has any man touched Donnie's bum. Never in his life has he exposed his arsehole to anyone. Surely he has not suffered all of this because of a fucking mosquito? But he is left with no choice but to meekly accept the antihistamine tablets and cream he is offered and get down off the table.

Bertha is sleeping when, by necessity, he swaggers cowboy-style back to the cabin. Just as well. He'll have to admit to her later that it is, after all, a mosquito bite. The room feels blissfully chilly, Bertha is lying naked, her body cool and inviting, there is a slight tang of her sweat in the air but the last thing Donnie wants right now is sex. His undercarriage is beginning to feel ticklish and this worries him. He forces himself to resist the irresistible urge to scratch. With every beat of his heart the pain throbs in his bottom.

Exhausted and tearful with the humiliating events of the day, he steps easily out of his shorts and leaves them where they fall. He scratches his armpit, sniffing his fingers to see if he really does smell as bad as the Egyptians. He is unable to tell but decides on a shower anyway, a cold one. After he has carefully soaped and rinsed he removes the showerhead from the wall and scooshes the cold water up his bum. The relief is instantaneous. He tinkers with the taps and produces a forceful jet that he aims at his rectum. This is ecstasy, not only is it taking the heat and the itch out of the bite but it actually feels really nice, sexy in a strange way.

But no sooner is he out of the shower than the heat and the bite start to bother him again. There is no point in getting dried, it will only make him sweat more but as he is about to return to the cool of the bedroom he spots Bertha's make-up mirror and has an idea. Although she's sleeping she could wake up and it would just be the icing on the cake if she were to catch him doing this. This has been the most shameful day of his life but it could always get worse. He slides the snib and locks the door as quietly as he can. Donnie places the small mirror in the middle of the bathroom floor and squats over it.

He has never seen himself from this angle before. It is not a pretty sight and, not for the first time, he wonders what women get out of sucking men's cocks. The idea is disgusting to him, especially from this point of view. He knew he was hairy arsed, he has explored it with his fingers often enough, but he had no idea it looked so bad. Coarse ginger hair sprouts from bluish puckered skin and, slap bang in the middle of this weird forest, a white pimple the size of a fingernail. Donnie laughs when he sees it. It's incredible to think that a thing this small can cause so much pain and burning mortification.

By the time Bertha wakes, Donnie has been in the bathroom three quarters of an hour and has scooshed himself three times.

'Let's go to dinner, there must be something we can eat,' says Bertha as she applies a sunburn-soother cream.

Donnie doesn't want to go to dinner. Why would he? The dining room is full of boring bastards, every one of them puffing themselves up about what good jobs they have and what posh areas they live in. And he can't even slag them off, Bertha doesn't like it when he talks people down, it's negative, she says. Daphne never seemed to mind, she quite enjoyed the names he invented. And anyway, most of those bastards were there today at the ruins, there's no way he's going to sit there while they laugh at him.

'I'm not actually that hungry, pet.'

'Well, I'm fucking starving. I need to get out of here, I'm starting to get cabin fever.'

Donnie has got the opposite of cabin fever, whatever that's called; he never wants to leave the cabin again. It is his place of security, it's out of the relentless sun, it's cool, if a bit noisy, the air conditioning machine seems to be getting louder, but he can do what he likes in here. If he wants to sit bollock naked with his legs open and the cool air circulating round his family jewels, he can. If he wants the relief of a scoosh up the arse he has only to go to the bathroom. Outside the cabin there are burns and bites and ridicule. Outside is dangerous.

'Come on love, get your kit on,' says Bertha.

Does she not realise how humiliated he has been today or does she just not care?

Dinner is not as bad as it might have been. The head waiter puts them at a table for two at the back near the kitchen. Donnie believes that this is not motivated by sensitivity to his embarrassment but revenge for not tipping. Bertha has the chicken and tells him it is delicious. Donnie requests bananas, unpeeled. Between them they drink two and a half bottles of wine. The wine has a tremendously relaxing effect, soon Bertha and he are laughing and for a while Donnie forgets about the bite. As they make their way back to the cabin there is a pleasant breeze in the night air and they stop to enjoy the view from the deck, strange beautiful Egypt, like nothing they've ever seen before. Throughout dinner Donnie has been as charming and as funny as he can be and it has paid off. Bertha leans in to kiss him. Her drawbridge is down and Donnie is confident of toe-wiggling tonight. As he opens the door to the cabin he wonders what kind of effect a blow job would have on his injury.

The air conditioning machine has stopped whining and the floor of the cabin is covered in two or three inches of brown dirty water. Bertha's open suitcase, which was underneath the air con unit, is saturated. Floating in the filth on the floor are some of Bertha's most expensive designer tops, the contents of his and her toilet bags, next month's *Vogue* magazine and lots of large dead insects. Bertha screams.

Donnie catches up with her on deck. She is leaning over the rail crying.

'I hate this place. I want to go home!' she wails petulantly. 'I can't go back in there. Did you see those bugs on the floor? What is wrong with this bloody country, and my *Vogue*, I haven't even read it!'

She hasn't seen her case yet then, thinks Donnie; wait till she finds out about that.

'Listen love, I'll try and sort it out. You go back to the bar and wait. Tell the steward what's happened, I think it's the air conditioning, but for God's sake don't tell them we had it on full blast.'

'You weren't supposed to have it on that high, did you not hear the noise it was making?'

Donnie can't believe she's trying to pin this on him.

'And did *you* not hear the noise it was making?'

'Oh fuck off!'

*

Donnie nips back to the cabin and paddles in. He has to turn the dial on the air con unit back to where the steward showed him to set it. The duty officer arrives and, despite Donnie shouting and swearing at him, is extremely apologetic. He leaves and comes back minutes later with two of the cleaning wallahs who set about sluicing the muck out of the cabin. When the water level drops and the bugs have been removed, Donnie goes in and starts clearing up, he doesn't want these Africans touching his wife's underthings.

The *Vogue* magazine is a goner; even if it could be dried out the pages are stuck together. The designer tops are woebegone rags, he wrings them out as best he can but, as far as he knows, all Bertha's clothes are dry-clean only. His shaving cream is probably saveable but the whole lot will have to be chucked out, they'll be infected with God knows what kind of horrible Third World diseases. As he is bagging the toiletries he spots a familiar plastic packet.

It is a month's supply of Neboxar, his brand of antidepressant. The pack is three-quarters full; he didn't know he still had these. Thank God Bertha never saw them. For a minute or two he considers salvaging them, the blister pack looks undamaged and if ever he needed alleviation from symptoms of stress it's now, but they'll be no use right now. Experience has taught him they take weeks to work. They'll be back home by the time the drug kicks in. Better to hold on and get an uncontaminated supply when he gets back. He quickly buries them at the bottom of the rubbish bag and hands them to the cleaning guy to get rid of. Bertha would go mad if she knew he'd been on prescription drugs.

*

Bertha can't stop crying. This has been the most miserable holiday of her life; all her clothes are ruined. She has spent the last three days in T-shirts supplied by the crew which read '*My parents cruised the Nile and all I got was this lousy T-shirt*'. She has no make up, no sunscreen, nothing. They are stuck with this smelly, bug-stained sweat-box of a cabin with the broken air con. The captain claims they don't have the parts on board to fix it, it is 'kaput', he says. The first cabin they were in, the perfectly good cabin that Bertha booked, is now occupied and there is nothing else available. Donnie has ranted and raved at the officers but he has only succeeded, with his hysterical empty threats, in making a complete arse of himself. Again.

And there is something else. The worst thing of all: her medication is missing. When the steward locked up the bar and there was nowhere else to go she was forced to return to the cabin. It was then that she realised that not only were the entire contents of her suitcase destroyed but her toiletries bag had been thrown out along with her antidepressants. She hates Donnie for this. He must have seen them, he must have picked them up and thrown them away but he's saying nothing. He has no right to do this to her. He's probably angry because she didn't tell him but what business is it of his? She needs those fucking pills.

She asked the first aid officer, she had to tell him but all he could offer was a mild sedative. The mild sedative turned out to be the same antihistamine he gave Donnie for his mosquito bite. She took them anyway, double the dose, and it did make her sleepy but it's not enough.

If only Donnie could be straight with her. It's always been the same. Bertha remembers when they first moved in together, all those years ago, when he hid in the bathroom to put his contact lenses in, when she sneaked into the bathroom to put hers in. She realised before he did when she found a pair of his glasses hidden at the back of a drawer. In five months of dating and nearly three months of living together neither had told the other that they needed help with their eyesight, it was pathetic.

She left her lens sterilising solution bottle in the bathroom deliberately to see what he would say but he said nothing. Then, one night after dinner, she took her glasses out of her bag and put them on to read the paper. Still he said nothing and continued to hide in the toilet putting his lenses in. Next time they were in Asda she lifted a bottle from the shelf and said, 'We need more sterilising solution, don't we?' Donnie, like a terrified rabbit, simply nodded and scurried away round the shop.

He made it so difficult to be honest. When they were preparing to get married she tried a few times to tell him something, something important, but he made it so difficult. She wasn't going to tell him at all, that was in the past and before she met him, but she knew he was going to find out. When they went to sign the register, he would see. He'd see that she had been married before. She nearly called the whole thing off but then it occurred to her that if she were going to call it off, she'd have to give him some kind of explanation. It was easier just to tell him. He took it surprisingly well. Never again did he mention it and never again did she.

He keeps disappearing into the bathroom. He refuses to leave the cabin although it's hotter than hell without the air con and it stinks. All she wants is a little comforting. She only wants him to put his arms around her and tell her everything's going to be okay, but he's not interested. He spends half the day in the toilet. She can hear the shower running but when he comes back out he's not wet. What the fuck is he up to in there?

*

Daphne's sick line has run out and she doesn't know what to do. She can't go back to work. The longer she stays away the more she doesn't want to go back. She *can't* go back. When she phones for an appointment the practice receptionist tells her that they have changed the system. It is an open surgery now, she can come down and she'll be seen but she'll have to wait and there's no guarantee which doctor will see her. She wants Dr Wilson. Dr Wilson is kind and understanding and quite handy with her pen at writing sick notes.

She knows, through her previous Internet research on Donnie's behalf, everything there is to know about clinical depression, but she's not so sure that the doctor will remain convinced enough to give her another month's line. She worries that she won't be able to squeeze out the requisite tears this time. Daphne has rarely had time off work sick, it always seemed like a complete waste of time. Until now her positive attitude has always ensured a robust immune system. She feels like a charlatan and wishes she had a bona fide illness or injury.

Daphne opens the front door carefully and listens at the stair. There is no one around. She puts her door on the latch and walks to the end of the corridor. Taking deep breaths she steels herself and visualises a successful outcome. Then she runs full pelt along the corridor. She's running hard, panting, leaning into the sprint, shoulder first, through the front door and along the hall, running at the inside wall. She closes her eyes and waits to hear the sound of breaking bone. But she can't do it. At the last moment she swerves and lands in a heap on the floor, winded but intact. Her nerve is broken but not her shoulder. Daphne doesn't feel a thing when, in an ecstasy of self-loathing, she bites her tight fist.

She tries on various outfits. A lot of her clothes look too cheerful but most of them don't fit anymore anyway. None of the things in her wardrobe say *I'm clinically depressed and about to top myself.* Finally she settles for a baggy grey sweatshirt she used to wear to yoga. It's too clean so she goes to the kitchen and carefully drips

136

a spoonful of soup down the front, a nice touch, she thinks. The weather is too warm for it now but she puts on a big woolly scarf along with the voluminous raincoat that she wears each night to the deli. The scarf is the final touch making her look like a recipient of care in the community.

Dressed like this she is mortified to encounter Carol in the doctor's waiting room.

'Daphne!'

It's a small room. She can't pretend not to have seen her.

'Hi Carol.'

Carol as usual is dressed to the nines in a figure-hugging biscuit-coloured dress that looks like it cost a fortune. Daphne pulls her coat tighter together trying to hide the soup stain on her sweatshirt but Carol has already seen it.

'How are you, love?' Carol asks, her voice dripping with pity.

'Aye, never better.' Daphne quickly replies and then bites her lip: she's here to throw a sickie. 'And yourself?'

Daphne didn't realise that they shared the same doctor.

'Oh God, it's a piece of nonsense, it really is. They've changed the system here and now I have to see the doctor to get my repeat script. I've had to take the morning off and I'm up to my neck in assessments. I could do without it, we're short-staffed at the moment.'

Ouch, thinks Daphne. Carol does a pretty good impersonation of being stupid and tactless but Daphne suspects she knows exactly the impact she has.

'Are you okay, Daphne? You look … different.'

Of course I look different you stupid cow, thinks Daphne, I'm dressed up as a Bag Lady.

'And you've put on a bit of weight, haven't you?'

No woman in the world tells another that she's put on weight, except Carol. But Daphne nods and shifts in her chair, pulling her coat even tighter, she didn't think it was that noticeable.

'So what are you in for?'

Daphne knew it was only a matter of time before she got around to that question and can't help but be impressed with Carol's brazenness.

'I'm not able to come back to work yet, Carol, I have free-floating anxiety.'

'Oh ho, you and me both, babes.'

There is a derisory tone to Carol's voice. Daphne is work-shy. She's using an easy excuse to dodge her responsibilities, she can't deny it. Carol has caught her red-handed and is laughing at her.

'And you Carol, what are you in for?'

Daphne really hopes it's something terminal.

'Oh just my usual, my antidees.'

'Antidees?'

'Yeah!'

Carol says this as though she is saying the word *dummy*.

'Antidees, you know, antidepressants. Listen Daphne, don't let them fob you off with any of those old tricyclics. They're a penny a pound, that's why they give you them, to keep their costs down.'

Daphne knows what Carol is talking about but pretends innocence.

'They're filthy; the side effects are horrible. Try and get her to switch you to an SSRI.'

Serotonin Selective Re-Uptake Inhibitor. Daphne is translating in her head the stuff from the Internet.

'But stay well clear of Neboxar.'

She looks Daphne up and down.

'Weight gain can be problem.'

She probably thinks Daphne is already taking the fattening antidee. Good, thinks Daphne, let her think that.

'Or even better an SNRI.'

Serotonin Noradrenaline Re-Uptake Inhibitor.

'God knows I've tried them all. I'm on a good one now though, a new one, the most expensive.'

Quelle surprise, thinks Daphne.

'But of course I was away on holiday, two weeks in Miami, it was such a hoot. I was having such a good time I completely forgot to stock up on antidees. I was down to my last tablet. As soon as I got back I asked Magda to ask Bob if he would lend me a packet, he's on the same ones, just till next week, to save me schlepping in here today when I've all these assessments, but he refused. He's such a dick.'

'Bob is on antidepressants too?'

'Yeah, but he won't share. Daphne, everyone's on them. Bob, Jo, Linda, Kevin.'

Kevin is the Head of Department.

'You know Lily in admin? We call her Lily of the Valium. Eh, who else? Oh yeah, me, you.'

But Daphne isn't on them; she didn't even get the prescription filled.

'You'll find that once you're on them and if you talk about it, people come out of the woodwork. And you don't hear of many coming off them. I tried to get off antidees last year, a bloody nightmare, believe me. I went on a detox diet and took up yoga and meditation but it wasn't any good. It was all weird positions and breathing in. I felt like I was spending half my life breathing in. '

Dr Wilson calls Carol's name and greets her like an old friend when she steps forward. She probably is an old friend. Within minutes Carol is back in the waiting room waiving her prescription triumphantly.

'Anyway, lovely to see you, Daphne. I'll tell everyone you were asking after them. I'll need to get back, I've got a class this afternoon, uggh! Bunch of lowlife loser junkies, honestly, hang on, didn't you have that class? I must have inherited them from you!'

Daphne nods. Carol is talking about Daphne's adult returners' class, the sweet serious students, her favourite class.

'They're quite a smelly bunch, aren't they?'

A few moments later Daphne is called by Dr Wilson and spends a similar amount of time in the consulting room. The doctor is kind but brisk and Daphne feels processed as though she were a sausage in a factory. She emerges with another sick line for a month and a prescription for more antidepressants. After everything Carol has said Daphne thinks maybe she should take them after all.

Chapter 20

The bite wound is getting bigger. What started out being fingernail-sized is now the size of a large fist. The idea of a fist up his arse is repulsive but fascinating to Donnie and spurs him to get into the shower for another scoosh. It is his only relief. Every time he comes out he has to face Bertha sitting crying in the bedroom. What the hell is wrong with the woman? He's the one with a fist up his arse.

She's crying over her ruined clothes. Bertha chucked everything in her case when they moved to the air-conditioned room and hadn't bothered to unpack again, so through some weird female logic it's all *his* fault. It's only clothes, he keeps telling her, but it's pointless. She has refused to throw them out. She won't even let him put them in storage and so her dry-clean-only designer stuff lies stinking in the open suitcase. Bertha sits on the bed glassy-eyed, silently weeping. Every so often she lifts something out of the case, a fungus-mottled silk blouse or a pair of now baggy-arsed, brown-stained linen trousers. She stares tenderly at them with tears rolling down her cheeks and wails, 'Oh, my nice things!' She sits up half the night refusing to go to sleep or even let him put the light out.

When the excursion has left for the day and the coast is clear Donnie goes everyday to the bar. He brings back bananas, packets of nuts and bottles of wine but she's not interested. As far as he knows, apart from a packet of cheese and onion Golden Wonder that was in her travel bag, she hasn't eaten anything for two days. But this is only as far as he knows.

She could be up to anything when he's sleeping or when he's in the bathroom, and he's in the bathroom quite a lot. He's in there for maybe an hour at a time and she never asks why. With the shocking trauma she's suffered over the loss of her beloved nice things she's completely forgotten about his arse. Donnie can't forget. No matter how many time he scooshes, the thing keeps getting bigger. Now it's the size of a dinner plate. He doesn't need to use the make-up mirror any longer, if he pulls his cheeks apart and turns his head he can see in the bathroom mirror that the inflammation is spreading out across his buttocks. And it itches like fuck.

The first aid guy is not much use. He is too busy denying, no doubt on captain's orders, the ship's liability for the effluent-flooded cabin. This is another thing the insurance will be paying out for, yes, Donnie thinks, the insurance will be paying out big time. The first aid guy concedes that there is always a chance of infection and gives him antiseptic antibiotic cream but insists that Donnie is just unlucky to have had such an extreme allergic reaction. Yeah, unlucky.

When he comes out of the bathroom there she is on the bed, with her face tripping her as usual. This would put years on you, thinks Donnie. He can't see, even with the make-up mirror, but he is sure something is going on with the bite. The centre of it, the place where the mosquito initially bit him, has become hard and very sore to the touch.

What if it isn't a bite? Sweat runs down Donnie's face as he contemplates another explanation. He has heard these stories about people being bitten in hot countries and then weeks later, thousands of tiny insects burst out of the host's skin. What if he's now incubating a nest of poisonous spiders up his arse?

Donnie doesn't want to alarm Bertha, she has been acting strangely as it is, as if she's going off her head, something like this could tip her over the edge. But on the other hand he needs to know.

'Bertha?'

'Hmm?'

'You remember, in the temple, I was bitten?

She nods her head slowly, rolling her eyes like some kind of imbecile but she might just be being sarcastic.

'Well I think there's a problem with the bite.'

'Oh yes?' Her tone is falsely enthusiastic, now he knows she's taking the piss.

'And I wondered if you wanted to have a look at it for me?'

'If I wanted?'

'Well maybe you don't *want* to, but I wondered if you would be good enough to, to do me the favour. I can't see it myself and I'm worried that a spider has maybe laid an egg or something.'

'Uh huh. An egg."

It's now clear that she doesn't give a toss.

'Well, will you or won't you? I don't want to have to go back to that first aid guy, not again.'

Bertha says nothing but she doesn't refuse. He'd like to ask her to come into the bathroom where the light is better but he doesn't want to give her any reason to say no and he doubts if she'll move off the bed. He drops his shorts and bends over, touching his toes, placing his perineum at a convenient eye level for Bertha.

'The middle of it looks different,' she says dryly.

'Yeah, I thought that,' Donnie says, his voice muffled by his legs, 'I could feel it. But what do you mean, in what way is it different?'

'Well, it seems to be moving.'

'Moving?'

'And. Oh my God!'

'What is it?' Donnie's heart is pounding; his skin is crawling.

'They're coming out! Hundreds of them!'

Bertha scrambles to her feet, she is standing on the bed, as far from him as possible, screaming her head off. Panic envelopes him and Donnie starts to scream. He instinctively goes to pull his shorts back up, to stop them coming out, but then he doesn't know what to do. He runs to the door of the cabin, shuffling with his shorts once again caught round his legs. He can't get the door open, he always locks the door from the inside and now he fumbles with the key until he drops it on the floor.

'Help, help!'

Bertha is jumping up and down on the bed.

'He's got spiders coming out of his arse!'

Bertha's wild screaming turns into hysterical screaming laughter. She is enjoying herself.

'Oh very good, Bertha, nice one.'

Donnie is angry and then immediately relieved. He isn't giving birth to baby spiders after all, it's just her sick idea of a joke. Still with his shorts at his ankles he shuffles to the side of the bed and sits down. Like a naughty child Bertha continues to jump on the bed. Donnie is being bounced around. His bum hurts every time it makes contact with the mattress. This is the most animated she's been since they got here. With a last final jump she flops down hard on the bed throwing Donnie several inches in the air and then down again painfully.

'Oh,' says Bertha, catching her breath, 'that's the best laugh I've had for ages.'

*

The holiday is nearly over, thank God, thinks Donnie, only one more night to go. Holiday, that's a laugh, this is the worst nightmare he's ever experienced. He's hardly slept a wink with the heat and the light on all night and Bertha crying all the time. Last night he almost slept. He had a dream, more than a dream; he likes to think that it was an alternative experience, that he was transported from this nightmare to a nice time.

He looked down and found he had broken ribs but it was okay, he was with Daphne. They walked to the park past the university. It's okay, he told Daphne, she doesn't work there any more; she won't see us.

They sat laughing in the park looking at photographs. Then they were in the pub and drinking. I miss you, he said, I miss your skin; the way you fill your bra. You always knew how to fill a bra.

They were in bed together, now his arm was broken, a football injury, but he was glad because he was with Daphne again. He held her and told her how sorry he was, that he didn't know what had happened. He didn't know what he wanted. It had all gone wrong.

Daphne was laughing at his shaven groin but then she stopped when she saw the card. She said, 'That's strange, here's a Purple Ronnie card which is black', but then she cried when she saw what Bertha had written in it. He offered to tear the card up but then she was in the bathroom pulling Bertha's toilet bag out of the cabinet, throwing it on the floor. Why? She asked him, but Donnie didn't know why.

Even though the dream ended badly, he'd like to dream it again, it's a lot better than this living hell. Bertha isn't crying for the moment but it won't be long. She's reaching down into her suitcase again. Any minute now she'll start on about her nice things.

Bertha, please will you leave it love, they're only things.'

'Yes, but they're *my* things.'

'Well we'll get you new things when we get home. The insurance company will have to cough up for this lot and think of the fun you'll have replacing them.'

'But you haven't lost any of your nice things. Oh yes, sorry,' she says, with her eyes almost closed in contempt, 'I forgot, *you* haven't got any nice things. That's why you're back with me, isn't it?'

'Just stop this Bertha, okay?'

'Stop what? It's true isn't it?'

She's screeching and it's making Donnie head hurt and his arse throb.

'You only want me for the nice things my income brings: my nice house, my nice car ...'

'Your nice holiday.'

This has momentarily shut her up, but it is only a brief respite as she wipes the spittle from the side of her dry mouth.

'Well maybe you would be happier with your old things, your scabby old flat and your plain, ordinary, low-income girlfriend.'

Yes, thinks Donnie, remembering his dream, his alternative reality. Maybe he would be happier, but he's too scared to say so.

Chapter 21

On the quayside Agnes tells Sean it was peaceful. Bernie asked for him, kept on asking for him. She made Agnes promise to have something hot ready for him when he came home. Then she just went to sleep. They have missed her by two hours.

Without thinking what he is doing, how he might embarrass his uncle, Pierce opens his arms and walks towards Sean. Sean sidesteps the embrace and, in the manner of a kindly doctor, gently but firmly directs him by the elbow into the arms of Agnes. With his plastered arm around her, Pierce holds Agnes and cries hard. He has known this woman as long as he has known Bernie and never realised before how precious she is; he loves her. He thanks God for her arms, her warm skin, her healthy beating heart.

No one else attempts to touch Sean. They follow at a respectful distance as he approaches the cottage. He doesn't invite them in, not even Pierce. The funeral party, along with Pierce, keep vigil next door in Agnes's house. Half an hour later Sean re-emerges and chaps the door.

He is taking it incredibly well. Though his voice is hoarse he actually claps his hands and rubs them together as he dispatches his willing friends to make arrangements. Bill will call the doctor to come and issue a death certificate. Roddy will arrange the drink and food from the Seaward Hotel for the wake tonight. Agnes and Jean, Bernie's friends, will get her ready for the party, Sean will choose her outfit. Jim will take the dinghy to the other side of the island and bring back those that are able to come. Bill will tell the villagers that don't yet know and invite them. Sean will phone the family on the mainland himself. Sean suggests, and everyone agrees, that it would be a nice idea if Pierce could compose a few verses for his Auntie Bernie. Pierce nods.

Something weird has happened to his breathing. He can take in breaths easily enough, gulping down the fresh island air, it's letting them go again that's difficult. Maybe he's developed asthma or a heart condition. Normally something like this would be worrying, interesting at least, but Pierce's head is crowded with ideas for the panegyric he's tasked to write for Bernie. Tasked. At last his skills have a practical purpose, at last he can provide a useful service. Pierce is going to write the poem of his life, no, not his life: Bernie's. Not for his glory – he won't even try to get it published – but for Bernie's. He'll squeeze out every drop of creative juice he's got. Pierce doesn't know whether creativity is finite or not but if it is he'll blow the lot. If blood was creative juice he'd gladly bleed himself dry. This needs to be the most beautiful eulogy ever written.

Everyone is doing their bit. Agnes, anxious to fulfil her promise, pleads with Sean to eat something but he refuses. Bobby offers to go and collect Charlie McGowan the undertaker from the next island but Sean declines.

'There's no rush. You're forgetting that now we have the big fridge we have time to wait for the mainlanders to arrive. I'll take her up there myself after the wake. Let's do this properly, not rush at it like we used to have to do.'

Every one agrees. This is an unexpected use for the refrigeration plant, one that no one had thought of until now. Sean claps and shoos and sends them all about their business. Only now will he let Pierce come next door and see Bernie.

'She looks fine,' Sean tells him by way of encouragement when Pierce lingers at the bedroom door. And he is right. She's thin and her skin is a funny colour but she looks fine. Pierce almost laughs to see how groomed her hair is. Agnes or maybe Sean has brushed it and it lies thick and smooth, neat beside her on the pillow, regal, like an Egyptian queen.

Pierce remembers how when he was a child she used to clamp him between her knees and, as best she could, with a lot of squealing and grunting from both sides, haphazardly drag the brush across his wriggling head. But she had to catch him first. The mad chase around the house was worth the pain. The child Pierce complained bitterly that she hurt him with her knee clamps and threatened to tell his mother but Auntie Bernie was never intimidated.

'Well sit still then and I won't have to.'

'Brush your own hair!' he shouted at her. 'It looks like a bird's nest!'

Bernie laughed. Despite her brutal manhandling – she brushed so hard Pierce swears she left permanent grooves in his scalp – Bernie accepted his cheeky retort as fair play. She couldn't argue; her hair did look like a bird's nest piled on top of her head with ineffectual hair clips and bits of ribbon or elastic. It was dark and curly and wild, and always falling in front of her face. Her bottom lip had a little line under it from years of puffing upwards, blowing stray strands out of her face when she was cooking or ironing or trying to brush his hair.

Pierce would like to see it like that now. He'd like to gently mess it up, break up the tidy waves into ringlets and place wisps across her cheeks and have her hand rise up to slap him off. But it doesn't seem right, Sean might not understand. Would it be a violation to touch her like that?

His room is made up for him; Agnes did it last night after they phoned. Pierce empties his rucksack and sits at the desk by the window. He tries to adopt the same businesslike manner that Sean has taken and sets to work with his notepad and pen. No opening line jumps into his head so he comes at it from another direction. He makes a list of all the things he loved about Bernie. He is trying to be as honest as possible. Sean will not appreciate mawkish sentimentalism.

Bernie was not exceptionally beautiful or talented. She was a competent housekeeper, a reasonable cook, a loyal family member, a good wife. But the list, when Pierce has finished it, could describe any woman, all women, all the girls he's loved before. They are all kind, loving, loyal, funny, sensitive, brave, etc., to one degree or another. There is nothing here that marks Bernie out from the ordinary.

Her relationship with her husband was not perfect; it had its ups and downs. They fought and sulked and chatted and laughed like any other couple. Pierce knows that Sean had an on-and-off thing with a woman on the mainland over several summers. He thinks Bernie might have known, too. But they stayed together. It wasn't until Bernie got ill that Sean really began to appreciate her. A few years ago he refused to let her buy a new outfit for a wedding and they argued bitterly for weeks about it. Now Sean has an expensive diamond eternity ring in his pocket he was two hours short of delivering.

There is of course a rich seam of material for the poem in the romance and tragedy of the too-late trip to New York but Pierce senses that this should remain a secret. Maybe he should focus on Bernie's ordinariness, or the ordinariness of their marriage. Surely there is poetry in that. It strikes him that there is nothing more eternal, and nothing more comforting, than the ordinary. He will write a poem about how lucky Bernie and Sean have been, despite the unexceptional quality of their life, to have had each other, for Sean to have had such a wife, such a plain, ordinary, good wife.

*

Sean laughs loud when he greets people at the door. It will be a miserable affair if he doesn't. By his laughter he sets the tone, giving permission for the fun to commence. But he does seem genuinely pleased to see them. He hasn't seen some of them since the last good wake. And this will be a good one. It has all the hallmarks of a long and memorable evening.

The Seaward Hotel has pulled out all the stops with the catering. It is a measure of the affection and respect that Bernie and Sean are held in that Harry, the owner, charges at cost price and throws in a crate of lager and the sausage rolls for free. There is plenty of good eating: salmon, venison, lamb. Someone has got hold of cherry tomatoes, a rare treat. Agnes halves them to spin them out a bit but this does not diminish their glamour. A cello has arrived by dinghy from the other side of the island and is stacked until later beside the black hard-bodied coffins of accordions and fiddles. Drink is plentiful and of top quality.

As people arrive they bring in the fresh evening air, they take off their coats and shunt along the overflowing couch, politely budging up to accommodate new arrivals. They ask Pierce about his broken arm and he repeatedly explains it away as quickly as he can. At first they talk in hushed voices but as the room fills the volume rises. The women catch up with each other's gossip: most of their grown-up children have left for university or jobs and they discuss with relish what the young folk are up to on the mainland. The men huddle round the sideboard laden with bottles of good single malts but although Sean is pouring large ones, everyone is taking it easy, pacing themselves.

As the food is cleared away and before the dancing begins, Pierce is called upon to recite his elegy. He raises his voice against the hubbub of clattering dishes in the kitchen. As he reads he is picking up reaction from the four corners of the room, in the form of sharp intakes of breath, and this excites him. The kitchen noise subsides and he is given the assembled company's full attention. People are leaning forward and listening hard. This is what poetry is all about, thinks Pierce, and when he stops there is silence.

The islanders stare at Pierce, waiting for more, waiting for revelation. Then they look at each other, a consensus of confusion gathering, building towards outrage. Agnes McConnell screams and lifts the first thing that comes to hand, a heavy model of the Statue of Liberty, and throws it at Pierce. It misses him by a two-inch margin and takes a lump out of the plaster on the wall behind his head. With a mad banshee glint in her eye Agnes rushes at him but three men tackle her and she is bundled, still kicking and screaming, out into the hall.

Even here, on the island, he is misunderstood. They have completely missed the point, missed the beauty of it. They've focussed only on words and not on what the poem is actually saying. They've latched on to words like: passable, adequate, average and humdrum and totally misinterpreted his meaning. Perhaps he should have gone with the mawkish sentimentality.

*

Next morning Pierce has trouble working out where he is. He still has his clothes on but this in itself is not that unusual and offers no clues. The room is familiar but what is foxing him is the quality of light. Then he remembers; he's on the island. He cringes and hides beneath the duvet. What was he thinking with that fucking stupid poem?

Until he read out that poem he had always held the privileged position of being Bernie's big boy. Last night, until he read the poem, he was Bernie's orphaned son. Now he's nobody, Bernie's friends won't give him the time of day, the steam off their piss. After the poem they were polite, but in a distant way, the way they are with the summer tourists. He has offended the whole island, he has insulted the memory of the best auntie he ever had and he has hurt his uncle with such a sharp deep cut that the wound might never heal.

A thick haar lies across the bay; it will be a lovely day if the sun gets strong enough to burn it off. He hears the diesel engine and metallic clunk of a van being parked outside. Pierce is too hungover to face Sean just now. He wanted to keep the vigil last night with him, he was desperate to, but Sean avoided him all night. Pierce spent most of the night down on the boat alone, rolling single-skinned joints, spinning out his hash to make it last.

Pierce opens the window and sticks his head out but if Sean has heard him he is not acknowledging him. Pierce wants to call out hello or good morning or something but everything he can think of to say sounds wrong. Sean opens the back doors of the van and enters the house. Pierce can hear him moving about downstairs, opening drawers in the kitchen, it sounds like he's looking for something. Pierce sees the bald patch on Sean's head re-emerging from the house and watches while he tosses his toolbox into the front seat and puts his big Maglite torch on the floor beside it. His heavy working boots clump up the stairs and within seconds back down again. Sean is spreading the quilt from his bed on to the floor of the van. Again Pierce hears the boots thud on the stairs and this time the door to his room is thrown open.

'Get up,' Sean says and walks out.

Pierce complies immediately. He feels guilty, caught kneeling on the bed with his head out the window as if he were spying on his uncle. Now Sean is in the bathroom throwing things into a plastic bag. Pierce, unsure of what to do, does nothing. Sean strides back into the room and Pierce straightens up, standing to attention by his bed. Sean pulls back the quilt from the bed, but it's the sheets he's after. The bottom one is giving him some trouble, the sheet is fitted and is tightly hooked over one corner of the mattress. Pierce moves to help but Sean growls, 'Leave it!' He obediently takes a few steps back and leaves it. With surly glances Sean examines the pale green sheets, apparently looking for something. Pierce is mortified; this inspection is making him feel like a wet-dreaming teenager. Thankfully the sheets apparently pass muster; Sean bundles them under his arm and thuds out. He's surely lost his mind, thinks Pierce.

Sean is downstairs again but now his movements are slower and quieter. He goes back out to the van and after a moment's hesitation Pierce chances a quick peak out the window. Sean has Bernie in his arms. With tiny sideways steps he is moving carefully round the door of the van so as not to bang her head against it. He bends his knees and his back to place her gently on the quilt. He takes time to smooth out her hair, breathing hard with the effort of carrying her. There is such tenderness and intimacy in the gesture that Pierce wants to go back to standing by his bed but any movement might alert Sean that he is watching. Please, please don't cry, thinks Pierce. He will not be able to bear it if Sean cries. But Sean doesn't cry. He wraps the quilt round Bernie, leaving her face exposed, and tucks her in. He stretches bungee cords across her body, attaching them to the sides of the van to keep her firmly in place, warm and cosy. Then he closes the doors and drives off.

Pierce doesn't know what to make of it. What is Sean up to? Does this mean he should leave? Pulling the sheets off someone's bed, especially when they are virtually still in it, is not exactly welcoming. He'll leave when Sean goes to collect the family from the mainland, if Sean still wants him to. Surely he'll let him stay for the funeral. For the meanwhile he'll just have to keep a low profile.

To stay out of Sean's way Pierce takes a long walk. Walking around the village is no fun; he's met at every turn with angry stares from people who were at the wake. He'd like to take a look at the new refrigeration plant but as he approaches he sees Sean's van parked outside. On a whim he walks all the way to the other side of the island, if he meets anyone, he'll tell them the sad news. It's almost dark as he makes his way back, without having met a soul all day. He's starving and can't stop thinking about soup.

He's going to have to start being nice to Daphne; you never know when you're going to lose people. When Sean phoned he dropped everything and forgot to tell her he was going away. Pierce groans when he thinks of Daphne and the lovely soup he could be eating right now. And the band, their big gig on Friday night and he's missed it. Tam will never forgive him.

As Pierce passes the refrigeration plant for the second time the lights are on inside and Sean's van is still parked there. He must be keeping her company, spending time alone with her until he has to say his final goodbyes at the funeral. It must be bloody cold in there.

As his thoughts turn to Bernie he remembers that he doesn't have any decent clothes with him, he'll need a good suit for the funeral. He'd borrow something from Sean but Sean will be lucky if he has a decent suit for himself and anyway Sean's clothes will be far too big for him. He'll phone his mother from the hotel and ask her to bring his suit with her. That way he can find out if he's welcome enough in the hotel to stay and have a pint and a plate of soup. It won't be as good as Daphne's though.

The public bar is warm and the smell from the kitchen is mouth-watering. Pierce asks Harry the barman for change for the phone and is treated civilly. No one actually spits on him but there is certainly an atmosphere. Pierce's face reddens with shame and anger.

Okay, he wants to announce to the pub, the poem was misjudged but that doesn't mean I'm not hurting just as much as any of you. If anyone speaks to him he'll tell them that, but no one does and they avoid eye contact.

'Hello, Mum?'

'Hi son, listen, me and your dad are just at our tea now, I've made him his favourite for a wee treat: mince and doughballs,' she laughs, 'can you phone back in twenty minutes?'

Pierce is speechless with fury at his mother's ebullience.

'Pierce? Hello, are you still there?'

In the background he can hear his father telling her to sit down and eat her dinner. He bangs the receiver down hard and then looks around guiltily to see if anyone has spotted him. Not only has he insulted his dead auntie; he's a phone vandal too. Pierce has to get his suit. There's nothing for it but to wait the twenty minutes and phone her back. He won't be speechless this time.

'Any chance of a plate of soup, Harry?'

Harry writes a chit and passes it through the hatch to the kitchen without a word.

'Smells brilliant,' Pierce says with a desperate smile. 'And a pint of lager too, please.'

The lager comes first, dumped gracelessly in front of him and Pierce knocks half of it back in a oner. It's quickly finished and he is three-quarters through his next one before the soup comes. Despite the fact that no one is speaking to him it's damn good soup. It's potato and leek, straightforward, with none of the fancy ingredients and embellishments that Daphne has and therefore none of the subtle nuances or delicate undertastes, but damn good soup none the less. His cheeks flush rosy from exercise and the lager as he carefully spoons the hot fluid past his lips. He takes his time with the last few spoonfuls, spinning out his time in the warmth and comfort of the bar.

'Hello, Mum?'

'Aye, hello son, what can I do you for?'

Her tone is too jovial by far for Pierce's liking.

'I need you to bring me my suit,' Pierce tells her curtly.

'Your suit? Bring it where? What d'you need a suit for? You're not in the jail, are you?'

'For the funeral! For Christ's sake, Mum!'

'Don't you swear at me! I'll get your father to you. And what are you talking about, what funeral?'

Now Pierce understands the jovial tone.

'Has Sean not phoned you?'

'Oh my God! Bernie.'

There is no ebullience now, no joviality, she breaks down and cries hard into the phone. He has to move the receiver away from his ear, her crying is too close and too painful, embarrassing in a weird way. Pierce hears her handing the phone to his father. He can tell by their breathing that his parents are standing close together. Mum's crying is muffled now, probably by Dad's shirt-front. Pierce wishes he could join their embrace.

'When?' says his dad.

'Two days ago. In her sleep. Tell mum it was peaceful.'

'Is Sean okay?'

'Yeah, yeah. Sean's good. He said he would phone you to let you know.'

'Well he hasn't phoned here and he hasn't phoned your Uncle Pat either. Pat would have phoned us.'

'He said he would.'

'When is the funeral, son?'

'Eh, I'm not sure. Sean hasn't told us.'

'Will you ask him to phone us? We'll need to make arrangements.'

'Of course I will. Can you ask Mum to bring me my suit and get me a black tie?'

Pierce is finishing his pint when Roddie and Bill come into the bar. They nod briefly in Pierce's general direction, which is encouraging and so he decides to approach them. He approaches slowly, carefully, ready to be rebuffed.

'Roddie. Bill.'

'Aye,' says Roddie noncommittally.

'Has Sean mentioned when the funeral is? It's just that the family, they need to know so they can make plans to come.'

'No, he hasn't said,' says Bill.

'Well, the undertaker, when is he coming?'

'He isn't,' says Bill. 'Sean hasn't spoken to him yet. The wife was on the phone to his wife this morning and they knew nothing about it.'

Pierce is perturbed. Sean seemed so organised the other day when he was delegating tasks to everyone.

'He took Bernie up to the plant this morning and when I passed tonight his van was still there. Do you think he's okay? He said he'd phone the family and he hasn't and he hasn't done anything about the undertaker. I'm a bit worried about him.'

Both Bill and Roddie stare at him.

Their silence implies that Pierce has no right to cast aspersions about Sean's organisational abilities. He's done it again. You can't win with these people, he thinks as he downs the last of his pint and leaves.

Pierce goes directly to the tiny harbour but *The Statue of Liberty* is moored and empty. He goes aboard anyway and sits below deck wondering what to do now. There is no sign of the van outside and the cottage is in darkness when he goes in, but Sean might be in bed. He wanders through each room looking for signs that Sean has been back but he can find none. Pretending to go to the bathroom, he peeks in as he passes his auntie and uncle's bedroom, listening for Sean's familiar fisherman's wheeze. He's not there either. The door is wide open the way Sean left it this morning. Maybe he's gone to visit friends who didn't make it to the wake, to tell them personally, or maybe he's having a pint now in the pub with his loyal mates, Bill and Roddie. Sean can't have gone to the pub, Pierce would have heard the van pass, and, although he's been alert for the sound of the diesel engine, no traffic has passed. For the first time ever on the island, he feels lonely.

Just for the hell of it Pierce decides to walk back to the plant. What harm can it do? It's not as if he's checking up on Sean, not as though he's accusing him of shirking his responsibilities. Sean is after all the man who got the refrigeration plant built for God's sake, if anyone on this island can make something happen then it's

Uncle Sean but it'll do no damage to take a wander up there. If he's there Pierce can tell him how sorry he is about the poem. He can tell him that his mum was asking when they should come. That's all.

The van is still outside but the plant is locked up. Maybe the van has broken down and Sean has walked back to the village and, by way of avoiding Pierce, has gone straight to the pub. Pierce can't help but get the feeling that Sean is still in there. He walks around the building looking for another entrance, hugging the walls to keep from tripping on rubble, but there is no other way in. The windows, such as they are, are too high up to see in. With his good arm he drags together five discarded wooden palettes and stacks them on top of each other. The rickety palettes retain a strong smell of fish, the whole place, even from the outside, smells of fish. Because of his plastered arm his balance is knocked askew and he is slow to climb the palette tower. He clings to the walls with his fingertips for fear of falling and slowly, carefully, raises himself up until he can see inside.

There is one light on inside which at first he takes to be a switch for the machinery but as his eyes adjust he sees that it is a strong beam pointing upwards. The light silhouettes a ragged outline in front of it. It could be sacks of oysters or something or it could be Sean.

'Sean! It's me, open up!'

The outline makes no move. Pierce bangs the window as hard as he can, nearly losing his balance on the shaky palettes.

'Sean, please, it's bloody freezing out here!'

If it *is* Sean the impudence of this remark will stir him to action, surely. But there is no response. Maybe it's just a bag of oysters.

Getting down off the palettes is easier than getting up except that Pierce grazes the side of his hand on the new pebbledash and it bleeds a bit. As he walks back to the cottage he has to lower his throbbing arm to stop the blood running up inside the plaster. His hand stings so much it makes him cry. Fat tears roll down his face and bounce off with the jolting of his hurried angry stride. There is still no sign of Sean at the house but Pierce is not surprised. Inside the bar he purposefully approaches Roddie and Bill, who stand with a few of the other men. When they see him Roddie and Bill immediately separate from the others and meet him in the middle. Pierce is grateful for this. If he's wrong this will bring down the wrath of the whole island on him.

'Have you seen him?'

They both shake their heads.

'Is there anywhere else he could be?'

'There a million places he could be,' says Bill sagely.

'Yeah, well he's not in the house, he's not in the boat and his van is still up at the refrigeration plant.'

Roddie and Bill say nothing. Pierce doesn't know what he wants them to say.

'I think he's up there. I looked in the window.'

'How the hell did you look in the window?' challenges Roddie.

'I stood on palettes, okay? D'you not believe me?'

Both of them are silent again. This is not getting Pierce anywhere; he came to ask for their help.

'Sorry, but I don't think Sean is coping as well as he seems to be. I need to borrow a key. I think he's up at the plant and I need to go and get him out of there before he freezes his bollocks off. Who are the key holders?'

'I've got a key,' Bill says slightly sheepishly before Roddie tugs his jumper and he is silenced.

'Oh for fuck's sake!' says Pierce through clenched teeth. 'I only need it for half an hour, I'll bring it straight back.'

Bill turns back to the other men and Roddie follows him. Pierce is left standing. He can't believe these small-minded tight-arsed fucks. He's only trying to help. He only wants Sean back here, safe and sipping a pint in the warmth and familiarity of the hotel bar. As his anger bubbles he marches toward the men who have now formed an exclusive huddle. This is pathetic, Pierce thinks. As he nears them Bill holds up his hand in a delaying gesture. He is close enough to them now to hear what they are saying. Surprisingly, Roddie is apparently pleading his case.

'The boy knows he made an arse of himself last night and he's sorry, he just said as much, didn't he Bill?'

Bill nods confirmation.

'There's been no sign of him all day. I say we go up there and take a look.'

There is a murmur of hesitation, which becomes general approval. Bill, with a wave, signals Pierce to approach.

'And I am really, really sorry about the poem,' confesses Pierce. 'I honestly never meant any offence.' Tiredness, frustration and unaddressed grief put a catch in his voice. 'Bernie is, was, one of the most important people in my…'

'We'll take the Land Rover. Tommy, you bring the rest of the lads in your car,' says Roddie, rescuing Pierce from encroaching tears.

Chapter 22

Pierce is proved right. Sean is in the refrigeration plant, but no one could have predicted the sight that awaits them.

The beam of light that Pierce saw earlier when he peaked through the window is still as bright, brighter now that he is inside and seeing it close up. It is held in the hand, from the outstretched arm, of a statue. The Statue of Liberty. Bernie, upright, barefoot and crowned, swathed in pale green sheets, frozen and hard as copper, stands posed before them.

In front of her, Sean is slumped on a plastic chair, lifeless.

Pierce touches the bare skin on Bernie's arm. Dead cold. He moves to Sean and puts a hand on his uncle's face. Not quite so cold.

'Sean! Roddie! I think he's alive! Roddie!'

'No way!'

'Uncle Sean, wake up!'

Pierce vigorously shakes him and Sean falls forward. Pierce is lying on the floor with him, his arms around him on the sub-zero concrete floor. Bill is pulling at Sean's neck, looking for a pulse.

'Get a mirror! Somebody, quick!'

There is no mirror but it seems there is a pulse, a faint slow pulse, but a pulse. The men, all fishermen, have seen death and dying before but even so they are panicking, crowding together to lift him. The beautiful sculpture he has created from his wife's body is ignored while they haul Sean between them out to the car. Once there, Pierce insists and has to fight off the others to get in beside his uncle.

Sean's skin is grey. Pierce puts his ear to Sean's lips and thinks he feels breath but it could be condensation from the white frosting that covers Sean's clothes. He slaps his face gently and then harder but Sean doesn't open his eyes. He shouts in his ear.

'Don't die, Sean, don't fucking die!'

It occurs to Pierce that if Sean dies it will be his fault. Too much time has been wasted and he's responsible. If he hadn't recited that poem, people in the village would still be speaking to him, they would have taken him seriously the first time. Roddie and Bill would have given him the key or come with him straight away. As a progression from this, another thought strikes him, a much worse thought.

Perhaps Sean modelled Bernie like this because he thought Pierce's poem labelled her, *damned* her, with ordinariness. Well she certainly isn't ordinary now. Amongst dead bodies she is quite spectacularly extraordinary. She looks amazing. This is a much truer reflection of Bernie's spirit than Pierce's piece of shit poem could ever be. What he'd intended as panegyric, a heroic eulogy for his gorgeous funny wonderful auntie, she who was so exceptionally herself, was no more than lazy thoughtless doggerel.

He sold her short. Sean knows it, and this is all Pierce's fault.

He lifts Sean's limp lifeless hand and begins to rub. Bill, from the driving seat turns and blasts him.

'For God's sake, don't do that! It's hypothermia; I've seen it before. You'll do more damage than anything else.

'Well what am I supposed to do? Just sit here and let him die?'

'Calm down. Everybody. Just calm down,' says Robbie. 'We have to keep him warm. Andy'll phone for the doctor…'

'The quilt!' Pierce shouts. 'He brought Bernie here in a duvet, it's probably in the back of the van.'

'Right. Tommy, can you see if it's there?' Roddie asks.

Tommy runs to the van but it's locked and as he runs back towards them Pierce is fumbling in Sean's trouser pockets. He passes the keys in to the front of the car to Roddie. Like a fire bucket, the keys are relayed to everyone along the route from Pierce to Tommy, as is the duvet on the way back.

'Get in beside him,' Bill tells Pierce. 'Give him your body heat, that's it, cuddle in to him, that's the best thing you can do.'

Pierce tries to cover as much surface area as possible, even pressing his face to his uncle's. Despite the circumstances, or perhaps because of them, a line from a song keeps running through Pierce's head.

When we're out together dancing cheek to cheek.

While they are in the car Pierce thinks he feels Sean eyelids flutter on his face. He tells Roddie this and for the rest of the journey they all, including Bill the driver, study Sean's face intently. It is not until they are back at the house that Sean does it again, this time witnessed and confirmed by the others. All three bars of the electric fire are turned on, an unheard of extravagance in this house. Like lovers Pierce and Sean lie under the duvet on the couch in the living room surrounded by middle-aged men. Pierce has another go at reviving Sean; he tries blowing on his face and surreptitiously flicking his ears.

'The doctor's on his way,' Andy reports. 'But he says it's probably going to be an air ambulance. And he says not to expect too much, if he's been lying in the plant all day the chances are not great.'

Pierce does not want to hear this and more vigorously pings his uncle's ear. He feels a little guilty, the ear is red now but at least it's keeping the circulation going. Sean's eyes open. He tries to say something. Pierce puts his ear to Sean's mouth to hear what he is trying to say. The men wait expectantly.

'He's saying his ear hurts.'

The others look slightly confused by this but everyone is relieved.

'How are you feeling, Sean?' Roddie bawls at him.

'He's saying: cold.'

This is generally interpreted as a positive response. The atmosphere becomes more relaxed and the men begin to talk amongst themselves. Within the privacy of the duvet Pierce asks questions by whispering.

'Sean, do you know where you are and what's happened?'

Sean holds Pierce's eye and slowly nods his head.

'Hypothermia,' he whispers. 'Nice way.'

'Did you mean it to happen?'

Again the slow nod, this time accompanied by a sensuous smile.

'Uncle Sean, I'm so sorry. Was it because of the poem? I never meant for any of this ...'

'Not the poem.'

'No?'

'No.'

Pierce hasn't time to enjoy the relief he feels when he hears this. Sean's speech is slurred and difficult to make out. He sounds drunk when he says, 'Did you see her?'

'Yes Sean. She looks beautiful.'

Pierce is not humouring a dying man when he says this. The image of Bernie in the refrigeration plant, noble, beautiful, everything she ever wanted to be, is very firmly imprinted on his mind, he thinks it always will be. As he sees the model of the statue on the mantelpiece, the one that Agnes threw at him the other night, he realises just how spot-on Sean has got it. Every detail, down to the folds of the statue's gown, Sean has lovingly recreated with Bernie, for Bernie. Pierce thinks she should be in a museum. He's going to talk to his contacts at the Arts Council about this as soon as he gets back to the city.

'A lot of work.'

'You've done a fantastic job, all the lads were saying so.'

Sean smiles.

'Tickets.'

Pierce is not following and communicates this in his expression.

'New York.'

'Ah right, the holiday.'

Pierce says this a bit too loudly and Sean warns him with a look to keep his voice down.

'You take them. You go.'

'Sean, you can probably get the money back on those tickets.'

'No. You go. Take a girl, a special girl.'

'Sean, thanks a lot, that's really kind of you, but ...'

Suddenly Sean grabs Pierce's arm with a strength that surprises them both.

'Could be my deathbed. Hope it is. My dying wish. Promise.'

'I promise, Sean.'

'The ring. Here.'

Sean indicates that the ring is in his trouser pocket and once again, Pierce, eyeball to eyeball under the quilt, must make intimate contact, rifling Sean's pockets, interfering in his groin area. Pierce finds the ring, opens the box, looks at it again and shakes his head. This is Bernie's ring. He can't take it and give it to some girl. But Sean is nodding yes.

'Take it, you need a wife. An ordinary wife. Passable, adequate, humdrum.'

But this is not, as Pierce immediately fears, an admonishment. The sly smile on Sean's face signals that it is a joke, a wind-up.

'Did you see her?'

'Yes Sean, she's beautiful.'

Sean smiles beatifically and slides back into unconsciousness.

Chapter 23

'Oh, definitely Marilyn Monroe,' says Carol.

'Yeah?' says Pierce.

'Definitely. Y'know, with the white dress? Like this,' she says, as she jumps up to demonstrate, legs straddling an imaginary subway vent. She lifts her brown frilled skirt, up and wide, to show even more of her long slim legs. Pierce and Tam are evaluating her pose and nodding approval.

Carol phoned last night and asked for help marking Daphne's student's end-of-term exam papers. Daphne's first impulse was to blow her out, she doesn't want Carol in her house, but she feels bad deserting the students. If it's left to Carol, she'll fail most of them and they don't deserve that. Since she's arrived Carol hasn't mentioned the absence of Donnie from Daphne's flat or conversation, but then Carol's too self-obsessed to notice anything that doesn't directly affect her.

Pierce is back. He came back late last night and chapped up this afternoon for soup as though he had never been away. He has given them a long account of his disappearance, describing in poetic detail the death of his beloved Bernie, his heroic rescue of his uncle and the bizarre sight of his frozen auntie. All the islanders came to view her in the refrigeration plant, bringing the kids, making a day of it. Pierce thinks it's a great business idea; he wants to set up a company styling dead bodies into famous poses. Daphne doesn't believe it but it's a good story. He is joking about it now but Daphne senses his laughter is brittle.

'What about you, Daphne?' says Tam.

Tam has also 'popped round'. He has popped round, uninvited, several times since the night of his famous gig. He no longer even pretends to be looking for Pierce. He has apparently forgiven Pierce for not turning up at the gig. The band has found new management anyway.

'A Teletubby,' says Pierce while she's still thinking about it. 'Tinky Winky.'

Yes, thinks Daphne, and laughs, that's exactly what I am, a Teletubby.

'Oh you!' Carol screams, with an ineffectual girly slap at Pierce's thigh. 'No. That photograph.' Tam says, as if they know what he's talking about. 'The famous American one, with the woman sitting down: legs open, arms covering her modesty, classy.'

'Oh yeah, *Nude* by Edward Weston, I can see you like that, Daphne, with your beard just peeking out between your legs.'

'You are such an ignoramus, Pierce. It's not pubic hair,' says Daphne, 'it's shadow: chiaroscuro.'

'Excuse me, I've studied that photo in some detail and I can assure you that it's definitely pubes.'

'And anyway,' she says, 'I want to be Boadicea going into battle.'

Pierce looks up from rolling a spliff. His arm is in plaster and his hand is badly cut but still he insists that he is the best joint-roller. He considers the suggestion and tuts.

'Full battle dress, a carriage and horses and everything,' he says as he crumbles hash into the tobacco. 'You're talking big bucks, Daphne.'

'Damn the expense, I've got a good insurance policy.'

'Well I'm sorted. I'm going to be James Bond,' Pierce says.

'Aw man! I was going to pick James Bond!' cries Tam.

'Too late, I got in before you.'

'That's not fair, you've had more time to think about it.'

'But you could be Keanu Reeves in *The Matrix*, Tam.'

'Oh yes! Cheers Daphne, Good one.'

Tam immediately stands up and strikes a martial arts pose.

Later, after the joint has been smoked and they have exhausted the possibilities for their modelled cadavers, Daphne goes to the kitchen to heat up the soup. She is tiring of their company; if she feeds them maybe they'll leave afterwards. Carol has hardly marked any of the exam papers; she's expecting Daphne to do it all. She can hear her in the living room giggling at everything the lads say.

As she's putting out the plates Pierce comes in and asks if she needs a hand with anything.

'No thanks, I can just about manage.'

Pierce turns round but instead of going back into the living room, he quietly closes the kitchen door. He shuffles from foot to foot until Daphne is forced to turn and give him her attention.

'Daphne, I want to ask you something.'

This is obviously serious. He better not try to hit on her for money. There's no way she's going to invest in any of his mad schemes, even if she did have the money.

'Ask away.'

'I've got two tickets for New York. You're not working just now. You could come with me.'

Daphne laughs.

'Come with you? What for?'

'For a holiday. We'll have to change the names on the tickets but it's only forty quid a head, I've looked into it, and it's a week in a really good hotel.'

Daphne has never been to New York. She wonders what the weather would be like at this time of year. New York would take her far away from Donnie, a different country, a different continent.

'That's mental.'

'I knew you were going to say that but think about it for a minute, there's loads of stuff we can do, we could …'

'Pierce. Thanks, I really appreciate the offer but …'

'Look, if it's the money, we can sort something out, fuck it, I'll pay your forty quid, and I've got spending money, enough for us both.'

'It's not the money.'

'Well what is it then? Is it Tam? You and him seem awful pally.'

'And? Your point is?'

'My point is nothing. You're right; nothing to do with me, but you could still come. Look, we get on well, right? We could have

166

a great laugh, paint the town, Empire State building, Statue of Liberty, separate rooms if you want.'

'Why are you asking me? There must be loads of other women you could ask.'

'Of course there are, what bird wouldn't want a free holiday in New York with me?'

'Pierce, I'm not one of your birds.'

'That's not what I'm saying. I *know* that. I don't want to go with a bird. I want to go with you. Please Daphne, this is really important to me. Just think about it, eh?'

'I'm sorry.'

'Aw for fuck's sake, Daphne! Are you still pining for that loser, Donnie?'

'Just shut it, Pierce, you don't know what you're talking about.'

'No, you shut it. I'm sick of this.' Pierce is shouting. 'So you were chucked, shit happens. Stop sitting about in your dressing gown and get a fucking life. Get over it and fucking move on. You think it's fun living below you moaning and greeting all the time? Worse things happen, you know, people you love die, good people, and you can't do anything about it.'

At this outburst Daphne's anger evaporates. She moves towards him and now he is in her arms, crying, sobbing hard on her shoulder. Daphne notices that the giggling from the living room has ceased abruptly. Tam and Carol are listening.

'You're okay, Pierce, you'll be okay,' she says softly.

And he is okay. After a few minutes he pulls himself together and with a sheepish laugh he helps her carry the steaming plates of soup into the living room.

*

The next morning Carol phones. Daphne knows what's coming. Carol accidentally on purpose left the exam papers with Daphne last night. She left after the soup with Tam and Pierce who were going to a poetry reading at a pub. Tam of course nagged Daphne

167

to come too but Carol didn't pressure her and Pierce didn't seem to care. For the first time in a long time Daphne thinks she might have enjoyed the pub.

'Daphne, I'm phoning to ask you a favour.'

Here it comes, thinks Daphne; she's going to ask me to finish marking the papers. She doesn't mind, at least this way the students will get fair grades, but it means that Carol will have to come round again to pick them up.

'Yeah?'

Let her beg.

'Could you mark those papers for me? You know the students much better than I do.'

'Yeah.'

'Oh thanks, Daphne.'

'When do you want to collect them?'

'Eh, well, that's the favour I wanted to ask you. Could you get them in to college? They have to be in by the end of the week.'

'I don't think so, Carol, I'm off sick, remember?'

'Yes but you could post them. I've spoken to Magda and she says she'll do the paperwork and make sure the students get them back.'

'But why don't you just take them in yourself? I can have them finished by tomorrow.'

'Well, I would but I'm off to New York! Pierce is taking me, he asked me last night, it's mad, isn't it?'

Daphne surprises herself by laughing.

'I know, it's great, isn't it? He's getting the tickets sorted out today and we're leaving tomorrow. By the way, I'm really sorry about you and Donnie breaking up.'

*

Spring has sprung. The leaf, which a few weeks ago was out of reach, is now knocking insistently on Daphne's window. She answers its call, opening the window and harvesting it. It is a lime leaf, a perfectly shaped heart, emerald bright on the tree. Now that it lies quietly on her kitchen table it is richer, darker without the light behind it, more serious. Daphne wishes she could stick it back on the tree. But she can't and now that she has taken it, what will she do with it?

She takes the long way home from the deli. This way is at least two miles longer and goes past Donnie's flat. It's nice to get a bit of a walk after being stuck in the house all day. She passes on the opposite side of the street looking up at his dark windows. This is what she expected. It's 3.30 a.m. and Donnie has to get up for work in the morning. After one more reconnaissance walk past, she climbs the stairs noiselessly and waits for a few seconds outside his door.

The leaf, which she has carried carefully in a reinforced envelope, she now takes out. It sits on her open palm and with her other hand she gently lifts the letterbox and slides the leaf through the door. She can't see it but she knows that it is floating down on to the carpet ready to greet him in the morning.

As she makes her way home she begins to feel much better about the whole thing. All day long she has been nervous. It looks bad she admits: a woman spurned, clandestinely putting garden refuse through a letter box in the middle of the night. But it only requires that two people understand the gesture.

The problem with the Asda incident is that it left no room for arbitration. Donnie's cowardice is a given and must be worked around. What if, after the Asda exposition and Donnie's inglorious retreat from the shop, Donnie wants to see Daphne but hasn't the courage to approach? What if he thinks, as might be a logical assumption, that she hates him and never wants to see him again? She doesn't know whether she hates him or not but she knows she must see him again. They have to talk. They have to talk and, by necessity, it must be Daphne who provides the opportunity. The time has come to put pride and cowardice away, they have things to sort out.

She can't phone, he probably wouldn't answer and even if he did she can't trust herself not to sound angry. She can't write, the last letter she wrote was from a position of ignorance and therefore invalid, any other letters would be the same. The leaf says everything.

Daphne feels relieved. It is the right thing to do, she is sure of it.

Chapter 24

'Well how was it?' asks Tam. 'The Big Apple, must have been brilliant, eh?'

Pierce gives an enigmatic smile.

'Oh ho ho! The Big Apple!' he replies.

New York was fantastic, wonderful, the best place Pierce's ever been. He couldn't get enough of it, didn't want to come home.

'You are one lucky boy, a holiday like that and a bird like Carol with you, must have been unbelievable.'

'Oh ho ho! Unbelievable!' Pierce replies again as if to confirm Tam's assumptions. His smile remains enigmatic. It is not his innate sense of gentlemanly conduct that prevents him from telling Tam the truth of the matter; it is more a question of losing face with his young admirer.

The truth of the matter is that although Pierce did not want to leave New York, he was enormously relieved to be shot of Carol. When, after a passionate and very public kiss at the airport, Carol climbed into her taxi, a rush of euphoric glee enveloped Pierce and he laughed until he almost cried, so glad was he that he would never have to shag the woman again.

The holiday had started promisingly enough. The day before he left he attended his Restart interview and, on the strength of having his arm in plaster, was excused taking part in the programme. Next stop was the hospital where they judged his arm to be well enough to have the plaster removed. The timing could not have been more perfect. Even Carol, unusually for a woman, turned up in good time to check in. Apart from her having what appeared to be fifteen stone of hand luggage, 'It's only my make-up,' she giggled, which Pierce was expected to lug around the airport, things were going pretty well. They had a few pre-flight drinks in the bar just to get them in the mood. On the plane Pierce went to the toilet and when he came back she was sitting with a bottle of champagne and two glasses

'Oh, it's just like blind date!' she squealed.

It wasn't until they were getting off the plane and Pierce was tapped firmly on the shoulder by the chief trolley dolly that he realised she hadn't paid for it. It took a largish dent out of his spending money but he didn't really mind, Carol was a classy bird and the way things were going he was guaranteed his hole. Not that he was expecting anything; he told her he could arrange separate rooms. 'I don't think that'll be necessary,' she said, all kittenish.

They were no sooner in the room than she ripped the clothes off him. Literally. His good Marco Polo shirt that he'd travelled in had three buttons missing and a torn breast pocket.

'Hang on love, we've got all week.'

But she was like an animal. She started with the little mewling noises that some women make which developed into a full-on lioness's roar. She wriggled and panted and groaned like some kind of porn star. Pierce was at first certain that she must be taking the piss and, just for a laugh, joined in with the exaggerated grunting. But she wasn't kidding and his response only spurred her on. Her face, not the prettiest at the best of times, became a frightening mask of lust, contorting into an ugly rictus when she came. And she came a lot. Over and over and over again. Now he knew she was taking the piss.

After, as she lay legs akimbo with her knickers at her knees, she had not even been able to wait until he had removed her clothes, he noticed that she had a thin paper liner inside her pants. Why did women wear those things? What was that all about?

After sex, while he was still in the toilet dabbing himself dry, Carol ordered another bottle of champagne from room service. This would have to be hit on the head. To be fair, he may have given her the wrong impression when he told her that he was managing editor of *Poyumtree*. Now he was forced to explain that the publishing house was a relatively new venture and still in the development phase, the investment phase, the non-profit-making phase. It was embarrassing but he simply didn't have that kind of money. She took it pretty well, although Pierce did note at the time that, rather than pay for the champers herself, she quickly got back on the blower to room service and cancelled it. They got cans of Coke from a slot machine along the hallway and drank the duty-free vodka.

Pierce was enjoying a dope-free week. He had been too scared to bring any into the country and too scared to ask anyone. It occurred to him that it had probably been years now since he had a whole week off the hash but abstinence certainly agreed with him as he now woke up with a long-forgotten sensation: vitality. He resolved when he went home to knock it on the head. He wasn't a teenager anymore.

New York City was phenomenal. Every morning Pierce was up at the crack of dawn ready to spend the day seeing sights. Carol was not so enthusiastic. It was usually nearer lunch before she could be winkled out of bed. To Pierce everything was so new and exciting and yet so familiar. Practically every time he turned a corner there would be another view, little changed since the first time, of many times, that he saw it in Bernie's dog-eared photo album. For Sean's sake, Pierce took photos of everything and tried to get Carol in as many as possible.

Her sexual exuberance had not waned as Pierce had hoped it might. She was constantly all over him. He couldn't even eat in peace. Carol would be giggling and groping him under the table regardless of where they were or who could see them. For all she had a posh accent, Pierce began to discover that Carol had little class.

Of course he pretended to enjoy it, but all the fake porn-star grunting was becoming very wearisome. He was baw weary. The rough animalistic sex did not give way to a more relaxed and gentle approach, if anything she became hungrier. Pierce began to wake up feeling afraid. That was half the reason he got up and out so early, if he didn't she would surely jump on him again and she was wearing his cock down to a frayed stump.

It wasn't just the sex. There were other things. For starters, Carol didn't have much of a sense of humour. She laughed all right, she laughed a lot. But it was usually *at* him. She laughed at the way he danced, she laughed at the few lines of poetry he had spontaneously come up with in Central Park. Once, when he rather vigorously blew his nose and a wee bit of paper hanky got stuck on his nostril, she screamed with laughter. It wasn't that fucking funny. Pierce liked to think of himself as the kind of guy who didn't take himself too seriously but Carol laughed at him once too often.

As usual, as soon as they'd returned to the hotel after sightseeing all day, Carol wanted a shag. He had managed to persuade her that there really was no need to rip the shirt from his back. He didn't have that many good shirts and he was quite happy to remove it. But she liked the rough stuff and insisted that he pull and haul her about like a sack of potatoes, it excited her.

Afterwards, as usual, he was sent along the corridor to the machine to get two cans of cold Coke. There he had to stand in a queue while a group of other British tourists fiddled about putting the wrong money in the machine. He showed them how to use it, but as he made his way back to the room he heard the tourists giggle and inexplicably this made him feel uncomfortable. He was becoming paranoid, he decided. This was until Carol saw him and fell on the bed in paroxysms of hysterical laughter pointing at Pierce's feet.

Even before he looked he knew what it must be. Now he came to think of it, he'd been aware of a slight adhesion to the carpet as he made his way back to the room. His worst fears were confirmed when, after a big breath, he looked down. Yes, indeed, he did have Carol's panty liner stuck to his shoe.

*

Carol has popped round and brought a bottle of wine. She has not been invited but Daphne doesn't turn her away. Carol knows now about Donnie and she will no doubt be full of girlie platitudes such as *que sera, there's plenty more fish in the sea, you're too good for him, I never liked him anyway* etc. Daphne doesn't mind that kind of talk tonight.

Donnie did not phone the next morning, or afternoon or evening or night. He's not going to phone. Fair play. The olive branch, or in this case the lime leaf, has been extended but not accepted or even acknowledged. Fuck him. He's had his chance and he's blown it, thinks Daphne, I never liked him anyway.

But Carol only wants to talk about Carol. And Pierce.

'Oh and he wrote me this really sweet poem when we were in Central Park. He's *so* talented. I don't remember how it goes but it was really sweet. He's crazy about me. And when we went to Times Square, which really isn't all that by the way, I wore my Versace, the brown one I got in Harvey Nicks, you've seen it haven't you? You haven't? Oh it's absolutely gorgeous.'

The conversation or monologue, for this is what it is, continues in this vein for some time with Carol giving a blow-by-blow, outfit-by-brown-designer-outfit, account of the week in New York. Her boasting does not surprise Daphne but she is surprised by how besotted Carol appears to be with Pierce. Daphne had assumed that it was a relationship of mutual convenience. When she spoke to Pierce yesterday over a lunchtime bowl of soup his New York stories were far more muted. Certainly he did not mention this love affair Carol is describing, but then why would he? After all, it's none of Daphne's business.

'God, he was all over me. Never gave me a moment's peace. But you know, it's weird to be back and not be with him 24/7. I actually miss him, can you believe it?'

Daphne can't believe it. This is a new departure for Carol, she has always treated them mean in order to keep them keen.

'Where is he tonight then, Carol, has he got one of his poetry things on?'

'Oh!' A rich dark laugh ripples out of Carol. 'No doubt!'

*

Pierce has arranged to meet Tam for a business meeting. Their *Poyumtree* project has been neglected over the past few weeks but now Pierce is bursting with ideas for it. He has been busy; first there was Sean and Bernie and then the New York trip. Tam has apparently not been idle either.

Last night when Pierce phoned, Tam was unavailable. He was busy, under instruction from the new manager of the band, to re-write one of his songs for an audition they have with a record company. The new manager wants Tam to 'joosh it up a bit', make it more accessible. Tam's soul has already been bought and sold and he doesn't even know it, thinks Pierce sadly.

'What we need is a competition,' says Pierce, after the pints have been bought and the meeting has begun in earnest.

'What kind of competition?' asks Tam, supping tentatively at his Guinness.

'A fucking plumbing competition you numpty, what do you think? It's a poetry magazine, isn't it? A poetry competition. Charge an entry fee. I've always thought that must be a right good scam. Advertise it widely, charge a fiver per entry, we'll make a fortune. Plough it back into the magazine, obviously, once we've taken our personal expenses...'

'Which are?'

'Consultation fee for the judges.'

'Who are...?'

'Us. Me and you. We can get a name on board too, that'll give it a bit more credibility, but basically it's down to you and me. If we advertise in the right places we can get, I don't know, say we get five hundred applications, a fiver a go, how much is that?'

'Eh, I'm not sure off the top of my head.'

'C'mon Tam, you're supposed to be the marketing manager. It must be, let's see. Yeah, if it was a thousand applicants then that would be five thousand pounds so half of that would be, man, we're looking at two and a half grand!'

'Brilliant!'

'And, and, it gets better: the competition will get us a bit of media attention and if we announce the winner in the first issue, all the punters who entered will have to buy a copy to find out if they've won. A guaranteed audience.'

'Fantastic.'

'And we can sell advertising space, or rather *you* can sell the advertising space based on our projected readership figures.'

'But what will we advertise in a poetry magazine?'

'All the usual stuff: other poetry mags, poetry courses, books, anything at all, it doesn't matter.'

'Oh man, it'd be great if we could get those adverts for legal weed!' says Tam. 'Maybe they'd send us free samples. I've always wanted to try that stuff but I thought it might be a rip-off.'

'Whatever.'

Their pint glasses have been drained in their enthusiasm. Tam, flushed with their forthcoming success, offers to get the next round in.

'How are you and Daphne getting on then, Tam?' Pierce asks as soon as Tam returns.

'Aye, fine.'

Obviously Tam is not willing to discuss it and this is probably a good idea, none of Pierce's business after all.

'So no…?'

Pierce inclines his head slightly to one side.

'Nah, snogged her once but nothing else so far.'

So it's not that Tam is being discreet and gentlemanly, thinks Pierce, he just doesn't want to admit that he has nothing to report.

'I thought you two were getting it on. You've been round there often enough.'

Pierce keeps his voice light.

'Och, she's not up for it. But anyway, I quite like hanging out with her, she's a miserable git but she's a laugh and her soup's not bad, and anyway, you were away all the time.'

'Aye, I'll say that for her, her soup's good.'

'How did you get on with the lovely Carol?'

'Aye, fine.'

'Aye, fine? So no…'

It is Tam's turn to incline his head.

'Oh aye, plenty, thanks for asking. That's me had my hole on two continents now, Europe and America.'

'When did you go to Europe?'

'We're in Europe, Tam.'

'Och, so we are. Two continents, eh? I don't think I've had my hole in two postcodes. So, what's happening with Carol then? Is she the new steady or what?'

'Nah.'

'Nah, I thought not. Too classy for the likes of us.'

'Classy? Fuck off. Jesus, Tam if you'd seen her. D'you know what she did?'

Pierce has not meant to tell this story but he can't keep it in.

'No, what?'

'We're out on the town this night. She's not really my type, Carol, talks a lot of shite, but she's okay, up to a point. So, we're out: couple of drinks, dinner, nice bottle of wine, both a bit pished. Back to the hotel room, the usual, I'm giving her it and she's fucking loving it.'

'Yeah,' says Tam.

'So, I'm getting a bit thirsty with all the work I'm putting in so I get up and go to the bathroom for a drink of water. I'm away a matter of minutes. I come back, back on the job and I,' Pierce is demonstrating by rocking his pelvis to and fro, 'stick my hand under her head, under the pillow, y'know, to get a bit of leverage and ...'

Tam is nodding, he knows.

'And suddenly my hand feels cold and sticky.'

'Eh?'

Tam is confused; the story has taken an annoyingly unexpected turn.

'So I pull back the pillow and, you'll never believe it.'

'What?'

'There's a big pile of red sick under the pillow.'

'No way, man.'

'Way. Red wine, bits of chicken, whole strands of spaghetti, fucking disgusting, man. While I was in the toilet she felt sick so she just puked under the pillow, just like that, and carries on as if nothing has happened.'

178

'That is gross, man.'

'And d'you know what she says to me, d'you know what she fucking says?'

Tam shakes his head in disappointment, disbelief and because he doesn't know what she fucking says.

'She says, 'What? The cleaners change the sheets every day, what's the problem?''

*

'Daphne, it's me. I need to speak to you.'

'What about?'

'I can't talk now, I can't talk about it over the phone. Can I come round, please?'

'Okay.'

Daphne is sick of these phone calls from Carol. She has phoned nearly every day for three weeks, sometimes more than once. She is using Daphne in the most obvious way. Her desperation makes her transparent and although it annoys Daphne she can't help but feel sorry for Carol.

Pierce is giving Carol the cold shoulder. He has seen her only three times since they've come back from New York, twice for lunch, on both occasions at Carol's insistence and she paid, and once for a coffee. He is apparently busy every evening.

Carol, always so cool with men, has become obsessed with Pierce and is now unable to comprehend what it means when he says he is too busy to see her. She is apparently unaware that she has been chucked. Nicely, in a *let her down easy* kind of way, but chucked none the less.

Daphne knows that Pierce knows that Carol doesn't know. She wishes he would just be man enough to tell her straight. Despite the fact that Pierce had his plaster removed weeks ago, the soup sessions continue and Daphne, unlike Carol, sees him every day. When the Carol phone calls begin to really annoy her, she berates Pierce for his cowardice and he is unable to meet her gaze.

Carol is dishevelled when she arrives. A shocking sight. Her eyes are red from crying and her clothes have not been ironed. Her T-bar is at least five centimetres wide. It gives Daphne no satisfaction to see that Carol's roots are coming in grey.

'Now he won't even answer the phone to me. I phoned him yesterday morning at five past eight, I mean, where is he at that time of the morning? I'm falling apart, Daphne. I'm up to 150 migs of Novazex.'

Carol says this as though expecting Daphne to be impressed.

'Dr Wilson has put me on the maximum dose. They're the most expensive, y'know.'

'Yeah, I know.'

'So I left Pierce a message to get back to me and then I had to phone again tonight and leave another message. He's not in; I buzzed his flat before I came here. Why is he doing this to me? What is it I'm supposed to have done? Can you tell me, Daphne, because I don't bloody know!'

'You haven't done anything, Carol.'

'D'you think he's seeing someone else?'

Carol is crying. Daphne wants to cry too. Not for Carol's pathetic unrequited love, but for her own. Okay, she acknowledges, there is a difference. She and Donnie were together for five years as opposed to Carol and Pierce's holiday romance, but it comes to the same thing.

Daphne puts her arms around Carol to help absorb the convulsive jolts from the weeping. Let her cry it out, and then when she has, she'll pick herself up, dust herself down, start all over again. Plenty more fish. Pierce is no great catch; he's an unemployed layabout with delusions of grandeur, she tells her. Carol is far too good for him. But just as Carol's weeping is running out of steam, there is a knock at the door.

Of course it's Pierce and Tam. While Daphne is answering the door Carol locks herself in the toilet.

'All right, Daffers? Just swung by to keep you company and help you scrape the arse out the soup pot.'

Daphne lets the lads settle in: take their jackets off, select a CD, begin to skin up, before she tells him.

'Actually, Pierce, I've got company.'

A look of panic crosses Pierce's face and Daphne smilingly nods confirmation.

'Yes, Carol popped round.'

Pierce is on his feet but it is too late. Carol has emerged from the toilet, fully made up and smiling.

'Hello Pierce.'

'Hi Princess, how are you doing?'

Pierce has crossed the floor towards Carol and gives her an innocuous peck on the cheek. He moves past her towards the door but Daphne is not letting him off the hook.

'Pierce and Tam want to join us in a wee bowl of soup, don't you lads?'

'Aye,' says Tam, 'the chip shop was shut.'

Daphne leaves the uneasy threesome playing music and rolling the joint while she goes to put the soup on. While she is in the kitchen each of them come to her, Tam is first.

'All right, Daffers?'

'Aye.'

'Need a hand?'

'Nope.'

'Sure?'

'Yep.'

'Okay. If you need me, give me a shout,' he says and retreats back to the living room.

Daphne deeply regrets ever having snogged Tam and is now uncomfortable when he is solicitous.

Next up is Pierce.

'What the fuck is she doing here?' he whispers.

'The same as you: taking advantage of my good nature.'

'T'was ever thus.'

'You better sort it out with her; she's making herself ill.'

'Och, you know I'm no good at this kind of thing, Daphne, can you not tell her?'

'No, I bloody cannot. For God's sake Pierce, be a man and just tell her, will you?'

'Okay, okay.'

Carol sweeps into the kitchen a changed woman. Make-up and the presence of the object of her love have transformed her. She is flushed and giggly, paranoid and conspiratorial with the effects of the dope.

'What was he saying about me?' she sniggers.

'Nothing.'

'I hope he wasn't telling you about what we got up to in New York.'

'Carol, I don't want to know.'

'Oh shoosh,' says Carol flapping her hands, 'God love him, you know, he makes out he's a sex machine but he's just a big teddy bear.'

'That's nice for you, Carol.'

Daphne has had to water the soup down to spin it out enough for four plates and now she is annoyed that it is too thin. She is boiling it hard in an attempt to reduce it but she's awful warm in her big baggy jumper, sweat and steam from the soup are making her face damp.

'Sex with Pierce is quite domestic, but in a nice way. I had to fake it a lot, but he's sweet and funny and ...'

But Daphne is not listening. The soup isn't thickening and the chicken chunks are becoming stringy. She tastes a spoonful and knows she has watered it too far, it tastes of nothing, dishwater. She has no fresh coriander left and is forced, something she hates doing, to add a stock cube and more salt.

'Can you pass me the cornflour Carol, please?'

As Daphne is putting the doctored soup in bowls, Carol is still hanging around, stoned and dithery, now intent on telling a joke.

'You'll like this, Daphne, this is a good one for that creep, Donnie.'

Carol has stopped even pretending to help. Daphne gathers the cutlery and plates on to trays. As she moves between the living room and the kitchen, Carol follows behind reciting the joke.

'Husband and wife are at the hospital. The wife has been in labour thirty-six hours when the doctor comes out and tells the husband he has good news and bad news. The husband says okay, give me the bad news first. I'm afraid the baby has ginger hair, says the doctor. The man is devastated but finally pulls himself together. Well, what's the good news?'

Carol, who has been sniggering all through her slurred telling of the joke, can hardly get the punchline out for laughing.

'The good news is it was a stillbirth.'

Pierce laughs first. He thinks it's hilarious. Carol joins him with hyena-like barking. So funny is the joke that Carol falls down on to the couch on top of Pierce who catches her and hugs her tight, both of them screaming and laughing.

Tam doesn't know whether to laugh or not. He's not sure, as he himself has ginger hair, if the joke is personally offensive. Finally he settles on an unconvincing titter.

'Right! That's it!' says Daphne. 'All of you out. Get out of my house.'

This only serves to make Pierce and Carol scream harder and Tam bray louder.

'I mean it. Get out! I'm sick of this, I'm sick of you people. I hate you! I hate you and your poetry and your joints and your seven shades of blonde and your stupid brown clothes and your pathetic gigs and your sad little band and your golden arm hair and, and, oh just get out!'

While the soup lies, thinned and thickened and steaming, on the coffee table, Daphne runs to her bedroom and bangs the door shut behind her as hard as she can.

It is several minutes before she hears them let themselves out.

Chapter 25

Daphne resolves not to answer the phone but even as she resolves she knows that she must. It could be the college, or Mum phoning from Australia. It could be Donnie. In the event her resolve is not tested because no one phones. Carol, now that contact has been re-established with her beloved Pierce, no longer has need of Daphne. Pierce, although she can hear him moving around below her, does not chap up for soup or knock her door. She is sick of soup anyway.

The phone does eventually ring and Daphne surprises herself in her keenness to get to it. It's Mum.

'Daphne, what's going on?'

'Hello Mum.'

'Look Daphne, I know all about it. I wasn't going to say anything but this is going on too long.'

'All about what?'

'You've split up with Donnie, haven't you? I could hear it in your voice the last couple of times on the phone but you didn't say anything so I didn't say anything. I'm worried about you.'

'Mum, there's nothing to worry about. These things happen. I'm absolutely fine.'

'You're not fine. You've been off your work for months. Ellen McNicol tweets me every day, her granddaughter is a student in the college.'

Daphne had forgotten what an insidious network of old-lady contacts her mother has.

'Agnes Preston was on Facebook last night and she says that she never sees you in Asda anymore.'

Hotmail, Twitter, now that Mum has got to grips with technology she's better informed than Interpol, thinks Daphne.

'What's wrong with you, pet?'

'Nothing Mum, honestly, I'm fine.'

'Now Daphne, you're going to make me angry. You wouldn't be off your work if you were fine. The doctor must have put something on your sick note. Please tell me, Daphne, I'm worried sick. I could email Janice Dickson, she works part time in the surgery, she would tell me quick enough.'

'I've got free-floating anxiety. At least that's what it says on the sick line, but there's nothing wrong with me, I just need a break.'

'Tell the doctor to give you Sevezonor, I was on that, it works pretty well.'

'*You're* on antidepressants, Mum?'

'Oh no, not now. I'm in Australia now.'

*

The weather is too warm now for Daphne's big coat but she hasn't got anything else to wear. On the other hand, wearing a big coat in warm weather will indicate to the doctor that Daphne is still ill and needs her sick line extended.

She has phoned ahead to check the doctor's availability and it's perfect. Dr Wilson is on holiday and a locum doctor will be taking the open session today. But when Daphne approaches the reception area the treacherous Janice Dickson is on duty.

'Oh hello Daphne, how are you, love? How's your Mum getting on over in Australia?'

As if she doesn't know. She's probably already compiling her report ready to email it as soon as Daphne leaves the consulting room. Mum will be up to speed on what diagnosis and treatment she is to receive before Daphne has even made to it to the chemist's. Janice Dickson will no doubt post it on the *Nosey Old Biddies* Facebook page

Entering the waiting room is another traumatic moment. She is stealing herself for an encounter with Carol but, mercifully, lightning has not struck the same place twice. Carol is not there. Daphne likes the doctor's waiting room, she likes the atmosphere of calm. The chairs are not hard plastic; they are old-fashioned comfy armchairs. The magazines are always quality. The radio plays quietly in the background, easy listening, Radio 2. The other patients wait patiently, reading the magazines. They look up briefly when she comes in then go back to their reading. No one notices her. Daphne begins to relax. Then Janice Dickson comes and speaks to her.

She whispers loudly, drawing the attention of the other patients who listen while pretending to read.

'Oh a bit of good news, Dr Wilson has popped in to pick up her mail and she'll see you.'

Daphne does not consider this to be good news. Dr Wilson is a good doctor. What Daphne wants is not a good doctor but a busy doctor, an unfamiliar, box-ticking, sick-line-writing, repeat-prescription-giving, no questions asked, doctor.

'How are you, Daphne?' says Dr Wilson.

'I'm fine. I mean. Still the same.'

Daphne's face is scarlet, embarrassed by such obvious lies.

'That's been a wee while now. The tablets aren't making a difference yet?'

'Eh, a bit, but I still feel... I don't feel ready to go back to work, I mean, it's not that I don't want to, I'm keen to get back but I'm just, I'm scared and I can't go back yet. Don't make me go back yet. I'll resign if you...'

'Daphne, nobody is going to make you do anything. And don't worry. I can see from your records that you have no history of absence. You don't have to convince me of your illness though I think you may have yet to convince yourself.'

Daphne begins to cry.

'I'm going to sign you off for another month. Now, can you roll your sleeve up please? I want to take your blood pressure.'

With the tears rolling down her cheeks Daphne complies. At least the sick line is secure; her humiliation has not been for nothing.

'Your blood pressure is a wee bit high. How are you feeling, I mean physically, Daphne?'

'Eh,' Daphne clears her throat, 'okay.'

'Your fingers are a bit swollen. Any swelling anywhere else?'

'No.'

'Let me see your knees.'

Daphne hauls her voluminous coat up around her waist and clings to it as she hoists up the legs of her baggy tracksuit trousers.

'Hmm, they're a bit swollen, too. When did you last have a period?'

Daphne thinks carefully before answering.

'Now. I've got my period just now.'

'Oh. Well, can you call the surgery when it finishes? I'd like to examine you. And I'll need a urine sample today. Here,' says Dr Wilson, fishing out a glass tube and handing it to her, 'just hand it in at reception on your way out. And Daphne, don't be so hard on yourself. We all get ill sometimes.'

Daphne can only nod, she is scared she'll start crying again, and Janice Dickson is out there.

There is a queue for the toilet. A wee boy is in front of her and while she is waiting a man comes and waits behind her. Pressure. Inside, the toilet is clean and comfortable and the wee boy hasn't peed on the seat. There are paper towels and a pump of liquid soap advertising a drug company. The soap is a lemon colour.

The first time she does it Daphne puts in too much soap. The mixture is bright yellow and a bit frothy. Too obvious. The next time she puts a much smaller amount in and pours the water in slowly so as not to cause any bubbles. It's perfect.

Daphne smiles as she hands the sample tube to Janice Dickson who calls out after her, 'Give my best to your mum when you speak to her.'

'Yeah,' says Daphne, sending Janice her fiercest optical death rays, 'you too.'

*

Donnie is sick. Sick and tired and baw weary although his balls have seen little action, save for the occasional lethargic wank, since he returned from Egypt. Since before Egypt, in fact, but Donnie would rather not think about Egypt. He would much rather sleep. His bed is warm and quiet and dark, he has pulled the blackout blind down, sealing the room against the harsh noise and light of the world.

He gets up to go to work and when he comes home he makes a sandwich and a cup of tea and stands eating it in the kitchen before laying the heavy burden that is his body back in the bed. He sets his alarm for work the next day, he has to, despite getting upwards of fourteen hours of sleep a day, he wakes up tired.

Donnie knows he should go back and see his doctor, not to show him his mosquito bite which has since completely disappeared, but for head medicine. He knows that the long sleeps are a symptom but he can't be bothered to make an appointment and anyway he likes sleeping. He supposes he should be disappointed that he is apparently unable to function normally without antidepressants but if this is what it's like, who wants to function normally?

Bertha refused to sit with him on the return plane journey. He pleaded with her but she instructed the girl at the check-in desk that she was to be seated as far as possible away from this gentleman. She held their British currency and forgot to leave him money for a drink. It was a long flight. He sat with a family, in a row beside a mother and a boy of about eight years old who didn't seem to understand that hitting air turbulence wasn't a fun thing.

While Bertha enjoyed one gin and tonic after another, the nearest Donnie came to a drink were the mini cans of Coke the kid next to him slurped noisily throughout the journey. During the flight, throughout several thirsty, terrifying and lonely hours, Donnie hated Bertha.

When the plane landed she waited for him to disembark and acted as if nothing had happened. She was cheerful, more cheerful than she had been throughout the holiday, making jokes, holding his hand and kissing him, as they waited at the luggage carousel for their bags. Donnie began to think that maybe they could put the ignominy behind them, forget about it. They had left Egypt and would never return, why not leave the memories and never revisit them? He certainly could if she could. Things could be okay again. He didn't hate her. He had given up everything to be back with her, how could he hate her?

'Right,' said Bertha on her return from the long queue at the ladies' toilet, 'I've phoned Mum and told her we'll be over, she's made us our dinner.'

'What, now? We have to go to see your mum now? We haven't even cleared immigration yet.'

'I know, I know, it's a nuisance, if it was up to me I'd go home first and get out of this hideous T-shirt, but she knows the problems we've had and she's worried. There's something at her house that I need to pick up, toiletries and stuff. And anyway, we have to go, she's cooked.'

'She knows the problems we've had?'

Donnie knew exactly how Gertie would react to the problems they'd had and how those problems will be portrayed. Gertie will eat this up and sook the bones dry. In her unstinting desire to belittle Donnie his mother in law will embroider the events, working the outlines into shimmering broad tapestries. She'll turn his every little mistake into a powerful legend: How Donnie Mistook The Tour Guide For A Terrorist, How Donnie Exposed His Cock In The Temple, The Strange Tale Of Donnie's Grossly Inflamed Anus, How Donnie Broke The Air Conditioning And Ruined Bertha's Holiday. And last of all, best of all, the story the grandchildren will crowd round her to hear at family gatherings: the hilarious When Donnie Had Spiders Up His Arse.

'Bertha, I'm not feeling well,' Donnie said sadly as he kissed her goodbye. 'I have to go home.'

He could see Bertha was confused. Gertie had cooked, they had been summoned, and here was Donnie refusing to attend. He was openly defying a Gertie edict.

Sleep. It's like getting really, really drunk without the expense, subsequent embarrassment, or shocking hangover. When Donnie is asleep he doesn't feel scared, or sexually frustrated, or a failure. The problem is that after more than a week of long sleeps, Donnie can sleep no more.

Instead he notices how grubby the kitchen has become. Also it occurs to him that he hasn't yet emptied his suitcase. At 4.30 a.m., after he has cleaned the house from top to bottom, he finds the leaf. He is scrubbing the back of the door and notices that on the underside of the metal box he has fitted to prevent the neds from torching his flat, a rotting piece of vegetation protrudes. He unscrews the box from the wall and finds two halves of the now dried out leaf. He knows instantly what it is, where it has come from and what it means.

Chapter 26

Pierce is having a shit time of it. Now that his arm is better the guy from the buroo is back on his case again. It will take every ounce of Pierce's imagination and creativity to avoid employment now. It would be less exhausting to just take a fucking job but he refuses to give in to the guy's bully-boy tactics. Pierce's attitude to paid employment is simple. It's like, for example, parachuting: he just doesn't want to do it. Some people like that kind of thing and good luck to them. It's still a free country and if Pierce wants to sign on he will continue to do so.

He hasn't been able to answer the phone for weeks. It could be the guy from the buroo chasing him up, asking him why he's not out job-hunting, or worse, it could be Carol. She got the holiday of a lifetime for free and shagged him till his baws were empty, what more does she want from him?

Tam is always practising with the band and has all but given up on *Poyumtree*. Pierce would replace him but he can't find anyone who'll take the job. He's asked just about everyone who comes to his various creative writing and poetry groups if they're interested, but none of them are. Oh yeah, they all want him to publish their stuff in the magazine but they won't lift a finger to get it off the ground. He has a good mind just to bloody well do it himself.

Daphne has taken the huff. He had got into the habit of going up there for soup. Fair enough, his arm is better now but it was after all her fault he had a gammy arm in the first place. On reflection maybe he should had chipped in something for the cost of the soup but if she wanted money she had only to ask. How much did a wee plate of home-made soup cost for fuck's sake?

She's avoiding him. He chapped up three or four times but she blanked him. Three times now when he's been coming up the stairs after the pub he's heard her above him on the stair. She waits until he goes into his flat before she comes down. She's fucking weird anyway. Who the fuck goes out to the shops at that time of night? And what is with that stupid big coat she wears all the time? She was well out of order that night she threw them out but she hasn't even acknowledged that she was wrong, far less apologise.

Sean is on the mend now, thank God, and has asked him several times about the ring. The ring is becoming a heavy load. Pierce has pulled loads of women at the disco since then; he has even abstained from shagging the better-looking ones to see if they turn out to be The Girlfriend. The ones he thinks have potential make excuses when he phones them again. It seems they're only interested in a one-night shag. Pierce begins to think that the after-pub disco is not the place to find Miss Right.

He owes it to Sean, and more especially to Bernie, to find a good woman, a woman worthy of wearing Bernie's ring. There aren't many of them to the pound, and certainly not at the after-pub disco. When he thinks about it, as he does a lot, Pierce likens himself to Frodo Baggins. For Bernie and for Sean, for honour, Pierce must fulfil his quest. The ring must find its rightful place. That's why he signs up for speed dating.

Pierce isn't embarrassed about doing it. It's not as if he's desperate, it's not as if he can't pull. His pulling power is beyond question but, like a Tolkien character, his powers are considerably weakened beyond the realm of the after-pub disco. Other forces are at work.

As he goes in, a matronly lady in her fifties, who introduces herself as Megan, meets him. He is relieved to discover that Megan is the organiser and not a potential date. She takes his money and talks him through the speed dating procedure, asking him does he have any questions and imploring him not to be nervous.

The event is held in the cavernous unheated function room of a local hotel. The venue is too big and although there is the full complement of ten men and ten women, Pierce has the feeling of having arrived too early, before the cool people have got

192

there. For the money Megan is charging he might have expected a three-course dinner and a four-piece band but there is only one free introductory glass of champagne. Pierce knocks it back and gets a pint in.

He is pleasantly surprised at the quality of talent. He had expected that some or most of the women would have something wrong with them but in fact they are all quite young and fresh. There are a few stunning looking girls and no absolute dogs. There is not one of them that he wouldn't shag.

The competition is a pushover too: specky geeks in sports jackets, nervous Normans hanging about at the back of the hall, crowding together for safety as if they were at a school disco. This is going to be a scoosh. In all modesty, Pierce is the best looking man here.

He has seven minutes with each girl and despite his natural advantage he surprises himself by being a bit nervous with the first one. She's gorgeous, Louise her name is, small and curvy but gorgeous eyes and a cute button nose. Louise puts her hand on his and tells him just to relax and enjoy it; she's a veteran of these do's. Her touching him like this, so warm and friendly, strikes at Pierce's heart and he thinks he's falling in love with Louise but all too soon the seven minutes are up. Pierce is concentrating hard on remembering names; he doesn't want to sign up for the wrong women. There is Phyllis: blonde, beautiful, quietly spoken; Lucy: redhead, likes hash, a potential soulmate; Alison: small, sassy, communist; Zoe: intellectual with fabulous lips and cleavage; Colette: slim, blonde and beautiful; Laura: too tall; Monica: dark, childlike, lovely; Elena: posh and gorgeous; and one rather exotic piece called Carmen: voluptuous with attitude.

After the third or fourth he is beginning to get the hang of it. He notices when he says, 'Hi, I'm Pierce, I'm a poet,' that the light goes out in their eyes so he has amended this to, 'Hi, I'm Pierce, I'm in publishing.' But the girls are not easily duped. In seven minutes they probe every aspect of his life. By way of an experiment he tells two of them that he is a double-glazing salesman. This is warmly received and not entirely untrue. He did once take a job in double-glazing when he was forced off the buroo but he only lasted two weeks.

After the last date, finishing with the less impressive Laura: too tall, baggy-eyed, Pierce signs up for the girls he wants to see again. He picks his top five, the cream of the crop: Louise, Colette, Zoe, Monica and Carmen. He doesn't want to be greedy.

There is much giggling as the girls fill out their forms and Pierce takes the opportunity to nip outside for a fag. Things happen faster than he expects and while he is outside some of them are leaving. Two of the guys, sports jacket lads, are smiling broadly and Pierce has a moment's worry that Louise has picked one of them. He nips his fag and hurries back inside. Pierce had hoped there would be more time after the formal dates but all speed-daters have received their form by now and are gathering their coats. His form is returned to him and he quickly scans it for the girls' names. Louise's name is not there. No girls' names are there.

'Megan, I don't know if I'm looking at this right, I can't see the girls' names.'

'Yes, this is your first time, isn't it?'

'Yeah. How do I find out what girls have picked me?'

'I'm afraid they haven't, Pierce. But please don't worry about it. It happens, you're new. Sometimes it takes a while to get into your stride.'

'*No* girls picked me?'

Megan nods sympathetically.

'The right girl is out there for you. You just have to find her. The thing to do is not to give up,' Megan says as she squeezes Pierce's shoulder. 'You should come again next week. If you pay in advance for the next four dates I can offer you a discount.'

*

'The good news is it was a stillbirth.' Sick. Sick sick sick. Why are people so down on red hair? Daphne doesn't know. She has tried to find out, she has consulted her best friend and oracle, the

Internet, her only friend now that she has blown out Pierce and his entourage. But it's all bad news.

Redheads are more susceptible to sunburn, insect bites, wrinkling and skin cancer. It's hardly surprisingly then that they're bad tempered and sexually brutal. As if that wasn't enough of a cross to bear they are also considered unlucky and untrustworthy. Judas was a redhead, a ginger minge, a fire crotch. In Corsica if you pass one in the street the custom is to spit and turn around. The Egyptians regarded the colour so unlucky that they had a ceremony in which they burned redheaded maidens alive 'to wipe out the tint'. *Alive*. But there is one ray of hope on the horizon. Despite red hair, or the genetic loss of function of MC1R having been around for a hundred thousand years, numbers are falling. People don't fancy redheads, don't mate with them and so fewer blighted red-haired kiddies are born.

In the wee small hours, after she's done the deli run and footered on the Internet for an hour, Daphne goes to bed but cannot sleep. She begins thinking again about what a terrible raw deal poor old redheads get.

What is more surprising to her is that, given their terrible reputation, red-haired people have not yet been rounded up and shot. Perhaps this tribe of uncouth ugly people should be locked in an abandoned warehouse, isolated from decent dark-haired society. Or better, bricked up in a ghetto, or even better: sent underground, they don't need sunlight anyway; it's bad for them.

There they can take out their bad temper and sexual brutality on each other. Used to only raging and grunting at each other, language is eventually lost. In the darkness their pale weak eyesight becomes vestigial, sight reduced to an angry red haze. In these difficult circumstances courtship becomes unfeasible and they begin to indiscriminately mount each other. The offspring of these bestial couplings have skin and hair that gets redder and redder with each generation until babies are born puce. Lack of sunlight makes their white translucent skin transparent, their blood vessels and organs visible to the sighted.

A few attempt to escape to the light. Stories, told through a series of grunts and tongue clicks, have been handed down through the generations of life 'above', but those who leave never return and those who are left behind have no hard evidence of the existence of 'above'.

Blind, dumb and grotesque, those who escape are quickly killed or captured and held in tinted glass cases as curios. A small minority of enlightened dark-haired humans try to help the captured puce people. Under cover of darkness they smash the glass cases and set them free. The puce people want only to return underground where it is safe and sex is freely available but they are ill-equipped and when dawn breaks they die in the pale warmth of the morning sun.

However, one does survive.

When the glass case is smashed the puce people run, overjoyed to be free at last, choosing death or glory over a life of captivity. Not all of them are brave. One puce male, the most stunted of them, is scared to leave the security of the glass case and lies quivering in the darkest corner. The dark-haired liberators are unsure of what to do with him, fearing he is a turncoat and may betray them to the authorities. The liberators feel that they must kill the stunted puce man if he will not escape but one of them, a beautiful dark-haired woman, offers to hide him. In truth she is not motivated by altruism but by the old legends she has heard of the sexual perversity of the puce people. She takes him home and after many patient hours of trying to tempt him with Kit Kat biscuits, he slowly, timidly, after tentatively sniffing her arse, is coaxed to mount her. He grunts and drools as he fumbles blindly on her. He pulls her hair and slaps her arse and his spittle drips down her back.

The dark-haired beauty is disappointed, sex with a Puce is not all that. She's had better. But she is kind and allows him to stay in a cupboard under the sink and feeds him bacon rinds and scrapings from the porridge pot. The cupboard is damp and smelly and cramped, even for his tiny dimensions, but it is safe from the harmful rays of the sun and the murdering Dark Hairs. The stunted puce man comforts himself by singing songs of his lost homeland underground. These songs sound, to the ear of the dark-haired beauty, like wailing and grunting, and after a time she tires of it.

One night another freshly escaped puce person, a female, hears his plangent cries and comes to rescue him. As he mounts her in the confined space of the cupboard under the sink he weeps with joy to once more feel beneath him pendulous breasts and turkey-skinned neck.

The lovers leave the house of the dark-haired beauty and travel throughout the night to where they hope to re-enter the underground. In darkness their blindness is an advantage and they move swiftly and easily. But they cannot find the entrance.

As the sun rises the first rays spread an unfamiliar feeling of warmth across the puce people's crinkly-skinned backs. It is a strange sensation to them, one of relaxation. As the sun climbs in the sky they cover themselves as best they can against the increasingly uncomfortable heat. Soon blisters appear on their thin puce skin, at first small and itchy but soon large and plasma-filled, swelling and popping as they scuttle blindly for shelter. They howl and grunt as their bodies run with seeping sores. Although they cannot see the sun burning through their transparent skin they feel and smell their organs cook and their innards boil. With dreadful screams they die under a vapid Scottish sun.

When the dark-haired beauty realises that the stunted puce man is gone she is relieved. No longer will she have to endure his groaning grunting singing. But although he is gone he has left something behind.

The dark-haired beauty is delivered of a baby, a daughter. Thankfully the child is normal, healthy, and within a year has thick coils of golden hair. The child has a quick wit and a lively intelligence and is loved by all who know her. Word spreads and, never having seen such a thing before, people come from far and wide to see the golden child.

It is at this point that Daphne wakes up, desperate for the toilet again.

*

Pierce has been invited to yet another book launch. Yet another shithead has somehow managed, no doubt by having a brother-in-law in the business and/or by arse licking, to get a book published. This particular guy, Frank, Pierce reluctantly admits, actually has a modicum of talent. Two or three years ago, until he began to move in more auspicious circles, Frank attended Pierce's Thursday night writer's group at the Clansman. Pierce had encouraged him; it was refreshing to have someone in the group whose work was actually readable. Frank paid attention and took on board every suggestion Pierce made. And now Frank was reaping the benefits.

Pierce liked Frank, it was hard not to: he loved Pierce's work. He believed Pierce to be an undiscovered genius. Frank was the first to admit that he himself was a beginner but he was keen to learn, grateful for Pierce's advice and he had tremendous energy and enthusiasm. Pierce tried not to dampen Frank's fervour but felt obligated to warn him of the realities of trying to make a living from writing. Frank had naively assumed that he would learn how to write a good book, then simply write one and sell it to a publisher, wasn't that what publishers wanted, he asked: good books?

Pierce is not sure whether or not he should go to the launch. He's embarrassed that Frank, who once sat at his feet, who had at one time referred to Pierce by his surname, talking about *McCormack's* new piece in the same way he might talk about *Roth* or *Murakami,* that Frank the disciple should have now so eclipsed him. But it is the free drink and schmoozing opportunities that finally swing it.

The bookshop is mobbed when he gets there. This is even more embarrassing. Pierce had assumed that it would be a modest little affair with a few bottles of Chianti and three rows of Frank's family and friends. There must be two hundred people here. It seems that Frank has had rave reviews, which have been blown up to poster size and are hung on the wall behind the podium from where he will read excerpts. The city's literati have turned out and Pierce recognises several agents and editors that it would be foolish to approach. Three have rejected his work more than twice, one that Pierce spilled a pint over and one whose top client's book Pierce insisted would make excellent material with which to wipe his arse.

During the reading Pierce lurks at the back, close to the wine table. He is surprised and not a little moved when Frank spots him and singles him out for praise.

'Ladies and gentlemen,' says Frank, 'if it hadn't been for the help and support I've had from so many of you, this book would never have made it. For instance, there's a man at the back there, Pierce McCormack, I'm sure he's a familiar figure to some of you.

'When I first began writing I was producing the worst kind of self-referential drivel, believe me, I'm embarrassed to think of it now, but Pierce, with his insight, constructive criticism and encouragement, kept me afloat.'

Frank then says a lot of other stuff about how much he owes his wife blah blah blah, but Pierce can't really take it in. This is the first time anyone, anyone in these snooty publishing circles, has acknowledged that he has insight, that his criticism is constructive, that he is encouraging. This is the first acknowledgement of Pierce's talent. It's just a pity that Frank has stopped calling him McCormack.

After the reading is the book signing and there is a long queue of people waiting. Despite this Frank calls out to Pierce and waves him over. This might be a little ticklish; Pierce never buys books at these readings. He rarely, if ever, pays full whack for a book. If he wants a certain book he'll request it at the library. If he can't get it there he'll try Bookcrossing, failing that, second-hand from the Oxfam bookshop, then Amazon. As a last resort he'll buy a new one, heavily discounted, in Asda.

'Pierce! Thanks for coming, it's great to see you, what are you up to?' asks Frank in one excited gush. Frank is a tall skinny young-old guy. He has the face of a pre-teen but the hairline of a pensioner. His face is chubby, unlined and darkly freckled. His hair makes a skirt around his head while his scalp continues the freckles theme. This makes him look as if a bird has shit on him. Frank has left an old lady standing at the front of the queue, a copy of his book in her hand, opened and ready for signing.

'Aye, y'know Frank, ducking and diving.'

'Here,' says Frank, reaching behind him and pulling a book from a huge pile of pre-signed ones, 'is there anything you want me to put or can I write it myself?'

'Actually Frank, I left the house in such a hurry to get here I've come out without my…'

'God no, I couldn't ask you to pay for it. This is from my own allocation. I hope you don't mind, Pierce, but I'd be really interested to hear what you think of it.'

'It doesn't make any odds what I think of it, Frank. You've got the reviews; you'll get the sales, you're going to be a big success.'

'I don't know about that, Pierce. Anyway, I hope you'll let me know what you think.'

'Sure I will.'

'By the way Pierce, what are you up to afterwards?' And without waiting for a reply Frank continues, 'There's a party, round the corner at the West Coast hotel, but don't mention it to anyone, will you? It's a private do, only *those and such as those*.'

In this elitist world of bona fide book publishing Pierce is now counted amongst *those and such as those*.

There is a wider range of drink at the private do, a free bar in fact, but Pierce takes the decision to pace himself. He has to treat this occasion as work, at least until he's schmoozed the agents and publishers, or everyone else is pished, whichever occurs earliest.

A horsey-looking woman accosts him at the bar as he is ordering a long drink, vodka and Diet Coke.

'So you're Pierce, then?'

'Yes, I am. But I'm afraid I don't know your name.'

'I'm Arab.'

It's always advisable to know whom you're dealing with at this type of bash, thinks Pierce.

'Oh,' says Pierce, 'and your name is?'

'Arab.'

'Oh.'

'Short for Arabella, but for God's sake, call me Arab.'

'Okay.'

Arab. She's got to be in publishing with a name like that.

'Are you a friend of Frank's? Arabel…eh, Arab?'

'I'm Frank's publicist, he's such a sweet boy.'

The conversation continues along the lines of how great Frank is while Pierce gallantly gets a double vodka in for Arab. He's finding it difficult to whip up the enthusiasm to fancy her. He knows that women know when he doesn't fancy them, it must show somehow, and he so wants to fancy her. Not a bad pair on her and good child-bearing hips but it's her overbite that's putting him off. He keeps trying to work out the logistics of kissing her.

'Pierce!' calls Frank.

Not again. Pierce is of course grateful to Frank for the mention in his speech and the invite to the party, but for fuck's sake. Can Frank not see he's putting the moves on the publicist?

'Pierce!'

As Pierce has made no move towards him, Frank has come to Pierce. He has propelled along beside him a small curly-haired woman. Tottering on ridiculously high heels, light brown curls are falling over light blue eyes and she's giggling. Pierce takes to her immediately, hoping she's not Frank's wife.

'Pierce. I want you to meet my editor, Daisy. Daisy, this is the Pierce McCormack I told you about. A great writer, our best-kept literary secret, you should snap him up.'

And Frank is gone.

'Can I get you a drink, Daisy?' asks Pierce quickly.

Daisy has had a few but none the less accepts a double vodka and Red Bull. Pierce tries to keep the conversation literary, discussing with his serious face the novel that he's working on, but Daisy is apparently more interested in whispering and giggling with Arab. Twice he has asked her if he can send her a few sample chapters but she appears not to have heard him. After ten minutes of this Pierce can schmooze no more. Daisy is the only person worth meeting here and she's not interested. He's tired now and just wants to get drunk on the free bar.

'Hey girls, I'm getting them in, doubles all round again?'

The girls readily agree and seem to be impressed with Pierce's ability, completely unabashed, to order so many free drinks in such a short space of time.

'I'm a bit behind you lot,' Pierce explains, 'I'm going to slam this one,' he says before he knocks his double vodka and Red Bull back in two gulps. Arab and Daisy attempt to follow suit.

'Put your head back and skelp it down your thrapple,' he advises as Arab chokes on hers.

'Whoa Tiger,' he tells her while she coughs exuberantly and eventually recovers, 'I thought I was going to have to give you the Heimlich manoeuvre there.'

'Yeah,' says Daisy, her cutsey blue eyes glistening, 'She likes it from behind.'

'Not as much as you though Daisy, eh?'

Daisy laughs. Now she's paying attention to him. Now Pierce is on solid ground, he's comfortably with this kind of slack banter, good at it, and, so it seems, is Daisy.

Two hours later Pierce is at the after-pub disco with a girl on each arm. He, slightly less drunk than the women, is nervous of what they'll think of the place. As they queue in the dingy hall-way, jostled by fat bouncers, their feet stick to the carpet. But they hardly notice where they are; they just want to dance. Pierce installs them in a booth; this will make it harder for other men, other lone wolves, to approach.

Pierce wants to show good manners and makes a point of dancing with each lady in turn.

'Do you want a drink, girls?'

Daisy and Arab have had enough, they are floppy and cling to each other, holding each other up. Drinks are expensive here.

'Yeah, cheers Pierce, get me double vodka and Red Bull.'

'Me too.'

When Pierce comes here he always gets a bottle of beer, he knows from trial and error samplings, which is the cheapest. He makes it last all night; never offering, never accepting drinks from anyone else.

'Hiya Pierce, how you doing?' asks a small voice behind him.

It's Julia, a girl he has slept with once or twice. As he recalls the separate occasions he realises it is actually four times.

'Aye, no bad, Julia, and yourself?'

'Aye. Okay.'

Pierce's heart sinks. Aye. Okay, means not okay. She wants to talk.

Julia is a lovely girl, a bright-eyed red-cheeked round-bottomed innocent. A single parent with twin boys. The twins must be three or four but Pierce can't remember their names so is unable to ask after them.

Julia's husband left six months after the twins were born. He phoned her from a friend's house to say that he wasn't coming back. When Julia asked him why he simply replied that he wasn't really enjoying it, married life was hard work and boring, he didn't want to do it any more. Pierce knows this because Julia told him. She has told him four times now. Pierce is sympathetic, he likes Julia and has tried with her but the most she ever wants, the most she says she can deal with, is a one-night thing. She only wants him to listen and then fuck her. She always puts him out early in the morning before the twins wake up.

'Listen Julia, I'm a bit tied up tonight, I'm in with a few publishing colleagues.'

'*Colleagues?* Is that what you're calling them?'

Pierce thinks this is a bit rich. She's the one who has repeatedly turfed him out of her warm bed at five o'clock in the morning after he's served his purpose.

'Sorry, I've got a bit of business to do. Another night, eh Julia?'

Julia peers up at him, her obvious annoyance at odds with her angelic features. Then she appears to accept it.

'Yeah, sure Pierce. No bother, another night. Phone me if you want. Phone me anytime.'

'Yeah, I will.'

Julia has never been so forthcoming before. He did phone her once and asked her out to the pictures but she sighed heavily and said she couldn't get a babysitter and even if she could, she couldn't afford one. Pierce put the phone down feeling vaguely guilty. But his being here with Daisy and Arab has obviously upped the ante.

He gets coppers in change from the tenner that he hands over for the drinks but he has to regard this as an investment. When he goes back to the table he will demand of Daisy that she let him send her his work. When he goes back to the table the girls are nowhere to be seen. They are dancing again.

He joins them on the floor and the three of them begin a slow wobbly jive. Pierce takes both their hands leading them towards him and away, turning them under his arms, into his arms, twirling them both to and fro as they giggle and stagger. He is good at this. Arab and Daisy are unfamiliar with this old-fashioned way of dancing, but they seem to like it. Although their co-ordination is shot, if he is slow and controlled, they keep up.

Other men are watching him. These girls with their posh accents and expensive understated clothes are something that most of them could never aspire to, and Pierce has two. If only Megan from the speed dating could see him now.

Pierce tries a new move, pulling one girl at a time in to him. As they curl their bodies towards him he nuzzles their neck. By his body movements he implies that this is part of the dance. This goes so well he is inspired to improvise. Now he's kissing their necks. It's actually a bit rushed and he is slightly nervous each time one of them crashes towards him but it looks good, and other men are watching. By the end of the record he has snogged both of them, full on the lips, mouths open, tongues. Surprisingly, despite her overhang, Arab is the more adept snogger of the two. But it is Daisy he wants; Daisy the editor.

'Daisy!'

'Pierce!'

'Will I send you my stuff?'

Daisy's face crumples and her hand waves in front of her face in a don't-let's-talk-shop manner but Pierce has come too far and spent too much to let it go. As they make their way back to the table, with his arms around both the girls, Daisy hooks her finger into the back of his jeans.

Arab wants to go to the toilet but Daisy will not go with her. She pleads for a moment and it seems that she really does need to use the toilet because without another word she stands up and walks away. Daisy has begun surreptitiously rubbing Pierce's back; as though he were a baby needing burped. When Arab exits, Daisy's hand hovers around the waistline of his jeans again. He turns towards her and kisses her again, this time a slow comfortable snog. Daisy's hand is now inside the back of his trousers. Her fingers are cold but he's not complaining. Her small hand only reaches the crack of his arse and she strokes. Pierce is thinking about what it would feel like if she wasn't quite so petite, if her arms weren't so short, if her fingers were a little longer.

Pierce is sipping his beer, he still has three-quarters of it left but the girls have finished theirs and want more. There is a moment's hesitation, a moment's expectation, and during that long slow-motion moment, he can only pretend not to understand that they want another drink and they want him to go and buy it. He has no more money left. Arab goes to the bar.

While she is gone Daisy resumes guddling around in the shuck of Pierce's arse. Pierce resumes kissing her. He comes up now and then for air and when he does, he looks tenderly into Daisy's eyes. His eyes attempt to communicate a complicated message: I've never met a girl quite like you before, you're special, this is not a drunken snog in a dance hall, this is the beginning of something important.

When Arab comes back she brings a barman carrying a tray, double vodkas and Red Bull all round. There has never been table service here before and Pierce is impressed by the power of a posh accent, a confident manner and a large tip. Daisy discreetly removes her hand from his trousers and puts it to her face. She is pretending to scratch her nose but Pierce sees very well what she is doing. She's sniffing her fingers.

In the taxi the three of them are squashed on the back seat together. Arab gets into a long and surprisingly erudite argument about football with the taxi driver. She leans forward, squashing Daisy and Pierce closer together. Daisy sits in the middle, she has switched sides and now her hand lies in Pierce's hand. In the darkness Arab doesn't appear to notice, she is too caught up in her debate. Pierce wonders why, other than for the sake of manners, he's not allowed to snog Daisy in front of Arab but every time he attempts to, she pushes him away. He hasn't asked if she has a boyfriend, girls like Daisy always do. She is not averse to a little covert action though and her hand slides, still in his, towards his crotch. His cock is solid and he is pleased that she finds him so. While Arab boffs on about Scotland's chances in the upcoming World Cup qualifier, Daisy is fingering his cock.

Crushed as they are in the taxi, Pierce's pants are cutting him in two. His nob strains against his Calvin Klein's as Daisy slowly, teasingly, rubs her thumb across his bell end. Predictably, she changes hands, why do women always do that? But Daisy has a reason. She's sniffing her fingers again. What does she smell? His maleness, his sweat heavy with hormones and pheromones and last night's curry, soap powder from his newly washed jeans, the faint whiff of hash, driblets of wine and piss. What is it that turns her on?

The seediness of being chugged off in the back of a taxi, by an editor, and the danger of being caught, heightens everything. For all the women Pierce has had, in all the strange situations, he has never had this. He's not sure if he likes it. What is it that she's trying to do? She's staring at him, what is she looking for in his face?

The taxi driver turns and asks him a question. Pierce is distracted, not sure what has been asked. He slides forward as if to better hear the taxi driver but also to move out of range of Daisy's hand.

'I'm saying it's got to lift the standard of our game, hasn't it?' says the taxi driver.

He is looking for a man's opinion.

'Oh aye,' says Pierce.

Arab is looking at him now too. She wants him to join in but he can't think of anything useful to say. Everyone is looking at him.

'Although I suppose the money could be better spent here, sports schools, that kind of thing.'

'My point exactly!' chirps Arab. 'We have to bring on our own young players!'

Pierce is off the hook with Arab. The taxi driver has given up on him as an ally. Daisy is back in control. She moves her hand over his cock and whispers to him.

'Will you come back to the hotel?'

She pokes her tongue into one side of her cheek, distending it like a hamster. She's offering to suck him off.

Pierce smiles. Daisy strokes.

'Nah, better not. '

Pierce can hardly believe he's saying this but he knows it's the smart thing to do. If he goes back with her now he'll never see her again after tonight. He'll be nothing more than a provincial adventure that she'll gossip about with her friends back in the metropolis. She'll be embarrassed to set eyes on him ever again, she won't even look at his book.

'But I'll call you.'

'Yeah,' she says, apparently unperturbed, 'Call me. And send me a few chapters, I'd like to read your work.'

Result.

Pierce doesn't care now that she's ploughing his crotch again. He puts his hand over hers to direct her and opens his legs a little wider to afford her better access. She has picked up a good rhythm again but now it's him that's running the show. Pre-cum juice is lubricating his nob-end, this is better, more comfortable. He reaches across and with a cheeky smile pinches her nipple. She likes that. Her thumb is working faster now. It's the smart thing to do, leave her begging for more.

As hand jobs go it's not ideal, he'd like her to get a proper grip, give him a good solid tug. But it is the very fact that she is unable to do this, the fact that they are in a taxi, right under the noses of two others that is keeping him hard. Now Pierce is staring at Daisy, not at her face, at the front of her blouse. Daisy likes it; she arches her back and pushes her tits out. She wants him to touch her again but he won't. He guides her to keep thumbing him, controlling the rhythm, faster, harder. The taxi is slowing down to stop at traffic lights; Arab is turning towards them.

'Don't stop!' Pierce calls out involuntarily.

It's too late to stop. He pinches her fingers tight around his cock, all the better to feel each quivering pulse of ejaculation.

Chapter 27

As Pierce makes his way home he's already deciding what chapters to send her. It was the smart thing to do. No longer caring that Arab was watching, Daisy fiercely snogged him as he got out of the taxi. 'Call me,' she said.

As he enters the close he hears her on the stairs above, breathing and shuffling. What the fuck is Daphne's problem? She's still avoiding him, up there on the landing waiting for him to go in so can she can scurry past his door without having to speak to him. Well she can wait. Pierce sits on the bottom stair; he's going nowhere. If she wants out she'll have to pass him. He sits quietly listening to her breathing two floors above him, amplified in the echoey hollowness of the stairwell. He employs his skill of silent breathing; maybe she'll think he's gone out again. But then she might get a fright when she meets him here. He doesn't want that. Daphne is of a nervous disposition at the best of times, always crying and throwing wobblies. No, it's better if she knows he's here. Then she can voluntarily come down and sort things out with him and get back to where they were, or not. She can go back inside her flat.

Pierce announces his presence with a theatrical cough. He hams it up, hawking and spluttering. So convincing is he that he actually produces a substantial piece of lung butter, which he gobs into a hanky. He knows that such an authentic impersonation of an expectorating consumptive will make her laugh. He imagines her up there smirking.

She doesn't go back into her flat, that must be a good sign, but neither does she come down. She's waiting him out. The cold from the stone step is creeping up through his bum and makes him shiver. What he poetically likes to think of as *his man juice* is coagulating in his pants, cold and sticky now against his belly. This is ridiculous, her hanging about up there and him hanging about down here. Fuck her, he thinks, it's quarter-past three in the morning, if she wants to play games good luck to her, he needs his bed.

But just as he stands up, he hears movement above. Feet are coming down the stairs, but not Daphne's, he knows her tread.

It's Daphne's old boyfriend, Donnie, what the hell is he doing here? Is she back with him?

'Oh hello Pierce!' says Donnie.

'Oh hello Donnie!' says Pierce with so much feigned surprise it sounds sarcastic.

And then the penny drops. Donnie has red hair, bright carroty orange, Pierce had forgotten that about him. Now he gets it. *That's* why Daphne threw them out, the joke about the ginger baby, of course.

She's still not over it. All these months of moping around in her baggy jumper, all these late-night deli runs, she still wants Donnie. The night-time crying binges stopped ages ago and Pierce had thought that her snogging Tam was an indicator that she had moved on. Why do women cling so much? And to a wee creep like this. Donnie is so ginger and hairy he looks like an orang-utan. And Daphne has taken this fucking simian back.

'I just popped round to see Daphne but I don't think she's in,' says Donnie.

'Oh yeah? Was she expecting you, like?'

'Eh, well, no, not really. But do you know where she is, Pierce? I'm a bit worried at her being out at this time of night.'

A snort of laughter bursts from Pierce involuntarily. He can't believe the cheek of the guy. Now he has a good look at him, what did Daphne ever see in this wee gnumf?

'Aye, she's out with her boyfriend.'

Pierce registers the look of fright that crosses Donnie's face and this encourages him further.

'I spotted them in town earlier. They were getting out of the

BMW and going into that really posh new restaurant on Glebe Street, d'you know it? '

Pierce is pleased with the effect this has on Donnie. It seems he can't even speak. His mouth is open and he's shaking his head.

'In fact, she doesn't even live here anymore, she's moved out.'

This should get rid of him.

'Really? But I don't get it. Her nameplate is on the door and it's the same curtains.'

Pierce hadn't thought of that.

'Yeah well, she's renting it out. To a couple, big Rottweiler dog. They must be out tonight. But I wouldn't upset them, mate, the guy's a bit of a psycho.'

Maybe that was a bit too much, Donnie is looking quizzical, but Pierce can't help it. When he starts a story he always wants to colour it in. If nothing else the psycho guy with his Rottweiler will be a deterrent for a fearty wee prick like Donnie, who is looking close to tears now.

'When you see her, Pierce, will you tell her I'm asking after her?' says Donnie, shoulders slumped, as he moves towards the door.

'Course.'

Pierce climbs the stairs to his flat. He fiddles with the keys longer than is necessary just to be sure that Donnie has left the building.

*

This one can't fail: Pierce was in the university two days ago putting up posters for his Wednesday evening Poetry and Pints. Usually he has to tear down other adverts to make space for the poster but this time the ad grabbed him. Of course he'd seen similar adverts before, years ago when he was a student himself, but he had no idea that they actually *paid* you for it. Once he realised the cash potential he looked up the phone book and was delighted to discover that there were six in the city. Six places where they handed out cash! And that was just Glasgow. It would be no bother to jump a bus to Edinburgh. He phoned and made appointments with all of them.

He had to write them down in his diary so he wouldn't mix them up but you had to be organised in business.

He has his first appointment today and is fully prepared; he put on clean pants and socks this morning.

'Ah, Mr McCormack?' says the woman behind the desk.

'Yes.'

'Lovely. Dr Morton is waiting for you. If you'd just like to make your way along to interview room four.'

Pierce is a wee bit dismayed to discover that Dr Morton is a woman, a girl really, a young attractive girl. She checks his name and asks him to fill in a long boring form with loads of questions about his general health: does he or anyone in his family suffer from heart disease, diabetes, etc. These questions are quite understandable and he quickly ticks through the boxes.

The form also asks about his lifestyle, questions that Pierce feels are a bit offensive: is he a practising homosexual? He certainly is not. Has he had sex with a prostitute? He's never paid for it in his life. Etc.

And then it comes to the interview.

'Pierce, may I call you Pierce?' she asks.

Pierce nods his head; of course. He likes being on first name terms with professional people. Her name badge says her name is Mandy.

'Thank you. Pierce, why are you interested in donating sperm?'

Pierce puts his head down and pretends to think what to say. After a suitable interval he speaks.

'I saw your advert in the university, I'm a lecturer there, and I became interested. I thought of all the young couples desperate for a family and my heart went out to them. My sister was in that position, her husband's testicles were faulty and it broke my heart. I believe, or at least I hope, that my semen is healthy and Mandy, I want to help.'

Dr Morton nods her head encouragingly; this is the right answer.

'Pierce, I'm obliged to inform you that current legislation makes donor identification compulsory. These means that there is the possibility that in years to come children may be able to identify you as their natural father and may wish to contact you. You must consider this before becoming a donor.'

But he already has.

Because he has never had a job Pierce has no pension. Unless he gets a big publishing deal he'll spend the rest of his life rooked, scratching out his last years in miserable poverty. Couples pay to come to these clinics. They pay big time.

The fruit of Pierce's loins, cuckoos in the nest, will grow up wealthy with a loving mummy and daddy who have invested heavily in them: private school, the best university, friends and family with connections, all willing to help Junior along. With Pierce's genes and those kind of opportunities Junior can't fail. This is the best start in life Pierce can give him.

As far as he is aware he has never impregnated anyone, never wanted to. He always uses a condom, no matter who it is. He knows, or did until Bernie died, that he wasn't ready for parenthood. Yeah, he's fallen in love a few times but even so, he knew himself well enough to realise that it wouldn't work. He'd get her pregnant and then a few years down the line they'd break up. He knows too many single parent girls, left with the kids, without enough money or support, and their kids who are denied enough discipline or attention or good male role models. He couldn't make a woman his baby mamma. No kid of his would live like that.

And besides, when he's a poor old codger and his grown up successful stockbroking children catch up with him, they won't let their old dad starve.

'Yes, Amanda, I can see that's a consideration but I'm not married, I haven't found the right girl yet. When I do she'll know everything there is to know about me, there'll be no secrets. And if the children want to find me I'll be pleased to see them.'

He has passed the interview and now it's the physical. This isn't as much fun, he's waiting in a cubicle freezing his bollocks off in a paper dress that has a split up the back. A brisk nurse eventually comes and parks him in another consulting room. He clenches his buttocks tight, he's been told to sit on the consultation couch but he's scared that his bare bum will leave skidmarks on it. It would be horribly embarrassing if Mandy were to see it. But luckily the doctor that comes in is not Mandy, it's a guy doctor.

'Mr McCormack? I'm Dr Grant. Nurse Scott will take some samples from you and I'll be along again to see you in a minute, all right?'

Pierce doesn't really have a chance to reply before Dr Grant is away. Nurse Scott sets to taking his blood, and so's not to look, Pierce makes a joke.

'So I suppose if this is a sperm bank then you must be a teller?'

'Ho ho,' says Nurse Scott unconvincingly. Her name badge says her name is Christine.

'Sorry. No doubt you've heard that one before.'

'Yeah, just a bit.'

She makes eye contact, friendlier now.

'I've pretty much heard them all. I'm going to need a urine sample too, Pierce, d'you think you can give me one now?'

Giving a urine sample is not as easy is it sounds and Nurse Scott is waiting. Pierce hopes this is not the shape of things to come and has a moment's anxiety about this whole sperm donation thing but then he thinks about the money. Cash in hand, tax-free and no questions asked.

After Nurse Scott has bled him dry – she's taken at least half a pint of blood and put it in lots of wee-labelled vials – Dr Grant comes back. Even through his rubber gloves his hands are cold as he fiddles with Pierce's cock, and it's a bit awkward that Nurse Scott is watching everything. Still, he's doing it for the children.

The rectal examination is not as bad as he was expecting. In fact once it's over Pierce becomes much more relaxed. He wasn't aware of how tense he had been but Dr Grant was spot on. He had somehow managed to have his finger up Pierce's arse without unduly hurting him or making it seem weird. Pierce has a new respect for the medical profession.

At last he's allowed to put his clothes back on and it's back for a final consultation with Mandy again. It seems that they don't want a sample today; they have to check the results of the tests and that will take three weeks. Three weeks? Pierce is gutted. He thought they were going to give him money today.

He hardly hears what Mandy is saying. She's boffing on in her medical manner about abstaining from sex three days before making a donation, sperm count having to be higher than 20 million, frozen within the hour, fifty per cent survival rate six months later. That's why payment is half the fee at time of donation and half six months later if the sperm survives frozen storage. Pierce is all ears now, half the fee? Oh well, the fee is pretty good so half a substantial fee is better than nothing but this is a lot more complicated than Pierce had originally thought. Six months to wait to see if his sperm can stand the cold. And she keeps stressing that only fifty per cent of men make it as donors.

'Ah I'm not too worried about that, Mandy. Surviving the cold is in my genes. My uncle nearly died of cold, twice, but we McCormacks are a hardy lot.'

Pierce is pretty confident he'll get his money and even if he doesn't he has six months to make as many donations as possible, getting in as many half-fees as possible.

'Let's hope so, we desperately need quality donors.'

Is she coming on to me? Pierce thinks, maybe I should ask her out.

Mandy boffs on a bit more while Pierce runs his sexy smile past her. She picks it up and passes her own sexy smile back. She's definitely interested. He leans in, all the better to hear her, and looks into her eyes. She meets his stare and holds it.

'Mandy, do you have plans for the weekend?'

'I'm afraid I have, Pierce. I'm going house hunting with my boyfriend.'

Bastard. He hopes nothing shows on his face.

'But I hope,' says the little tease, 'that we'll see you again when your results come in.'

*

Donnie is back on the full dose. He went to the doctor yesterday but it's going to take weeks before he sees any effect from them.

What will he do until then? He can't clean the house anymore. He can't shred any more paper, he's already shredded things he shouldn't have, insurance documents and stuff, he has to get a grip.

What's eating him up is that it's a BMW. She's doing it deliberately, going out with some creep just because he's got a BMW, just because that was the car Donnie always wanted. She's even started with the silent phone calls again, knowing full well the tables have turned. Thumbing her nose at him. And if she's living with him that means she must be sleeping with him, doesn't it? The very idea of it, he retches when he thinks of it.

The neds have started harassing him again. They threw a brick through his bedroom window a week ago, he could have been killed but he was out at the shops at the time. That's why they threw it then. Neds prefer guerrilla tactics, they're too scared he'll catch them doing it and come after them. They must have known he was out, they must be watching him. He's phoned the factor three times a day every day but no one has come to fix the window yet. The factor, or rather the fucking ditzy receptionist at the factor's office, because that's the only person he ever gets to speak to there, doesn't seem to understand the risk a broken window poses to his personal security. The alarm and the triple locks on the front door do not offer sufficient protection. He's only one floor up; they could get a big ladder. So he has foiled their plans.

He has made a fortress of the flat. Yesterday he mixed Polyfilla and spread it across the external window ledges. He wrapped six milk bottles in a newspaper and smashed them with a hammer. He bought seventeen packets of razor blades from the 99p shop and made an attractive design, *a mosaic of menace* as he likes to think of it, by placing the blades and the sharp shards of glass in the drying cement.

The sun glints on the shiny steel and glass, reflecting light into the room, he's pleased with his creation; it looks like one of these arty-farty art installations Daphne used to drag him along to. But his at least serves a practical purpose, it's cheaper than a window box, less maintenance and with a bit of luck it might even kill any bastard ned who tries to gain entry. Let them get past that.

He wishes they would try. It would be good if the neds got hold of a big window cleaner's ladder and, on a moonless night when they can't see, reach into the window. He'd watch as they slashed their puny ned arms to rashers of streaky bacon. He'd laugh. And then he'd push the ladder away. Only protecting his property, nothing wrong in that. He could pour boiling oil on them too, he could easy enough buy a can of Castrol but that might be construed as assault.

But they won't climb the ladder. Unfortunately they know the hazard's there. Or two of them do, the big skinny blond one and the wee runt, the two he got with the Super Soaker, they were standing in the street, watching him, as he went about his legitimate home improvements. They won't be long in telling their ned pals. The two looked up and sniggered and mouthed things, no doubt obscenities, and Donnie whistled while he worked. There's nothing they can do; he is unassailable but he still doesn't feel secure.

He has never spent this amount of time in the flat before, and the walls are closing in on him. After Bertha left him the first time, he bought this flat but it wasn't long before he met Daphne and spent most of his time at her place. Hers was a much better flat in a much better area, not as good as the home he had shared with Bertha but still, a lot better than this shithole. Bertha's new place was even better, nice neighbourhood, nice neighbours. Why did it all go wrong with Bertha? Again? Had he not learned his lesson the first time? Obviously not, that's why he was back on his own in this dump. What a fucking stupid fucking prick.

Donnie has a constant background level of self-loathing which he can just about accommodate, but a few times a day the needle swings violently across the scale and he would like to punch himself hard in the face. At other times, when he realises that no one is going to get him out of here now, panic electrocutes him. His nerves jump, his muscles shake, his skeleton dances.

But he knows why he had to end it with Bertha. Apart from the fact that the fat old cow Gertie had made his life a living hell, apart from the fact that at some point during the Egypt fiasco he realised that he didn't love Bertha after all, apart from all that, he realised that he was also partly to blame. He was just too greedy.

It's not his fault, as a child, when other people at school had new football boots he had none. He asked his mum and dad for them but they said there wasn't the money. There was always the money for fags and drink but not for boots. His was a childhood of austerity. He swore as an adult he would never go without. Semper apparatus. If he needs football boots, he buys them. Daphne accused him of being selfish and materialistic and perhaps he is but she doesn't know how it felt to be the only one in class whose parents obviously didn't love him.

But maybe she was right. Maybe this obsessive acquisitiveness has led him to make a dreadful mistake. Whoever made up that cheesy expression a bird in the hand is worth two in the bush got it absolutely spot on. He had been happy with Daphne, what did it matter that Bertha had once been his wife and they had lived a luxurious lifestyle? It wasn't bricks and mortar that made you happy.

The bricks and mortar of his flat are making him miserable, particularly in comparison to the comforts of Daphne's flat. Donnie remembers how cosy it was, how lovely she was, how warm and welcoming her thighs were, how he was her ginger baby, how much she loved him, how much he loved her.

Chapter 28

When she opens the door she hardly recognises him, so dishevelled is he. He's unshaven and the orange twizzley hair that grows up the back of his neck is poking out of his T-shirt.

'Hello,' he says, fatalistic and pathetic.

'Hello Donnie.'

She doesn't immediately let him in.

'Can I talk to you?'

'What about?'

'Not here.'

'Come in then.'

Within a few weeks his shoulders have sagged even further. His shoulders are now so rounded that his jackets hangs out wide of his waist. His head is sinking into his neck as if being sucked there by the vacuum created by his emergent humph. This combined with the tuft of twizzley hair that runs down his spine makes him look like some kind of medieval goblin. She won't be surprised if he soon begins to drag his leg. He is not aging well. Despite having several years on him, she looks a lot fresher and she knows it.

She has taken the precaution of closing off the kitchen door before answering the front door. Bertha sees Donnie's eyes flit towards the kitchen and knows what he's thinking. Let him think. She would offer him a cup of tea but that would mean opening the kitchen door and anyway, she doesn't want him to get too comfortable.

'Can I sit down?' he says. He says it jokingly as if of course he can sit down, things haven't come to that, but perhaps they have, thinks Bertha.

'Help yourself.'

There is a long silence. Bertha is not sure whether he is gathering his thoughts or waiting for her to start. She's not going to start; he's the one who came round here. The silence lasts so long that Bertha gives in.

'What is it you want, Donnie?'

'Just to see you.'

'What for?'

'And to apologise.'

'There's nothing to apologise for.'

'No, I was a complete nightmare on holiday, I know I was, and after all the money you paid …'

'Forget it, Donnie.'

'Oh Bertha!' sighs Donnie, 'I've fucked everything up!'

Bertha says nothing to this.

'I'm a total fuck-up.'

Clara her therapist, her mum and all her friends have told Bertha how damaging it is to have these negative thoughts about yourself. Clara has started her on something called *cognitive therapy* where Bertha must prove through the assessment of evidence the validity of what she is feeling. This appeals to her scientific mind and has been a great help. Clara says that she sees no real need for Bertha to continue with the antidepressants.

Of course she will have to be weaned off, her dosage stepped down gradually, but although she was initially terrified of the idea, she's working it through with cognitive therapy. She's thinking about it from every angle, thinking about panic and why she feels it, about where the panic comes from, about how she can positively address it. She's filled in all the columns for and against, what are hard facts and what is perceived, what is the negative way of looking at it and what is the positive, what is the best course of action for her. Bertha is looking forward to coming off them.

In Donnie's case, given the disastrous holiday and the more damning evidence of his subsequent refusal to talk to her, it would be reasonable to conclude that he has indeed fucked everything up, he is indeed a total fuck-up. In Donnie's case perhaps self-loathing is justified.

'Can you forgive me, Bertha?'

He doesn't look at her when he says it. But she wants him to look at her. She says nothing until he raises his eyes to her and then when she speaks she holds his eye contact, to let him understand that this is for real.

'There's nothing to forgive,' she says gently. 'Everybody make mistakes, we're no different. We mistook who we used to be for who we are now. As for myself I was lonely and frightened. It's understandable that I would seek the comfort of the familiar.'

As well as her cognitive therapy, Bertha's mum has helped her come to this conclusion. Mum had been great. Although she had never liked Donnie and could not hide her distaste of them getting back together again, she accepted it as what Bertha wanted. She was as supportive as any mum could be. She was big-hearted enough to welcome Donnie into the family for the second time despite the acrimony of the divorce.

When everything fell apart Mum didn't judge or blame. Even when Bertha told her, through hiccupping tears, the way he behaved in Egypt, she didn't say anything. Her face was red and she tutted a lot but that was indignation on Bertha's behalf for the humiliations he'd forced her beloved daughter to endure, there was nothing personal against Donnie. The first time they split up Mum said she'd punch his face if she could get a hold of him and Bertha was grateful for her fierce loyalty. This time and the last there was never a word of reproach for Bertha, only support, and Bertha thanked God she had Mum.

Cognitive therapy had helped with that too. She had come to realise that Donnie probably didn't hate Mum at all, what was there to hate? More likely his insecurity, jealous of the close mother and daughter bond, drove him to demonise Mum. And even if he did, that was his problem; she could not take responsibility for the way he felt. It didn't mean that Mum was bad or even that Donnie was bad.

'Bertha, can I come back?'

There is a crashing noise in the kitchen and Donnie looks to Bertha for explanation. She is disinclined to explain, reeling from the upfront cheek of him asking to get back, after Egypt, after ignoring her phone calls for weeks, after everything she's just said.

'You've got someone in the kitchen, haven't you Bertha?'

'Yes.'

Another long silence and this time Bertha waits him out.

'Can I come back?'

Bertha has already workshopped this scenario in her head. She has worked out clearly what she feels and has no hesitation.

'I'm sorry, Donnie.'

She will not change her mind again.

'Okay,' he says and tries a smile.

As she is seeing him out there is another loud crash from the kitchen but he doesn't ask, he is too beaten. At the door the hug is brief and final.

'It's okay Dave, you can come out now,' says Bertha as she opens the kitchen door.

Dave rushes towards her, delighted to see her, his tail wagging and his sweet little puppy-dog ears flapping.

*

Pierce is now registered at all six sperm banks and is making regular donations. This is giving him a very healthy bank balance but a sore nob. Well, if not a sore one then a very tired one. He's lost all interest in recreational masturbation; it's just no fun anymore. He's getting run down. And now his old war wound, the broken arm he received while attempting to keep Daphne from topping herself, is playing him up. In this warm humid weather he can hardly sleep at night and wakes up with his arm throbbing.

He has decided that after today he's going to have to give it a rest. Every time he goes he expects them to tell him that his sperm count has nose-dived but they still seem happy enough. Superspunk that he is, even he has his limits.

How did he, with all the promise he showed at university, end up doing this? People he knew at uni, people with shit grades compared to his, have good jobs. They have offices and secretaries; they have cars and property and pensions, wives and children. He never wanted any of that but the glamour of being a professional wanker is wearing thin.

So, no more. The monkey-spanking has to stop, at least for a wee while. He'll have a few days off, stock up on steak and milk and get to bed at a reasonable hour. This will be his last professional engagement this week and then he can relax.

Iris, the receptionist, greets Pierce warmly as he picks up his specimen bottle and brown paper bag and is allocated a room. He quite fancies Iris, or he would if she didn't keep mentioning her fiancé with depressing regularity.

The clinics range in their facilities from top rank to piss poor. Top of the range have home cinema and 3D porn movies so real they nearly poke your eye out. You can rewind and freeze-frame any scene you want. He saw a good one the other day. A demure looking woman shoe shop assistant working alone in the shop goes up a ladder to get shoes for the only customer in the shop. Pierce knows what must come next and porn rules dictate that she must have prosthetic tits, he must be hung like a whale. On the ladder, whoops! She nearly loses her balance and the guy, a gentleman of course, catches her and then holds the ladder steady while she climbs. From beneath he can see up her skirt. She's wearing black stockings and suspenders, what did Pierce expect? Granny pants? The well-hung guy begins immediately to feel up the hot sexy bitch. She's moaning and before you can say Humpty Dumpty, they're at it. If only real life was like that.

Pierce replays one particular scene. It's not the bit where the guy is giving her it doggie style or the cum shot at the end where he unloads a glass and a half of full cream custard on her face. These scenarios have their charms of course, but his favourite is at the beginning, before any of the malarkey, when she nearly falls off the ladder. The guy's lightning reaction rescues the woman from a nasty fall. Then she trusts him to hold the ladder steady. The initial act is not one of lust but one of gallantry. Pierce likes this bit the best.

Sadly this particular clinic doesn't have 3D porn. All they have are dog-eared well-thumbed sticky-paged spank mags. The donors keep stealing the good ones, Iris says, by way of an apology. Once the door is securely locked behind him Pierce sets to flicking through the mags looking for an image that will engage him. With his other hand he unzips his jeans and gets out The Monster, as he has come to call it. He finds that giving it a job description and impressive job title helps their working relationship. The Monster is slow to respond and although Pierce is putting a lot of effort in, The Monster isn't even trying.

He has found a picture that is of some interest to The Monster. Weirdly it is a reader's wife. Approximately eighteen stone of sheer blubber is spilling out of a peephole bra and pants. The bra and pants are a vivid puce colour and both Pierce, and The Monster, find this captivating.

Perhaps he is greedy. He is after all, here to do a job of work but Pierce usually likes to take The Monster to the tickly bit at least two or three times before allowing him to gush. The build up of a tease, even if it's only himself, still makes for a better cum.

The first tickly bit comes quite soon, almost as soon as he sets eyes on the puce playmate, but The Monster is lagging so he gives him time to catch up. This is shortly revealed to have been a mistake.

Pierce has always given free reign to his creative right brain and has been rewarded with the ability to turn on something akin to a computer-aided design programme in his head. This he presses into service by revolving a fully-fleshed 3D image of the eighteen-stone stunner, posing her in many quite undignified positions, the more undignified the better. Then he tries the more pervy stuff: bagpiping, felching, frogging, tromboning, he slaps her wobbling arse and rides the waves, but he rides alone. The Monster is not with him. He should have milked the bastard the first time and got the hell out of here.

Try as he might he cannot produce any love juice, his pips are dry.

Luckily Iris is on the phone, no doubt to her fiancé, as he approaches the front desk. Everybody has off days, he imagines her saying in a sympathetic tone. She gives him a preoccupied smile as he leaves the empty bottle in the brown paper bag on her desk and skulks out.

*

Antsy, that's the best word to describe it, thinks Daphne. Ants in her pants: bored and angry and anxious, all at the same time. She can't sit down. Every time she sits down she has to stand up again, she has to pace around the living room, she's wearing a path in the carpet. She looks out the window, looking for something in the street, she doesn't know what, just something.

For some weird reason she can hardly breathe and keeps taking big gulps of air and sighing. It's as though there isn't enough space in her lungs. This air swallowing will not help her delicate digestive system. Her tummy has been giving her gyp all day. She took two paracetamol tablets earlier, something Daphne has for the last few months studiously avoided, but they made little impact on her bellyache. She's been constipated for days and has drunk so much sweet black weak tea that she has to go to the toilet every fifteen minutes or so. At this stage she's peeing clear water. She knows this because, alarmed at the volume she was producing, she investigated by holding a whisky glass under it. Not only does it lack colour, it doesn't smell of anything either. This is surprising, she thinks, Daphne thought that pee always smelled.

And she's sweating, bucketloads. It is a warm night but surely this isn't normal. This state of mental and physical turbulence is making Daphne cry. For no good reason she can think of, she is very weepy. Daphne is losing moisture from every pore and orifice. She can't keep this up; she'll fall on the carpet a desiccated husk, she'll turn to dust like a vampire and be blown out the window.

This is not a bad option. Considering the things that she obsessively tries not to think about, her past, present and future, this might be the ideal solution. It's the future that's the scariest of all.

Daphne drank the last of the whisky hours ago. There was only three fingers worth left in the bottle. That's what comes of being an excellent hostess, she thinks, that bastard Pierce has drunk all my good whisky and now I've none left. This strikes her as bitterly unfair and sets her off crying again.

After all these months of shunning everyone Daphne suddenly feels very alone. She craves company, she wishes her mum was here and not on the other side of the planet. Mum would help, she'd know what to do, why has she not spoken to Mum before now?

*

Donnie is vaguely aware of something having woken him.

Dates: 12th of January, 25th of April, 6th of October, these dates are significant but he can't remember why.

His tucks his chin into his throat, stretching out the tendons in his neck, feeling that any minute they'll ping, rupturing so that he'll no longer be able to support the weight of his head. His head is heavy with unfinished thoughts, thoughts too scary and confusing to complete.

He's upped the dose to three Valium but he still can't sleep. He lies curled on the couch watching old football videos. He can't get organised enough to record the current matches but it makes little difference. He's stopped even changing the tape, playing the same one over and over again. It's soothing, knowing what's going to happen, knowing the score. The commentators make the same predictions, tell the same jokes. He slides in and out of dreams that he can't quite remember but disturb him none the less. It's an alarm, a really loud one that has woken him.

It doesn't stop and Donnie begins to wonder where it's coming from, it's really loud. When he makes it to the hall he realises it's coming from the bedroom. That can't be right. He opens the bedroom door. It is right. On his sweat-sour unmade bed a ball of fire is scorching through the sheet and tousled quilt. The smoke is blackening the wall. Why is his bed on fire?

He should do something; he should put out the fire. He stumbles to the kitchen to get water and stumbles back again empty-handed. He doesn't want to throw water on the bed. The fireball is made up of a large brick wrapped in newspapers. Black slivers of soot fly up the way, the opposite colour and direction of snow. They fly up towards the jagged-glass broken window. Ah, now he's sees. The neds have done this.

Understanding galvanises him. He takes a corner of the quilt and beats out the flames. More soot flakes rise but it only take a few beats and the fire is out. What is left is a charred brick, fragments of newsprint and the remains of what looks like a dog turd. That old trick. With beating the flames out the shite has been smeared on the quilt, on the bed, on his hands. And then he is sick.

A few hours later he wakes up again, back on the couch in front of the football video. He scrubbed his hands as best he could but he can still smell the dog shit. He would take a shower but the towels are in the bedroom. He can't go back in there again.

*

Pierce is celebrating. He's had an email from Daisy. She says she is 'excited' by the three chapters he sent and would like to see the complete manuscript as she has a commissioning deadline at the end of the month. 'Excited', I bet she is, thinks Pierce, I bet she's creaming her pants. What a masterstroke that was, holding out on her.

The one slight problem might be that there is no complete manuscript; three chapters are all he has. Three chapters are all he's ever managed before getting bored with the project and ditching it for a new idea. Pierce is really a poet; he finds it difficult to rattle out pot-boiler novels to order. In fact he has found it impossible. So far. But he has not had this kind of motivation before. Daisy has practically said that if he can give her a novel she'll buy it.

So fired up by this offer is Pierce that he resolves to get stuck in, get the head down and just work, all night, every night if necessary, until he has a complete manuscript, he'll start it right away. Right after he's had a few celebratory pints with his mate. Just to lubricate the knuckle joints and the wheels of his imagination.

For once Tam doesn't have a gig or band practice. He gives Pierce a congratulatory high five as soon as he walks into the pub. He is so pleased for Pierce it is shining out of him.

'Aw man! How good is that?' Tam says repeatedly as Pierce tells him about the email.

'I always knew you were going to do it, I fucking knew it!'

Pierce is pleased and grateful but he recognises Tam's relief.

Tam has been a bit strange with Pierce recently. Not unfriendly in any way but shy, reticent. Ever since his band was signed he's been modest, reluctant to tell Pierce of his good fortune and how much money he's about to be paid. He has a big-shot music business lawyer now who has cut him a fantastic deal with the publishers, but Pierce did not hear this from Tam. It was the other band members who boasted on his behalf.

This had saddened Pierce. It put distance between them, the distance was how far Tam was travelling towards success while Pierce stood still. Just like Frank at the book signing, Tam was embarrassed at leaving his friend and mentor behind. As things stood Tam would move on and away from Pierce, it was inevitable. But now with Pierce's publishing opportunity they are fellow travellers again.

The evening is going well. Pierce and Tam are back to where they used to be, Pierce at the helm and both seem more comfortable with that, but a few pints in, Pierce has to sound a warning note.

'Tam, I can't be out all night. I'll need to get back and get stuck in, I've got a tight deadline, the end of the month, I'll need to go some to do it.'

'Aye no bother, Piercey, whatever you like. I want to get up early tomorrow as well. I've got a riff I need to work with, I just made it up on my way here, want to here it?'

'Fire away.'

'Well, it's nothing fancy but I think it'll work really well for a song I've just finished. It's like, *dum dum dum dum, do do do* then it changes *dum dum dum dum dum do do do*, d'you hear it? *Dum dum dum dum do do do*, then it goes back to the start again.'

While he is demonstrating this Tam is playing an air guitar, plucking the strings with one hand while the other slides up and down the imaginary fretboard. He makes a tunnel of his lips as he hums the notes, unselfconscious, completely taken up with what he's doing, creatively in the moment. Pierce nearly cries with the beauty of it. To stop himself from crying, and after he has told Tam how good the riff sounds, he gets the next round in.

Now that Pierce is no longer to be left behind in the fame and fortune stakes, an element of competition creeps in.

'Mind you,' he says, 'I might not get the groupie action you'll get but still, at least mine'll be posh tottie, with a brain in their heads.'

'Who cares about brains? As long as they get their drawers off.'

'Well said that man!'

'Once your book comes out the two of us'll be baw deep in starfuckers, whoooeeee!' Tam shrieks.

And the celebrating continues.

Chapter 29

Daphne makes a succession of phone calls, the first one to her mum. The phone rings five times and then the answering machine clicks on. It is her brother Albee's voice, in the background she can hear his kids. The baby, Daniel, is howling while Albee's little girl Eva is singing. She sounds so Australian. Even Albee sounds Australian. 'Hi!' Albee chirrups, 'You've probably just missed us but leave a message and we'll get back to you! Don't be a stranger!'

Mum is so proud of her successful son and his lovely family, she sends new photos every other day by email. It is all Daphne can do to send back gurgly one- or two-line responses agreeing how lovely the kids are and how fabulous the house is. But when she hears the voices she wants to cry. Albee's house is so full of fun and love and Australian sunshine.

'Hello Albee, long time no hear, eh?' Daphne is waiting for them to answer. She has no idea what time it is in Australia but she's hoping that the family are out in the garden having a barbie, cracking open a few tinnies, that they'll get to the phone before she cracks.

'Hello Esther and Eva and Daniel, hello Mum. Hope you're all well. I got the photos, you're all looking great as usual. Just phoned for a wee chat. I'm missing you all. Mum, phone me back. I'm missing you, I'm so missing you.' Daphne catches herself sighing, a deep lonely sorrowful sigh, and realises how pathetic she sounds.

'Oh well, nobody home. Phone me, Mum, when you get this message. I'm not feeling well, I want to talk to you.'

It is a good ten minutes later before she regains her composure and makes the next call. Also an answering machine.

'Hi, Carol here. We're not able to take your call at the moment blah blah, leave a message.'

We're not able? Who is we? Daphne had intended to ask Carol to come round. She would have begged if necessary, and knowing what a selfish cow Carol is, it probably would have been. She knows it's hypocritical to call on the help of someone she despises but Carol is the only woman available and she needs a woman now. But Carol is not answering, the self-centred bitch probably has a man there with her. She's probably giggling and shooshing him right now while she listens to the message and he removes her clothes. But it's the blah blah that really gets to her.

'Carol? Are you going to answer? No? Just as well because I phoned to tell you what I think of you. Yes, it's me, Daphne, re-member? Just phoned to tell you that no matter how many shades of blonde you dye your hair – oh and by the way, I know it's grey, I saw it the last time you were here – no matter how much you spend on your turd brown clothes, no matter how sassy you think you are, at the end of the day I pity you, yes, I pity you because you're a selfish self-obsessed fuckwit and …' Daphne is crying now, 'and nobody loves you!'

She bangs the phone down. Her heart is racing and her face is hot. She'll have to get a grip, she's has no idea where that poisonous rant came from. It's too late to do anything about it now, Carol will have heard it or will hear it when she comes in. So be it.

She takes five big breaths before dialling the next number. She has to look this one up in the phonebook. She really is scraping the bottom of the barrel now. But it's another answering machine.

'Hi, Pierce McCormack here, Editor in Charge, Poyumtree Publishing. Sorry I'm unable to take your call at the moment but please leave your number and I'll get right back to you as soon as I return to the office.'

A snort of laughter escapes Daphne when she hears this and softens what she was about to say.

'Pierce, it's me, Daphne.'

She keeps here voice bright and hard like glass.

'Just wondered if you fancied coming up for a wee plate of

soup. I've made too much and I hate to throw it out. If you're not otherwise engaged with laydeez, would you pop up and see me when you get in? I'd really appreciate it. Eh, don't bring Tam or anybody, just come on your own.'

She returns to pacing the floor but her tummy is sore and the panic is getting worse. There is no one left to call. Everyone is out. Everyone else has a life. There is one call she hasn't made and she still remembers his number, but no. Not now, not yet.

She needs to go to the loo again and while she is straddling the toilet pan, her distended belly pushed out in front like a bad case of kwashiorkor, terror overwhelms her. Something terrible is going to happen if she stays here. She has to get out of the house.

She'll go to the deli, buy stuff for soup. That way if Pierce comes up she really will have soup to give him. Stick to the routine, that's the thing to do. She grabs her big coat though she's sweating and it's a lovely warm night. So eager is Daphne to get out of the house that she nearly forgets her purse and has to go back to the kitchen to get it. Everything's going to be fine, she tells herself, but she knows deep down inside with the rumblings in her belly, that it isn't.

*

Instinctively Donnie dials a number. He doesn't even know what number he's dialling, he should call the police, but when the answering machine clicks on he knows. Daphne sounds cheerful *Hi, I'm not here just now but leave a message. Cheers.* She says.

'Daphne it's me. Pick it up Daphne, pick it up.'

Donnie's crying now but what does it matter?

'Please. Pick up.'

She doesn't pick up and Donnie smashes the receiver on to the cradle. Probably out with the BMW bastard, he thinks. I have to go round there, I have to tell her, she'll understand, unconditional, she said.

The phone rings. It's her. She's not saying anything but he can hear her breathing.

'Daphne please, speak. I love you. They threw a shitty brick through the window, those fucking neds, there's shite all over the bed, I don't know what to do, Daphne, please, speak to me!'

But she doesn't speak. A voice laughs, a man's voice and Donnie throws the phone across the room.

*

Daphne keeps having to stop in the street. She leans against a bus stop shelter, a shop window, a car. She leans into the pain, curling like a hedgehog. She crosses her legs tight, locking them, one foot hooked behind the other knee. The pain consumes her, the only thing in her life. It is always the same, a white hot heat that floods her body and arrests her brain, a religious experience in its intensity, demanding all of her attention. While it's upon her she doesn't know where she is, who she is, who she was, who she will ever be again. It is not that she has forgotten it's just that these things are now of no consequence. The pain is a bottomless well of searing agony, timeless and infinite, and yet it does end, and Daphne staggers on.

This is embarrassing; people will think she's on heroin. No one approaches her and she is glad of it. She is slick with sweat. Her face is shining and her clothes slide, lubricated, across her body as she walks. When she gets to the park she is going to roll in the cool grass. Now she understands why horses do that. This is the best idea she has ever had and it drives her on. She is walking smartly now, every step tugging at her intestines, gravitational force pulling her guts out of her body.

In the park she reaches the long grass and the trees but the pain comes at her again and she must give in to it. She has no idea how long it has lasted but when it has stopped and she is able to take stock of her surroundings, she finds she has locked her arms around a tree. She has slid down into a squat with her knees wrapped around the thick trunk. Holding hands, holding her own hands, feels okay. The tree is warm and alive, it's mature, all grown up, it's roots are deep and solid. The bark has dug its impression into her thighs and her face but it is not an unpleasant sensation and she must cling on there.

Treehugger, that's what Donnie would call her. *Treehugging hippie,* as though treehugging was a bad thing. Daphne has never hugged a tree before, never felt the need, never saw the point, but now it feels good.

*

He has unplugged everything and then as he's locking the front door it occurs to him that it would be a better idea to leave it open. The keys are left dangling in the door and the alarm system switched off. Downstairs as he comes out of the close he hears a phone ring and wonders if it's his but it's too late for that now.

It's a warm night and they'll probably be drinking Buckfast up at the railway embankment. Or what used to be the railway embankment and was remodelled, at great expense, as a cycle path. Or what was briefly a cycle path until being once again reclaimed as exclusively ned territory.

He walks along the path, his feet making a satisfying crunch on the broken Buckie bottles. In the light of the bright full moon he picks out an empty can of cider and kicks it along, clattering it until it disappears into the undergrowth. The steep embankments on either side of the path are a jungle of bushes and thistles and wild flowers. Their perfume combine to overwhelm the smell of piss except when he enters tunnels. In the tunnels he hums loudly and swings his arms as he walks. Come and get me.

It's a lovely night for it. Funny he thinks, the way things turn out.

There are no other people on the path. Tunnels and more tunnels, he passes the bridge over the river. If he met them now he'd throw them one by one into the shallow river and watch the water turn red with their blood. He imagines their gurgling screams as they lie, bones smashed, unable to move, drowning in knee-deep water. And then he hears them.

Instinctively he darts into the bushes but halfway hidden, as his feet become enmeshed in nettles and sticky willow, he reconsiders. Better to meet them head on. No, stupid to give them an advantage. Keep the element of surprise; wait till he can see the whites of their eyes. He pushes further in. Except that this has been a tactical error.

In the bright moonlight he sees that he is standing on a narrow shelf. There are only a few feet of mossy earth and then a twenty-foot drop to the river. Another foot and he'll fall into the gorge. He crouches and clings to a young tree. The neds stop and sit or otherwise lounge around the broken bench that overlooks the river. Panic rises in Donnie's chest: If they find him they could easily push him over the edge, and no witnesses. It'll be his blood running in the river.

He can hear the usual ned noises: laughing, bellowing, swearing, they're close enough for him to make them out. They're wearing the uniform, the usual neddy sportswear, trainers and caps. They are typical generic interchangeable neds, four of them, but amongst them there is a tall gangly blond one and a wee red-haired runt. These are *the* neds. The ones who hang around the close mouth at the door of the sun tanning shop, the ones he squirted the piss-filled Super Soaker at, the ones who, no doubt, by way of retribution, lobbed the blazing shit brick though his window.

'Heh Doyle!' he hears the red-haired runt call to the big lanky one.

I knew it, Donnie thinks: a Catholic, a typical dirty bog-trotting Tim. Doyle looks about sixteen, with blond bumfluff on his chin, but he's a big bastard, big feet and long arms, and young, he'll be quick on his feet. But it's a relief to know he's not a Protestant; Donnie would be uncomfortable killing a Protestant. At this thought Donnie's legs feel weak and he wonders if he has taken on more than he, one man alone, can achieve.

'You coming tae Spud's hoose? He's got an empty.'

'Naw,' says Doyle. 'Too late, man. I've got my work in the morning.'

A ned with a job? Donnie can't believe it.

'Aw c'mon,' says the runt, 'Sally telt wee Shug she fancied you, you're in mate!'

'Aye but I've got mah day release and I've no done mah home-work, ah'll need tae get up and dae it in the morning.'

A ned who goes to college and turns in homework?

Any kind of coherent discussion peters out after this as the neds revert to their more usual mode of communication: dummy fighting. Donnie's legs are sore with squatting so long. He'll have to make his move soon. But they'll hear him coming, they'll be ready, there are four of them. They'll hurt him. Donnie desperately tries to invoke the mad burning rage that drove him here, the fearless fury, but it has run out on him. It has changed to a sickening terror of the damage four pairs of Doc Martin boots might do. He wanted to kill them he wanted them to kill him. He wanted an end to being frightened.

'Fancy geein' the wee man a bell?' says the runt, laughing.

'Aw man, whit a laugh,' says Doyle. 'We've been phoning him for months and the cunt never says nothing, he just breathes, *hhh hhh hhh*, like a fucking paedo in a playground. But the shite bomb cracked it. He's howling like a wean doon the phone. Doyle affects a nasal whine at this point, '*There's shite all over the bed, I need help,*' he says!'

The other neds are laughing.

'Too right he fucking needs help, needs fucking locked up,' says Doyle to general agreement.

*

The pub is shutting and Pierce tries to talk Tam into coming to the disco with him. He begins by reassuring him that this is a cost-effective venture.

'It's filthy cheap, cheaper than buying pints here. Five pounds to get in on a Monday and the beer's two pound a bottle. You can sook the same beer all night if you're careful.'

Despite now being a big time rock star, money is always Tam's first concern.

'But we're not buying any more pints here, the bar's closed.'

Pierce tries a different angle.

'They play all yon pop music, all the latest from the hit parade. It's good research, you need to keep your finger on the pulse, Tam. You need to know what the pop pickers are dancing to.'

'Your patter's rotten,' says Tam, but he laughs anyway.

Even Pierce can see that this is not a convincing argument and in desperation must state the crude, unvarnished obvious.

'Monday, book ladies'll be in, the place is hoaching with fanny.'

Tam says nothing; he seems disinterested. Pierce can never understand Tam's reluctance to accompany him on these Monday night fanny missions.

'C'mon, live a little, for fuck's sake. I know loads of women that go on a Monday, they're gagging for it, I'll introduce you. You're guaranteed your hole.'

'Cheers Pierce, but not on a school night.'

'School night nothing, you don't need to get up in the morning. That's the beauty of us working for ourselves, Tam, we make our own hours.'

'Yeah and I've got things to do tomorrow, I want an early start, busy day.'

'But it's not as if you have to, you said you were going to work on that riff, you can do that anytime. We're artists, man, we work when the muse moves us.'

'*You're* an artist, Pierce. I'm just trying to make a living. No, that's not right,'

Tam's voice has risen and his face is getting red.

'I'm not just trying to make a living, I'm trying to make a career.' Pierce holds up his hands.

'Fair play to you, Tam, fair play.'

Tam has never been this strident with Pierce before and they are both surprised and a little embarrassed by it.

'I've got a good chance this time, I could do well at this, I'm good at it, I know I am.'

'I know you are, mate,' Pierce agrees, 'I told you that from the start.'

'I know you did, and I appreciate it. But my days of sitting in the pub talking about it and lying in my bed dreaming about it are over. I'm not like you, Pierce, I can't afford to piss about.'

At this Pierce stops indulging Tam's burgeoning ego.

'What the fuck d'you mean by that?'

'I don't mean anything, I'm just saying …'

'That I *do* piss about?'

'That's not what I said.'

'It's what you meant.'

Pierce expects another hasty denial but Tam only shrugs.

'Take it any way you like.'

They sit in shocked silence for a few minutes while the pub empties and the barman lifts chairs around them.

'I know how talented you are, Pierce, you've told me often enough.'

Pierce bristles at this, this kind of cheek from a young upstart is intolerable, but Tam's weak smile indicates that it was meant as a joke.

'Look, the publisher bird, Daisy or whatever her name is, she knows you've got talent. They wouldn't want to publish you if they didn't think you were good. They believe in you, maybe it's time you started believing it yourself.'

*

What seems like a long time later, after the neds have left and he is no longer privy to their boastings of delinquency, acts of delinquency perpetrated against him, and him hiding in the bushes like a prick doing nothing about it, Donnie decides to get up. What's the point of sitting here? He's not going to go after them, he's never going to attack them, he hasn't the balls, why not just admit it? Why not just accept it: some people have tiny balls. Some people are born beautiful or rich or clever or poor or deformed or Catholic, and some are born without courage.

Donnie would give anything for courage, swap it for a limb, well maybe not a limb, he wouldn't want to have only one arm or even

237

worse one leg, but he'd swap for an organ, one he had two of, like a an eye or a kidney. He could manage okay with one kidney and he would be no less of a man.

He knows he can't afford self-loathing, knows it's dangerous, but sometimes, times like now, it's the most powerful emotion he has, the only emotion he has. Here he is, hiding in the bushes, letting a bunch of fucking Catholic neds throw shite at him and laugh.

It wasn't Daphne who phoned. All these months he thought she was still there for him, still keeping the door open. Somebody else, the dirty BMW bastard, is accessing Daphne's letterbox and she won't even pick up the phone. What the fuck is he going to do now? Might as well top himself.

Take the coward's way out; that would be the best solution. He could go home and take all four packets of the antidepressants, wash them down with a few beers, stick the video on and float away. Someone else can clean the shite off the bed and the smoke off the walls. He can snooze while Rangers score and never have to wake up again.

But what if he did wake up? He doesn't know enough about it and he's heard stories about drugs ripping up your guts. He could wake vomiting up his own stomach wall, taking days to die, in agony. Not nice. And he couldn't face his mum and dad at the bedside saying: why, Donnie?

Sliding off this precipice is another option. With a bit of luck his head would hit a boulder and it would be goodnight Vienna. He wouldn't feel a thing after that. But maybe he would just get all smashed up, and not knowing for sure, those few seconds before impact … nah. Donnie shivers involuntarily.

There must be easier ways. He could look it up on the Internet, there's bound to be a site, *How to top yourself in three easy steps*. Three steps is two steps too many. Donnie hasn't the resources for more. That's the irony, he thinks, I would commit the ultimate act of cowardice if I wasn't fucking paralysed by fear.

So he gets up. Or he tries to, but his legs, having crouched so long, are numb. He punches them and this induces an unbearable sensation of pins and needles. He needs to get out of here.

He puts one leg out in front of him and tentatively balances his weight on the other, which seems to help. He hangs on to the sapling tree and pulls himself up, hand over hand. The tree is a bit shoogly, its roots infirm on this rocky platform. His legs are still dead, he'll have to stand a while but as he's transferring his weight, he slips. His legs slide away from him and his body drops. He grabs for the young tree and makes it, holding on tight.

Thank God for that.

Donnie laughs, what a revelation! How weird is that? Within two seconds his perception has completely changed. He doesn't want to die. He didn't know that.

He knows it now.

He'll wait a minute, get his breath back, get the strength back in his legs and climb up out of here. Okay, the house is a mess but it's not the end of the world, it can be cleaned, things can be sorted. He really, really, doesn't want to die. He's not ready.

He's sobbing now, this ledge is pretty fucking dangerous.

Chapter 30

What a fucking cheek he has, thinks Pierce. Hits the big time and five minutes later he's telling everyone how to run their lives. Well he's not going to tell me, I go my own way, Pierce McCormack is his own man. And after all that, after falling out with his best mate over it, the disco was rubbish anyway.

He hates the snooty bitches who won't return his eye contact, sniggering into their Red Bull and vodka, whispering to their mates. He knows what they're thinking. They see a guy out on his own on a Monday night, a lone wolf, slightly overweight, slightly too old for this. A sad unemployed loser, that's what they think.

And the ones who do make eye contact, whose gaze he can hardly escape: the ones who have been dumped. Other men's rejects who, desperate to prove they can still pull, lower their standards and slum it on a Monday night. He despises them too.

That only leaves the Monday Book Ladies. God love them. He doesn't have the energy or the semen to go home with one of them tonight, what's the point? He'll only get kicked out before the alarm goes off. They have lives to get on with, kids to get ready for school, packed lunches to make. He's not part of that life, real life.

He's too drunk for it anyway. Above the noise of the pumping music he speaks to a big-toothed, small-breasted woman. She's not smiling but she is nodding agreement at what he's saying so he gently pushes back a lock of her hair and whispers in her ear, letting his lips, softer than a kiss, brush her skin. This wee tenderness is one of his trademarks. He looks into her eyes to register the effect of the intimacy but the girl looks slightly scared. She's left her big teeth out to dry and forgotten to take them back in again. He must have on his drunken sneery face, he realises. It's time to go home.

Chapter 31

Donnie's face is muddy. He would spit the dark mouldy earth out of his mouth but he's frightened of any movement. He tried a few minutes ago to pull himself up, scrabbling and swimming, and now his legs are dangling over the edge. His hips and the tree are the only things holding him, and his arms are tired. He has to move, he has to try, but he's scared.

He can't stay here all night. If he doesn't move he'll surely fall. The only thing that will save him now is guts. Balls. Cojones. The lack of which got him here in the first place. If ever there was a time when Donnie had to be a man it was now when his life depends upon it.

The wee tree is not secure. He has experimented, one hand at a time, for something more solid to hold on to but there is nothing. A tumble of earth to fill his open mouth and the disturbance further weakening the tree was all it got him. A taste of things to come, if this goes badly his mouth might be permanently filled with earth.

The tree is loosening. Clean white roots, like bones, are visible now at the bottom of the tree. The weight of Donnie's body is pulling it out as he slides. He tries to use his ribcage as a brake, burning as it scrapes the rocky ledge.

It's too late to try. Whatever he does now will only hasten his fall. He wants another minute, another second, before the pain.

Chapter 32

As Pierce makes his way home he reflects on what Tam said. Every word, every nonchalant shrug is imprinted on Pierce's brain and he recalls and scrutinises them one by one. After a fair and through analysis he concludes that Tam is an arse. He thinks about what he now considers his book deal, and knows he must knuckle down. This is a good chance, the best opportunity he's ever had. But the days of sitting in the pub talking about it and lying in bed dreaming about it have to be over.

Although he's a bit tired and more than a wee bit drunk he could make a start tonight. He pictures himself at the computer, his fingers a blur on the keyboard, smoke rising from the overloaded machine due to the complexity and profundity of his ideas and the rapidity with which he records them. It's like a movie with the ashtray filling, the manuscript becoming a tower of paper and the sun slowly creeping into the sky. He sees himself type the words 'the end'. These visions suddenly give tremendous urgency to his mission and he rushes home to make a start.

Chapter 33

The tree is now only loosely attached to the ground. It begins to slide. It is a hopeless equation. The looser it becomes, the further off the ledge Donnie slides, putting more weight on the tree, making it looser. A downward spiral, but finite. For the first time in his life Donnie questions gravity, why must things fall down? Who made up that rule? Could it not, just this once, work the other way around?

Another inch, another couple of inches, Donnie accepts it. What else can he do? He wishes he'd taken more Valium before he'd left the house, all of it. Every second is a bonus, one in which he might be rescued, one in which he is not dead, his guts are not splattered on the sharp river rocks.

Please God don't let it hurt, he prays, don't make it sore, don't let my eyes pop out the sockets or anything gross like that. Don't let my body buckle, my leg twist round my neck, no ugliness, no bones sticking out, please God, please. But he knows it's got to hurt. Anticipation of the pain weakens his remaining strength.

Now the tree has lost its hold on the earth, and so will Donnie. He knows it's pointless but Donnie continues to hold fast to the slim trunk, he needs to hold on to *something*. The young tree, so green and fresh, full of life, so full of the future, slides with him, slowly, slowly, into the gorge.

Chapter 34

It is at this very moment that something slides out of Daphne.

Slides is not the word Daphne would use, implying as it does, ease. Her teeth are still gritted, her jaw locked, her face purple, her muscles juddering. A long time has passed since she first hugged the tree, the full moon has climbed up and across the sky, time enough for her to pass out at least three or four times, she doesn't know for how long. Time enough for her to be wakened by the torture of her body being ripped in two, for her to change position, sometimes squatting sometimes kneeling, but always holding tight to the tree. Earlier on she did let go of it but only to pull her wet and bloodied jogging pants off and make a little nest beneath her clenched bum.

The nest is filthy now, bloodied by the mess of organic stuff she has voided but there is more to come. Another dump, but this time it passes easier, it is not so solid as the last one. As it flops on top of the earlier load she sees that it is a big, dark, red, jelly thing, which could be her liver. But Daphne knows it is not her liver. With the bark biting into her face she passes out again.

Chapter 35

Right, he thinks, computer, check. Paper, check. Ashtray and fags, check. Chocolate Digestives, check. Having gathered the accoutrements, Pierce has to gather his thoughts. The answering machine is blinking. Should he find out who it is?

No, ignore it and concentrate on the work. It's probably Tam phoning to apologise. Well fuck him, he can wait, in fact, he's not going to see or speak to Tam now until the book's finished. See how he likes them apples.

But what if it's Sean? If it is Sean it'll only be to tell him that now he's fully recovered from the hypothermia, he's planning suicide again. Pierce thinks now, after the event, that it was perhaps wrong to stop Sean leaving with Bernie. He would be much happier dead. Pierce should never have intervened. If Sean says he's going to top himself it's going to give Pierce a bit of a moral dilemma and he's got a book to finish. He can't speak to him either.

It could be a burd. Pierce checks his watch, the disco is coming out now, maybe one of the girls hasn't pulled anyone else and is calling him in as back up. It wouldn't be the first time. The fourth emergency (shagging) service. Pierce's baws are temporarily empty but anyway, he's sick of being used by women. Fuck them too, he thinks, or rather, don't fuck them.

He listens to the message. It's Daphne. Pierce smiles to hear her voice, to hear her pretending nothing's wrong. She's trying to keep her voice light but she's fooling nobody. How conveniently she's forgotten turfing him out of her flat, embarrassing him in front of his friend and making him spend another night with that nympho Carol. Not once has she offered him soup or as much as a cup of tea since then and now she's on the phone all palsy-walsy. Fuck her.

He goes upstairs and chaps her door anyway, but she's not in. She's probably out prowling the park in her big coat in this heat. More likely she's away to that deli buying lemon grass or some such shite at three o'clock in the morning. She's a weird one. *I'd really appreciate it*, she said on the phone. She's never said anything like that before. She normally makes out she's doing him a big favour. Maybe she's finally realised how much she blew it by not coming to New York. Well, he's generous enough to let bygones be bygones. And now that she's ready to apologise he's happy to restore the soup status quo.

The thought strikes him that maybe that fucking ginger chimp Donnie has been round here again. She's obviously not interested but maybe Donnie's stalking her. Underneath her cheery message Pierce could hear anxiety in her voice, fear even.

Just to be on the safe side he'll take a stroll through the park and see if he can find her. He'll use the time constructively, he can plan the next chapter and the walk will sober him up. It's not right this, a woman alone in the park at night, there are a lot of weirdos around. And if the gimp chimp is giving her any hassle this will be a good opportunity to deck the wee bastard.

Chapter 36

He nearly trips over her. A woman hunched against a tree. This is trouble, foul play, and makes Pierce's heart hammer in his chest. He puts his hand on her shoulder.

'Are you all right, love?'

A stupid question, she's alone in the woods at night slumped against a tree, she's obviously not all right, but it is not until he sees her face in the light of the moon that he realises that the woman is Daphne. She has been stripped naked from the waist down, there is blood on her legs, she is woozy and doesn't seem to recognise him. She's been … the taste of sick rises in Pierce's throat.

'You're okay, Daphne, you're okay, I've got you.'

Pierce leans down and hugs her. She clings to him, shivering and sobbing. She is saying something, mumbling into his shoulder.

'I'm sorry', she says.

She is pulling her jumper down over her knees to cover her nakedness. It's a warm night but she is shivering. She's in shock. He pulls away from her, pulls his jacket off and wraps it around her and as he holds her he feels her warm wetness, she's bleeding. He has to get help, get an ambulance. He wants to shout for help, run and phone an ambulance but he's scared to leave her, he can't leave her here alone again. He doesn't know what to do. He sees the bundle of her blood-soaked trousers beside her and reaches across her to them. He has to get her dressed and get her out of here, get help. The weight of the trousers surprises him, there is something on them. Then he sees what it is but it makes no sense. Tiny, naked, blood-streaked.

It is a dead baby.

'Daphne?'

She only lifts her head and nods. A tear drips off the end of her nose. He recoils from the corpse, pulling Daphne close to him, away from the dreadful sight.

'Oh my God.'

'I'm sorry,' she says again, 'Donnie, I'm so sorry.'

Donnie she calls him. Pierce is amazed and guilty that he can be so stung by such a triviality at this moment. With Daphne resisting he gently but firmly untangles himself. She's sobbing and hugging her knees as he gets to his feet and walks around her. Now that his brain understands what has happened, he wants a closer look at the foetus.

It's a perfectly formed little person, a baby girl, not frightening to look at, just really, really sad. The moonlight throws leaf shadows across its pale and motionless body. Poor wee thing, dead in a city park, a pair of stained jogging trousers for a crib. Tenderly he touches its poor little dirty face, wiping blood and mucus from its cheeks. Poor wee soul. Poor Daphne.

As he rests his hand on the tiny white chest, the baby's arms and legs spasm as if it has been electrocuted. The tiny body jack-knifes and it coughs. It is alive. It was dead and now it's alive. He touched it and it came to life.

Now he has it in his arms. It has stopped moving again. He puts his finger in and scrapes out a blob of something from the tiny warm mouth. It's still not moving or breathing and Pierce can't see what else to do. A mixture of instinct and what he's seen on telly tells him to smack the baby's bottom. She's slippy; he's scared he'll drop her and kill her before she gets a chance to take her first breath. Carefully, trying not to damage her, he locks his fingers between her centimetre-sized ankles and lifts her.

Silhouetted against the full moon, before he has a chance to smack her, she fills her lungs and howls. It is surprisingly loud. In a small patch of forest in the middle of the city the baby girl's angry bawling bounces off the trees and brings her mother to her senses.

Epilogue.

Three years later.

Daphne has been up and down this aisle three or four times and still she can't decide what to have for tea. It took her a long time to set foot inside Asda again. Even months after the funeral she still felt creepy in the shop. But she's over all that now; that was a lifetime away. Asda feels good again, it's the highlight of Daphne's boring day.

She picks up a tin of pink salmon, running through recipes in her head, pasta maybe, but the metallic taste floods her mouth again and reluctantly she replaces the tin on the shelf. She turns back to the trolley. Where is she? The wee one has disappeared. She shoves as fast as she can, dodging other trolleys, hurrying to the end of the aisle. Puffed out with the effort of her dash, Daphne rests her belly on the trolley handle and stretches out her spine. It's okay, Holly Louise is here, she's fine, she's standing waiting for Daphne holding her dad's hand while they both admire the Easter eggs.

'Please Daddy, please!' begs Holly Louise, pointing to the giant Kinder eggs on the display.

Daphne sighs; she spent fifteen minutes this morning putting Holly Louise's hair up in a princess bun because she insisted on wearing her new Barbie clasps. Now she's pulled the clasps out and her golden curly hair is falling in untidy ringlets over her face.

'Well, we better ask Mummy,' says Daddy.

'Pierce, no more, you've already bought her enough sweets,' says Daphne firmly.

'Och, but these ones have a toy inside; they're educational.'

'Look how dear they are!' Daphne protests. 'We can't afford it.'

Daphne turns and heads towards the fruit and veg aisle. Pierce and Holly Louise trail behind her, the toddler dragging her feet and whining. Daphne has a moment's hesitation when she almost gives in before her hesitation hardens to resentment. Why is she always the one who has to say no? He spoils Holly Louise, but he won't be able to for much longer, not once there's another wee one howling for attention. The new baby is going to change the dynamics, thinks Daphne with some satisfaction.

Pierce has a great talent for spending money, particularly when it comes to Holly Louise but he's still not very good at earning it. Unlike his pal Tam, who's now living a rock star lifestyle in America, Pierce is still waiting for the royalties to come in from his first book even though it came out nearly two years ago. His editor, Daisy, says that despite superlative reviews a first book is rarely a money-spinner. She has high hopes for this next one. So does Daphne.

She has nagged and wheedled him to get a proper job but he continues to resist. He needs time to write, he insists. And, he freely admits, he'd rather spend this time with Holly Louise before she has to go to school, she's growing up so fast, he says, he wants to savour it. Pierce revels in all the kiddie stuff: breakfast at 6am, the swing park, teaching her to swim, days out at the beach, bath time, bedtime stories. But they need money more than ever now. Daphne's maternity pay will only last a few months after the baby is born and then one of them will have to work.

Unlike her last one, this is a planned pregnancy. Planned like a military operation, by Pierce. He wants this baby as a playmate for Holly Louise. He doesn't want her growing up an only child. And there is something else, something neither of them has ever acknowledged. He wants this baby because it will be his. Daphne, although constantly worried about money, had agreed. She knows Pierce is right, it'll be nice for Holly Louise to have a brother, nice for all of them.

More often than not, Daphne likes being a mum but a lot of her time is wasted being annoyed with Pierce, who every year gets a little fatter and balder and lazier. She never expected life to turn out like this.

She only agreed to marry him for Holly Louise's sake, and because he was desperate for her to wear that huge diamond ring. It was a low-key affair. Mum came back from Australia, thrilled to meet her granddaughter. Pierce's Uncle Sean was the best man.

'It's a grand thing to see two young people so in love,' said Sean.

Daphne had to look away. Sean came to visit the following Christmas and helped Daphne wash up after dinner.

'It's a grand thing to see two young people making a life together,' he said into the basin, 'even if it isn't perfect, I suppose there's a lot of everyday joy to be had.'

At the fruit and veg aisle Daphne sees something she can work with, a large bunch of leeks. They look fresh and green and wholesome.

'Is it soup again, Daffers?'

'Uh huh. Got a problem with that?'

'No, no, you fire in, love.'

'Cheers,' says Daphne cheerlessly as she weighs out the leeks in the hanging scales.

'We had *soup* yesterday,' Pierce says in an exaggerated fairy tale way to Holly Louise, 'And *soup* the day before that.'

The little girl is holding her daddy's arm with both of hers and jumping as high as she can every time he says it.

'And *soup* tonight,' Pierce continues.

'And soup tomorrow!' Holly Louise shouts in joy.

Daphne stops putting the leeks in the poly bag. This isn't fair; they are ganging up on her again.

'Look, if you don't want it, you only have to say so. I can't find anything I want, I've been round the whole shop and everything makes me feel queasy.'

'Everything but soup?'

'Yeah,' she laughs, realising how ridiculous this sounds, 'Everything but soup.'

With a toddler's passion Holly Louise lunges forward and wrestles her mother's legs. Daphne gently peels her off and enjoys the unspeakable pleasure of one of Holly Louise's soft and chubby little hands in hers. Holly Louise giggles triumphantly when Pierce accepts her other hand. They all know what must happen next.

'Swing!' cries Holly Louise.

They look at each other, sigh, nod, and on a silent count of three pull her up by the arms.

'Well then, *soup* it is my dear! *Soup* it is,' shouts Pierce, with their ginger baby swinging joyfully between them.

THE END

Reading group questions

What is the significance of the title?

Is Daphne's reaction to breaking up with Donnie a normal response?

Why does she drop her friends and stop going to work? Is she depressed?

How does Daphne feel about Pierce at the beginning of the story? In the middle? At the end?

What is it that attracts Daphne to Tam?

Why doesn't Daphne develop a relationship with Tam? What does she mean when she says he's 'a few months too late'?

Is Daphne ignorant of her condition or in denial?

Why does Pierce change his mind about having a steady girlfriend?

Do you think Bernie and Sean's relationship is a good model for a marriage?

Do you think Bertha's mother, Gerty, is actively working against Donnie or just supporting her daughter?

Bertha has resolved to come off the antidepressants. Will she end up the same as Donnie?

How many romantic liaisons/relationships are there in the story and how do they end?

Is the story pro- or anti-romance?

Do you think Pierce and Daphne will be happy together or have they both 'settled'?

Did you feel any sympathy for Donnie? If so, why?

Do you think Donnie and Daphne would have got back together if things had ended differently?

What do you think Daphne will tell Holly Louise about her father?

Acknowledgements

Laura Marney gratefully acknowledges the support of the Scottish Arts Council when she was writing the first edition of this book. Without invaluable inspiration from the Inch High Private Eye and the Roly Poly Wannabe, this book could not have been written.

Why I wrote *Nobody Loves a Ginger Baby*

LAURA MARNEY EXPLAINS THE INSPIRATION FOR THIS NOVEL.

You know these people you see in your doctor's surgery waiting room? You know the ones: a suit with a briefcase, free Post-its and a smarmy line in patter? They're obviously not patients, they're too smiley, so they must be 'medical reps': sales representatives hawking drugs to your GP during her coffee break. I used to do that.

I answered an advert for Medical Sales Representatives. They sought graduates in biological science, nursing and chemistry, pharmacology degrees or doctorates. I had a biology 'A' level. Beyond that I knew nothing whatsoever about science, but I was desperate. I was a penniless single parent of two bright-eyed kiddies and it was November; I needed money for Christmas presents. I reckoned that if I could tell whatever lies were required to get the job, by the time the company trained me, realised how useless I was and then fired me, they'd have to pay me a month's salary – enough to ensure that Santa would come to our house. I called the recruitment line and blagged an interview.

On my first day I left the price tag on my M and S suit tucked inside. That way I could return it and get my money back as soon as they fired me. A young woman was training us new recruits on the antidepressant we were to sell to GPs. Her sales graph looked none too healthy, it had nosedived, but she was optimistic.

'As you can see we've not yet been able to maximise our sales of this excellent product, but as it's now winter we believe things will begin to change. After the Christmas holidays the general public will have nothing to look forward to except their credit card bills and more miserable weather,' she said chirpily, 'so the good news is, we anticipate increased demand for our antidepressants.'

I realised then what a snakepit I had fallen into.

The more I talked to friends, the more it seemed that everyone and their granny were on antidepressants, not just folk with actual clinical depression. What had gone wrong in our society that so many seemingly ordinary people were having to numb their pain?

Were the drug companies exploiting our misery? Or did we feel entitled to be happy all the time? Was not being constantly happy making us miserable? Why were we thinking antidepressant and not pro-joy? This fascinated me and I resolved to write a story around this theme. I wanted to help people stop being dependent on chemical happiness, and I'd be more effective working on the inside. Hah! The drug company who employed me would unwittingly sponsor their own downfall!

As I began the novel, Daphne's neighbour Pierce was a minor character, a bit of local colour. I modelled him on an unemployed but charming poet I knew. He was fun to write, and his sweary voice was one of the loudest in my cast. I named him Pierce, meaning 'rock'. I felt poor old Daphne needed someone to be her rock, and so his role took on even greater significance. Obviously another word for pierce is penetrate, something that Pierce was particularly fond of doing to ladies. It tickled me to make his name a verb describing his favourite activity. I confess that as he developed and showed himself to be a compassionate if hapless individual, I fell a little in love with Pierce.

The ending was supposed to be so much darker too. I never told my editor this, sparing her delicate sensitivities, but the episode in the park was going to have a much grizzlier outcome. Except that when I came to write it, I couldn't do it. I'm too nice, that's my problem. As I approached Donnie's denouement I noticed that my writing had slowed down to a few hundred words a day. I was dreading the moment when Donnie, well, you know. And if it was hard to do it to Donnie, how could I do it to an innocent?

In the end, not only had I fallen in love with Pierce, but despite the shortcomings of pathetic Daphne and selfish Donnie and everyone else, I found it hard to hurt them. Once I had finished the novel I saw that what I had produced was not what I had originally intended to write at all. What began as an over-optimistic plan to bring down the pharmaceutical industry became a story about people who were selfish and fragile and pathetic and foolish. A lot like me, and maybe a little bit like you, too.

DAVID RAMOS FERNANDES

About the Author

Laura Marney tries to do a good deed every day. Occasionally bad deeds do accidentally slip in, but there you go, nobody's perfect. She is the author of five novels: *For Faughie's Sake, No Wonder I Take a Drink, Nobody Loves a Ginger Baby, Only Strange People Go to Church* and *My Best Friend Has Issues.* She also writes short stories and drama for radio and the stage. She lives in Glasgow and holds a part-time post at Glasgow University.